An
ANGEL
in TIME

OTHER BOOKS AND BOOKS ON CASSETTE
BY DAN YATES:

Angels Don't Knock

Just Call Me an Angel

Angels to the Rescue

An Angel in the Family

It Takes an Angel

An Angel's Christmas

Angel on Vacation

An
ANGEL
in TIME

a novel

Dan Yates

Covenant Communications, Inc.

Covenant

Cover images copyright © 2000 PhotoDisc, Inc.

Cover and book design ©2000 by Covenant Communications, Inc.

Published by Covenant Communications, Inc.
American Fork, Utah

Printed in the United States of America
First Printing: September 2000

07 06 05 04 03 02 01 00   10 9 8 7 6 5 4 3 2 1

ISBN 1-57734-724-2

Library of Congress Cataloging-in-Publication Data

Yates, Dan, 1934-
    Angel in Time / Dan Yates.
        p.   cm.
    ISBN 1-57734-724-2
        1. Time travel--Fiction. 2. Angels--Fiction. I. Title.
PS3565.A763 A53 2000
813'.54--dc21   00-043055

I'd like to dedicate this story to my friend, Dorma,
and to her Gerald, who waits on the far side of forever.

After that first kiss, when the two of you meet again,
tell him I think he's a most lucky man.
And then—kiss him again.

I would like to thank those of you who read my stories.
It is my sincere hope that in some small way
my stories may brighten your lives.

Thank you, Lord, for everything You have given me.
Mine has truly been a storybook life.

PROLOGUE

Howard Placard was first mentioned in *Angels Don't Knock* when Samantha Allen—who was still a mortal at that time—went with Bruce Vincent on a date to Howard's private beach. This was the same beach onto which Bruce later parachuted from the sky and proposed to the woman he was destined to spend forever with—Arline Wilson. His love story is told in *Just Call Me an Angel.*

Not until the book *It Takes an Angel* was the man behind the name unmasked. In this novel, Howard was introduced as a motion picture magnate whose obsession with a woman nearly destroyed the lives of three people: Lori and Brad Douglas, and Howard himself.

Because of Howard's interference, Lori and Brad spent ten years separated from each other. During those ten long years, Brad remained hidden from the world on a lonely island in the Caribbean Sea. Although Lori still loved Brad, she had no idea where to find him, and all this time Brad thought Lori had left him for Howard. Things might never have been straightened out if it hadn't been for the intervention of Samantha and Jason Hackett, two angels in the business of repairing broken hearts.

With a little help from Samantha and Jason, Brad finally returned home and found that Lori had remained faithful to him all the years he had been gone. When Howard saw that Brad and Lori were getting back together, he took drastic steps to prevent this from happening. With all the power and wealth behind his efforts, he might have succeeded—if he had been up against anyone other than Samantha and Jason Hackett.

In the end, Brad and Lori's marriage was saved, and Howard lost everything. He could even have been sentenced to a ten-year prison term for tax fraud, even though it was his accountant, not Howard himself, who was guilty. But in a surprise move, Samantha turned the tables and came to Howard's rescue—sort of. She arranged for his prison sentence to be suspended on the condition he spend time on the very island on which he had caused Brad to live all those years.

No one could understand why Samantha would do such a thing, but she just said it was because she saw something in Howard that was worth saving. The higher authorities approved of her plan, because they understood the reason Howard had been attracted to Lori Douglas in the first place. It was a secret kept hidden from the world for more than a century, one that could be revealed only when the higher authorities decided the time was right.

Howard's fate was sealed and he was banned to the island. There Samantha left him in the capable hands of a crusty old sea captain named Horatio Symington Blake. Captain Blake was a seventeenth-century seaman, who for personal reasons had remained on earth after his death, haunting this tiny island for the past three hundred years. Captain Blake and Brad had become fast friends during the years Brad spent on the island; now it was Howard's turn to become acquainted with the captain.

A year and a half had passed since the day Howard first arrived on the island shores. The experience of this year and a half had left Howard a changed man—more humble, and as Samantha put it, more teachable.

And so, in the pages of *An Angel in Time*, we'll see what closely guarded secret made Howard the man he had become. As you read on, see if you agree with Samantha's appraisal of Howard. Ask yourself if Howard will be able to rewrite the pages of history—to become the man destiny had intended him to be?

CHAPTER 1

Howard Placard woke to the sound of the howling wind. He sat up in bed and listened as the heavy rain pounded against the old house with cruel vengeance. Through the one window in the room came the brilliant flash of a lightning streak as it danced across the stormy Caribbean night sky. Howard glanced quickly at the ceiling to see whether his effort at patching the leak from last night's storm would hold this time. Not that it really mattered all that much. Even if this patch did hold, he knew another leak would break out somewhere else. For more than a year and a half now, he had been patching holes in the old roof trying to hold out the water brought on by one storm after another. And for that year and a half, as soon as he got one leak patched, three more would show up to take its place. Such was his curse since being banished to this desolate island by that busybody lady angel, Samantha Hackett.

So far, so good. His patch job seemed to be holding. Maybe, with a little bit of luck, he could pull the covers over his head and make this storm go away. Wouldn't it be nice to get one uninterrupted night's sleep?

As was so often the case, this pleasant idea didn't even have time to take root. At first it was a trickle, a few isolated drops striking him on the crown of his head. But in the time it took him to look up, the trickle had grown into a steady stream of icy cold water.

"NO!!" he cried. "NOT OVER THE BED!! NOT AGAIN!!"

In an instant, his feet hit the floor and he leaned his weight against the bed, shoving it out from under the drizzle. This done, he grabbed one of the buckets he kept on the nearby night table and set it on the floor under the new leak. It took only a second to realize he was completely drenched.

"So much for getting any sleep tonight," he grumbled to himself.

Throwing on a robe, he shoved the door open and stepped into the hallway that led to the front part of the house Brad had built when he'd been living on the island. Howard stomped past the bucket that sat under the leak in hall, and through the living room, at last entering the kitchen, which was the driest room in the house. There he pulled out a chair and flopped down at the table, pulling his robe tight around his neck in an effort to make himself a little warmer. After the life of unlimited comfort Howard had managed for himself back in the days of his empire as a tycoon motion picture producer, this is what he had come down to—sitting out a midnight storm in the cold, dingy kitchen of another man's cast-off house.

Howard leaned back in the hard wooden chair and covered his ears against the dreadful sounds of this cruel night. Try as he might, he just couldn't drown them out. The howling wind roared in its fury. The driving rain against the time-worn roof pounded harder than ever. Another flash of lightning lit up the room, followed almost instantly by a maddening clap of thunder.

"THAT'S ENOUGH!!" Howard shouted fretfully. "STOP IT!! PLEASE STOP IT!"

Leaning forward, Howard buried his head in hands. "What have I done to deserve this?" he moaned. Never had he known a moment of greater despair than this one. If the valley of life had a floor—he had found it.

* * *

Far from Howard's island, and with him far from her thoughts, Lori Douglas pressed the garage door opener and drove into the driveway. Once the door was open, she slid the red Porsche into the garage and shut off the engine. Lori loved this car. It was a gift from Brad when the two of them had resumed their marriage after being apart for ten long years, thanks to Howard Placard's meddling in their lives.

Picking up the two bags of groceries from the front seat, she walked into the house, made her way to the kitchen, and set the groceries on the counter. She smiled, thinking about the secret she was dying to share with Brad. She'd tell him tonight. Maybe right after dinner. She couldn't wait to see the expression on his face when she broke the news.

Taking the milk from the grocery bag, she moved to the refrigerator and opened the door. As she did, she noticed something lying on the kitchen table that she hadn't noticed before. It was a stack of papers. She wondered if Brad had left it there. *Probably a script for a movie he's working on,* she thought. She shoved the milk inside the refrigerator and closed the door, then stepped to the table and looked at the cover sheet of the manuscript. *An Angel in Time,* she read, noticing that the type was faded and hard to read, and the pages of the manuscript were yellowed and worn.

Funny, Brad hadn't mentioned directing a film about angels—and he seldom kept anything about his work from her. Then she noticed something else on the cover page. Near the bottom, the author's name appeared. But—what was this?

This manuscript was written by L. Parker. Lori was L. Parker, or at least she had been before marrying Brad. Parker was her maiden name. But she certainly hadn't written any angel stories. Not now and not back when she went by the name Parker. "What is this?" she muttered in confusion.

"Maybe I can explain," came a familiar male voice from behind her.

Lori turned to see who had spoken, and her face broke into a smile as she recognized him. "What do you mean sneaking up on a lady like that?" she scolded. "And what are you doing here?"

"I see you've already noticed the manuscript lying on your table. Well, I'm here to explain it. And I think you're going to be very surprised at what you're about to learn, Mrs. Douglas. Very surprised indeed."

* * *

Howard was sure there was no place on this earth left for him to sink any lower. He had most certainly descended to the very depths. "What have I done?" he cried out again. "What have I done?"

But, just when he was sure things couldn't get worse, he heard her voice. "I think we both know what you did to bring this on yourself, Howard. And I think we both know you deserve everything that's happening to you, don't we?"

Raising his head, Howard groaned and parted two fingers, which allowed him to see her with one resentful eye. "Wonderful," he grumbled. "As if this miserable storm wasn't enough, now you have to show up to torment me. How many pounds of my flesh do you need to extract before you'll be satisfied, lady angel?"

Samantha folded her arms and glared at Howard. "Is that any way to talk to the one who kept you out of a cold prison cell? You may not like living on this island, but it beats the heck out of the alternative, doesn't it?"

Howard knew she was right. Bad as this island was, a ten-year prison sentence would have been, by far, a worse penalty. But he certainly wasn't going to admit it to this pesky angel. In fact, he really didn't deserve the prison sentence she kept holding over his head at all. Granted, the evidence did point to his being guilty of tax evasion—but it wasn't his fault. Not entirely, it wasn't. Except for his stupid mistake of trusting his finances to his uncle, he would never have had problems paying his taxes. It was only when Samantha had confiscated his records from where he had them supposedly hidden safely away, that he had learned of his tax problem. He had fully intended to set the matter straight by having an outside accountant firm audit his books to determine exactly how much he did owe in back taxes—and by seeing to it the taxes were paid. But he never got the chance. To his horror, Samantha had given the files to Bruce Vincent, to put in the hands of the IRS—and the rest was history.

If only I'd listened to my instincts instead of taking Mother's advice about using Uncle Rudy's accounting service, I wouldn't be in this predicament now, Howard fumed silently to himself. He had known better than to mix business with family, but he had given in to his mother's pressure. Dear old Uncle Rudy. Every time Howard thought of the man, it made his blood boil.

Raising his head from his hands, Howard looked Samantha in the eye. "You talk about what we both know," he said, accusingly. "We both know the excuse of my committing tax fraud has nothing whatsoever to do with your banning me to this island, don't we? The real reason you've done this to me is Lori Parker. Admit it, woman. It's true and you know it."

"Her name is Lori Douglas," Samantha corrected him. "And yes, she is the real reason you're here on this island, Howard. I could clear your name of the tax charges in a heartbeat, if I wanted to. But I figure as long as I hold the tax evasion thing as an ace card, it'll keep you from doing something stupid, like trying to escape from this lovely little island and going after Lori again."

Howard knew Samantha was right. On two counts. First, Lori's last name really was Douglas, not Parker. And second, he knew he couldn't take the chance of escaping from this island, as this would leave Samantha an opening to send him to prison. She had him over a barrel and he knew it. "So what are you doing visiting me in the middle of the night? Guilty conscience keeping you awake? Or am I assuming too much in thinking angels ever sleep?"

Samantha grinned. "Do angels sleep? Sorry, Howard. That's a question you'll just have to wait your turn to learn for yourself. Some things the higher authorities won't permit us to tell about life on the far side of forever. As for your other question, what am I doing here? That one I can answer. I've been keeping a close eye on you, Howard. I've been waiting for you to reach the point where you've grown humble enough for me to try to straighten out your destiny. Tonight's storm seemed to do the trick. I'd say you're ready now."

Howard stared at her. "I hope you'll pardon me for not having the slightest idea what you're talking about," he grumbled.

"I know you don't, Howard. But what I'm talking about is your obsession with Lori Douglas," Samantha said deliberately.

Howard threw up both hands in disgust. "We're back to that subject, are we? Obsession indeed! I happen to be very much in love with Lori Parker, and you know perfectly well I'm speaking the truth. And something else you know, when I do get off this disgusting island, and when I do get my life back, I intend to convince Lori that there is no way a loser like Brad Douglas can make her happy. She deserves me, and by heaven, I intend to give her what she deserves."

Samantha shook her head, although his words didn't surprise her. "You never give up, do you, Howard? I suppose you'd even like to send Brad back to this island again while you're at it, even though, thanks to you, he's already spent ten years here."

"Brad Douglas deserved every minute he spent on this island," Howard retorted. "And would I send him back here again? In a heartbeat, lady angel. All I need is the opportunity."

It was roughly twelve years ago that Howard had contracted Brad to direct a film in Acapulco, Mexico, for the sole purpose of getting Brad out of the picture long enough so Howard could make a play for Lori. It hadn't mattered to him that Lori was Brad's wife. In Howard's mind, he was the right one for Lori; he was the one who could make her happy. Even though Lori had finally and firmly rejected Howard, Brad had seen them together the night he returned from Acapulco and believed she had chosen Howard over him. That same evening, Brad learned that his sister, Shannon, was planning to leave her abusive husband, James Baxter, so Brad decided to hide his sister and niece on a secluded island in the Caribbean Sea. Thinking that his own marriage to Lori was over, Brad accompanied them to the island, where he could care for them.

Brad built a house, planted a garden, and even found ways to provide hot and cold running water, electricity, and virtually every other convenience he and the girls had left behind when they came to the island. For ten years, the three of them lived on the island—or rather, the four of them, if you counted the ghost of Captain Blake, who had remained on earth after his untimely death, watching over a fortune in gold, until it could be safely delivered into the hands of its rightful owner.

After ten years of searching for Shannon, James Baxter finally located where she was hiding. His intention was to bring her home where he could make her pay for leaving him all those years before. But with the help of Samantha, Jason, and Captain Blake, Baxter was defeated. The three castaways then returned to the United States and the lives they had left behind so long ago.

Although Lori was thrilled to have a second chance with Brad, Howard was furious at his return. Howard had never given up that someday he might win Lori for himself. What right did Brad have to show up, after all those years, and try to take Lori back? But under Samantha's guiding hand, Brad and Lori were reunited in the end.

And as for Howard—well—Howard was banned to the same island on which Brad had spent ten long years, having inherited Brad's old house.

Unfortunately for Howard, several severe storms had taken their toll on Brad's house. The electricity was gone, as was the running water. Even the structure of the place had been greatly weakened, which was why Howard constantly battled the leaking roof—among other things.

All this was fresh in Howard's mind as he sat, still damp and uncomfortable in his kitchen, glaring at Samantha, who had engineered the whole setup. "Brad Douglas isn't worthy of Lori!" he growled. "I'm the right man for her, and you know it, Samantha Hackett."

Samantha shook her head. "Wrong, Howard. Lori and Brad are destined for each other. She couldn't be happier than she is now with him."

"Nonsense!" Howard grumbled. "Utter nonsense!" He stood to face her. "As long as you're here, maybe you can tell me why I haven't seen that pesky old sea captain in the past few days. I know he's not much company, but he's better than no company at all."

Howard had gotten to know Captain Horatio Symington Blake quite well over the past year and a half, which was a bit ironic, since Captain Blake had also been close friends with Brad Douglas during the ten years Brad spent on this very island. When Samantha had banned Howard to this island, she felt it only fitting that the captain should become his watch keeper.

"The captain is part of what I'm here to talk to you about," Samantha explained. "I'm pulling him off the job. You won't be seeing him anymore."

This revelation came like a slap in Howard's face. Granted, he and the captain were constantly bickering one with another. And it was true, in the beginning neither had any liking for the other. But in spite of all their bickering, over time, they had softened toward each other and had actually become warm friends. Not that they would show it, mind you. But the friendship was there, nevertheless.

"I won't be seeing the captain any more?" Howard grumbled. "Preposterous! Blake's been on this island forever. Why take him away now?"

"I'm retiring the captain," Samantha explained. "He's earned it. Ever since he crossed the line to my side of forever, I've been using him in one assignment after another. It's time he had a break."

Howard scowled. "A break? What do you mean?"

"The captain's a sailor, Howard," Samantha reminded him. "It's the love of his life. I've talked with the higher authorities, and he's been cleared for a new job. The captain's about to set out on a grand new journey that will take him places he can't even imagine now. He sailed these mortal seas more than three hundred years ago. This time he'll be sailing across vast galaxies to worlds beyond mortal description, and his old crew will be joining him. I haven't told him yet. We're having a surprise party in his honor early next week. I'll tell him then."

Howard felt a twinge of sadness at this. "So he won't be here on the island with me anymore? Well, more power to him. Tell him I said good-bye, will you, Sam? And tell him I wish him Godspeed."

"I'll tell him, Howard. It'll mean a lot, I know."

"So," Howard asked, after considering this new information. "How will this affect me? Am I on my own now or will you be overseeing me personally?" He grinned and then added, "Heaven forbid that thought."

"No, Howard, you won't be on your own—nor will I be overseeing you personally. I'm sending in a new angel. One who shares my belief that it's time to go to work on your true destiny."

"Oh, marvelous," Howard responded, rolling his eyes. "You're about to play more games with my life. What, pray tell, do you have in store for me this time?"

"I'll leave the explanations to your new angel, Howard. I think you going to like who I've chosen. She's a very special lady."

"She?"

"Yes, she," Samantha responded. "Do you have a problem with that?"

"Humph! I do if she's half as obstinate as the one female angel I've had anything to do with."

Samantha laughed. "I love you, too, Howard. I'm not sure whether you'll find this lady obstinate or not. I guess it's all in how you perceive her. And just for your information, she's no stranger to you. You've known this lady for a very long time."

"How is that possible?" he asked. "With the exception of you, I've never met any female angels."

"She wasn't an angel when you knew her, Howard. And by the way, she has a pet name she likes to call you."

Howard's eyes shot open wide as a thought struck his mind. "A pet name?" he asked, almost afraid to voice his suspicion. "That name wouldn't happen to be . . ."

"Hello, Peaches," came a lovely female voice from across the room. "I can't believe what's become of you. You're a sight for sore eyes."

Howard spun to face the lady. His mouth dropped open, and for a very long time he could only stare at her. At last he spoke. "Annette?" came his feeble question. "Is it—really you?"

She smiled but said nothing. Howard looked back to where Samantha had been standing only seconds before to discover she was gone. "Oh my . . ." he gasped at the realization of what had occurred here tonight. "How can this be happening?"

CHAPTER 2

Lori was still smiling from her excitement over her unexpected visitor. "I can't believe this," she exclaimed. "It's not every day I walk into my house to find an angel in my kitchen."

"True," Jason agreed. "But just because you don't see an angel doesn't mean there isn't one nearby most of the time."

Lori couldn't help being excited at the thought of Jason Hackett paying her a visit again. It had been through the efforts of Jason and his vibrant wife, Samantha, that Lori's marriage to Brad had been saved. When Sam and Jason had said good-bye, she had assumed she'd never see them again. Not in this dimension anyway. And here he was in her kitchen. She was dying to learn why, but too intimidated by his presence to come right out and ask.

"I've never played hostess to an angel in my kitchen before." she said uneasily. "May I offer you something to drink?"

Jason laughed, sensing her tenseness. "A drink sounds nice," he responded reassuringly.

Lori opened the refrigerator and pulled out two bottles of ginger ale. "Is this okay, Jason? I can make up some lemonade, if you prefer."

"Ginger ale is perfect," Jason smiled. "And never mind the ice. I like mine straight."

"It's not every day I get to entertain an angel," she said as she handed him a bottle. "Shall we sit down?"

"Am I making you nervous, Lori?" Jason asked. "We should be old friends by this time."

"I don't know," she said, feeling very foolish. "It's just different, you dropping in on me like this. Does my nervousness really show all that much?"

Jason shook his head. "Not really," he said, "and speaking of angels appearing unexpectedly, have you ever heard the story of the first time I appeared to Sam?"

This caught Lori's interest. "No, I haven't, Jason. Tell me."

Jason leaned back in his chair, letting the memory fill his mind. "You know the story of Gus' typo," he said, dreamily. "The darn guy wouldn't let me cross the line to the far side until the matter was cleared up. That meant I had to wander the earth as a first-level angel for some twenty years, just watching Sam grow from a child to the elegant woman she became." Jason sighed. "I loved her from the first time I laid eyes on her. Which was only natural, since we were contracted for each other."

"That must have been hard for you," Lori observed. "Watching Sam grow up and not being able to let her know you were there."

"One of the hardest things I've ever done, Lori. But the time finally came when the higher authorities approved me to appear to her. It was in her apartment in the old Anderson Building. Room 707." He smiled, just remembering. "She used to hate that old building. The elevator was on the blink half the time, and she had to climb seven flights of stairs."

Lori nodded. "I've heard that part of the story."

"Well, one night my chance finally came. I appeared to her, right there in her apartment." Jason paused to look at Lori. "If you think you're nervous having me here drinking your ginger ale, you should have seen Sam that evening. She even pulled a gun on me."

"You're kidding," Lori laughed.

"Nope. She pulled out a rusty old revolver her granddaddy had given her. I knew the darn thing wouldn't shoot, but she didn't. Then, when I walked through a wall to prove I was an angel, she was so shook up she actually passed out." For a moment, Jason looked a little nervous himself. "She'd bust me if she knew I was telling you this," he admitted.

"Your secret's safe with me, Jason. I love hearing little tidbits like this. Is it true she wouldn't call you by name at first?" Lori asked eagerly.

"Oh yes, that's true. And she liked to call me a ghost. That doesn't bother me anymore, but back then I hated being called a ghost.

Anyway, that's what happened the first time I appeared to Sam." He paused a moment, looking at Lori. "I hope my story helps put you at ease," he said at length.

"It does," she laughed. "Thanks, Jason."

"Yeah, well, I suppose I should get to the real reason I'm here, huh?"

"I have been wondering about that," she admitted. "What is it? I know it must be important to warrant my seeing an angel again."

"Yeah, you could call it important," Jason nodded. "But I'm not sure you'll be all that excited to see me once you learn what it is."

Uh oh. That didn't sound good. In her jubilance at seeing Jason, Lori hadn't considered it might be something bad that brought him to her kitchen. Her smile diminished. "Okay, I give up. Why won't I be excited?"

Jason took a drink and set the bottle back down. "I can answer that with just two words," he said. "The first one's Howard, and the second is Placard."

A chill passed through her at the sound of Howard's name. It had been a year and half since the day on Howard's yacht when she had finally become free of him—and when her long, lonely years of separation from Brad had ended. It was also the last time she had seen Sam and Jason, whose work was supposedly finished, with Brad and Lori's marriage saved and Howard out of their lives forever. Or so Lori had assumed until now. Why would Jason reappear in her life talking about Howard Placard?

"What possible reason could you have for bringing his name up again?" Lori asked coldly.

Jason fidgeted with his bottle. "I'm sorry, Lori. I wish I didn't have to bring him up. Believe me, I know what a thorn he's been in your side."

Lori felt her face grow hot. "A thorn in my side? That's what you call him? That's putting it a bit mildly, if you ask me, Jason Hackett."

"Okay," Jason conceded. "I agree Howard's a first-class reprobate." He leaned an elbow on the table and rested his chin in his hand. "But even reprobates can change," he added.

"Howard Placard change?!" Lori couldn't believe she was hearing this. "Ha! The Cheshire cat will wear a frown before that happens."

Jason sat back up. "What if I told you the higher authorities have enough faith in Howard that they're about to provide him with a chance to prove he's changed?"

Lori's eyes narrowed. "Exactly what is it you're getting at, Jason?"

Jason rubbed his chin thoughtfully. "You know what, Lori. I think I'll just set that part of the assignment aside and let Sam explain it later. She's better at this sort of thing than I am."

Lori didn't know what to say. Jason showed up in her house, mentioned Howard Placard, and implied that the man was somehow going to pop back up in her life—then he dropped it. That would have been disconcerting enough, but her mind took hold of something else Jason had suggested. "You said Sam will explain?" Lori asked. "Are you telling me I'm going to see Sam again, too?"

Jason winked. "Thought that might get your attention. Yep, you get to see Sam again. She's the one who'll be working the closest with you on this assignment. But, since one of the unchangeable laws of nature is that even second-level angels can only be in one place at a time, Sam couldn't be here to get the ball rolling on your end. She had to take care of another end of this assignment, so I came for this initial contact in her place. Make sense?"

"No, not really. But if it means getting to see Sam again, as well as seeing you, Jason, then it's worth whatever else it brings."

"Even Howard Placard?" Jason asked, smiling.

Lori winced. "I don't know. Maybe I spoke too soon. I guess that will depend on whatever it is you're leaving Sam to tell me."

"Okay, that's settled," Jason said. "Let's get on with the rest of the reason I'm here drinking ginger ale at your kitchen table." Jason picked up the manuscript and handed it to Lori. "This is the rest of the reason I'm here," he stated.

Lori took the manuscript from him. "It wasn't Brad who left this here; it was you, wasn't it?" she asked.

Jason nodded, smiling.

"Okay, you have my attention," she said. "It's obviously a manuscript for a story about angels. But why does it have my name on the cover, Jason? I didn't write it."

Jason reached out and let his finger trace the author's name on the cover of the manuscript. "Think about it, Lori," he said. "Parker is your maiden name, but were you the first L. Parker in your family?"

Jason was right. There had been another L. Parker in her family, a Loraine Parker, who had lived a long time ago. Lori looked again at the age-worn pages of the manuscript. Could it be that Loraine Parker was the author of this? She looked back at Jason. "You mean my distant aunt, right?"

"Loraine Parker," Jason responded, smiling.

Lori examined the manuscript more closely. It was about three inches thick, and though it showed definite signs of age, it was nevertheless in very good condition. "I don't understand, Jason. If Loraine Parker wrote this, why have I never seen it before?"

"Let's just say it's been hidden from the eyes of the world since Loraine Parker's death. You're the first to see it, Lori—and you'll be the first to read it, too."

Lori was confused. "I still don't understand, Jason. You're saying that no one has seen this before. Why not?"

"That's a good question, Lori. And one that deserves an answer. But we're putting the horse before the cart. You need to understand some things that are in the manuscript, before finding out why no one has seen it until now. I know you had some other things planned for today, but I'm asking you to put them on hold." Jason paused a moment, then with a smile, added, "Except the news you're planning to tell Brad, that is. No need putting something that good on hold."

Lori's mouth dropped open. "Then—you know about . . . ?"

Jason grinned. "Yeah. And like I was saying, everything else but that goes on hold so you can spend today reading the manuscript. You and Brad, too. You can read it together."

"I don't see how, Jason. Brad's at the studio working. He won't be home until late."

"There's been a change, Lori. Actually, he's on his way home, even as we speak."

"He is?" Lori asked, surprised.

"Learning what's in the manuscript is just as important for Brad as it is for you, Lori. Let's just say a very good friend of his put a bug in his ear that he was needed at home more than he was needed at the studio."

Finishing off the last of his ginger ale, Jason set the bottle back on the table. "Thanks for the drink, Lori," he said. "It was great. I give you five stars for your performance at entertaining an angel."

Lori couldn't keep from laughing. "Thank you, kind sir. That's a nice thing to say."

Jason stood up. "I have to be going now," he said. "Pressing business at the office, you know. This Special Conditions Coordinator thing keeps a fellow jumping. You and Brad get started on the manuscript, and Sam will fill in the gaps a little later on." With a wave of his hand, Jason was gone.

After a minute or so to let her head clear, Lori finished putting the groceries away. Then, taking the manuscript, she moved to the family room, where she sat down on the sofa and thumbed through the pages. Part of her was excited to learn what was in the manuscript, while another part of her remained concerned at the yet unexplained mention of Howard Placard. Turning to the first page, she began to read.

CHAPTER 3

Howard stared in astonishment at the young woman standing before him. He had to swallow away the lump in his throat before he could speak. "Are my eyes deceiving me?" he struggled. "Or is it—you . . . ?"

"Of course it's me, Peaches. Don't tell me you're not happy to see me. I suppose I can leave, if you like."

"No! Please don't leave! It's wonderful seeing you, Annette. It's just that . . ."

She waited for him to finish, but he was having difficulty forming the words. "Why does it bother you to see me like this, Peaches? So I'm an angel. You've been working with angels for the last year and half. You should be used to us by now."

"Yes, but—you're not supposed to be an angel. You're a real person, Annette."

Annette raised an eyebrow. "Sam, Jason, and the captain aren't real people? They're going to be quite disappointed when I tell them."

"You know what I mean, Annette. They're real people, but they're not . . ."

She finished his sentence for him. "They're not your sister. Is that what you're saying, Peaches?"

"Stop calling me Peaches! You know how I hate that name."

She ignored his remark. Opening her arms, she asked, "Haven't you got a hug for the sister you haven't seen in twenty years?"

Howard was overwhelmed. Learning to accept those angels who came to him as strangers had been hard enough. Now he was looking straight into the eyes of the little sister he had so dearly loved . . . The sister he had seen buried after that horrible plane crash . . .

A combination of feelings assailed him. Feelings of elation at seeing her so alive and so lovely. Feelings of doubt that what he was seeing was real. That it was perhaps a dream or a trick of the mind brought on by the wretched conditions his life had deteriorated to. He wanted to wrap his arms around her in a loving embrace but feared she would vanish if he tried. Struggling to control his emotion, he managed to say, "Can I hug you? Is that possible?"

A warm smile filled her whole face. "I'm a second-level angel, Peaches. Now are you going to stand there staring at me, or do I get that hug?"

Howard had little trouble understanding the difference between a first-level angel and a second. A first-level angel, Captain Blake couldn't so much as shake Howard's hand. He couldn't pick up a rock, open a door, or even straighten a picture hanging crooked on the wall. But Samantha and Jason were different. They were second-level angels. They could do all sorts of things a first-level angel couldn't.

It wasn't enough that Howard was looking at his long-departed little sister as an angel. He was looking at her as a second-level angel. He opened his arms, and darned if she didn't come to him with one of those special hugs she had given him so often when they were young. And darned if she wasn't crying even. What's more, Howard felt his own eyes grow moist as well, something completely foreign to the hardened man he had become over the years.

"I—I can't believe this," he stammered, squeezing her ever so tightly. "You really are an angel, little sister. A second-level angel."

Annette stepped back and wiped her eyes on her shirt sleeve. "What's with that awful beard you're wearing? And your hair is down to your collar. You look hideous like that."

Howard felt his beard. "Shaving isn't exactly convenient on this primitive little island. I have to heat my water over a wood fire, and it's not worth the effort just to shave every day. But I keep my beard trimmed as best I can. And it's easier to cut my own hair when I leave it a little longer. I keep myself presentable," he defended himself.

"I don't like it," Annette said firmly. "And neither will a certain other party I have in mind to introduce you to very shortly. The beard goes, and so does the long hair."

Howard shook his head. "Same old Annette. You always did think you had to dress and groom me. I'm a grown man now, little sister. If I want to wear a beard, I'll wear a beard."

Howard's mind really wasn't on his grooming at all. He was wondering how much Annette knew about the reason he was on this island in the first place. For the most part, Howard didn't care what anyone else thought about his past actions, but this was his little sister. With her, it did matter. He wondered if she knew why he had been condemned to this island.

Gathering his courage, he asked, "How much do you know about my life on this island, little sister?"

She folded her arms and scowled at him. "I know it all, Peaches. I've been keeping very close tabs on you these past years. And you have to understand, I have some miraculous technology at my disposal for knowing your every move. My first five years on the other side of forever, I spent working in the Celestial Records Department."

Howard was stunned. Nothing he had done, it seems, was hidden from her eyes. "What is a Celestial Records Department?" he asked sheepishly.

She explained. "On the other side, Peaches, we record everything. Not one act in the mortal world goes unrecorded. And we do our recording using high-tech methods that put the motion picture industry you're so familiar with to shame. You like to brag about your wide screens and special effects. Well, let me tell you this, Peaches, my recordings make that stuff look like kiddie games. Have Sam or Jason ever treated you to a holographically enhanced recording of an event?"

Howard shook his head no. "I've heard about it from Captain Blake, but I've never actually seen one myself."

"Then you're in for a very special treat, big brother. I've been approved to use some holographs in this assignment. And when you experience one of these holographs, you'll understand a little better about our record keeping on the other side."

Howard cringed at the thought his sister had seen his every action since her death. He held his breath as she went on with her explanation. "I was able to keep track of you even after leaving my job in Celestial Records," she said. "I had friends in the department who kept me up to date. And you know what, big brother? I didn't much like some of the stupid stunts I watched you pull. You've turned into a real jerk, you know that?"

Howard suddenly felt very uncomfortable. The thought of Annette knowing what he had done was almost unbearable. Annette was his sister. No one before or after Annette had held a place so close to Howard's heart. She and he were more than best friends. They had been inseparable since birth, and even then they were apart only three minutes. Howard was born first, and Annette came along three minutes later. Although separated by only three minutes, Howard had always thought of himself as her older brother, which had irritated Annette to no end. That was the main reason for what she had done to Howard that left him tagged with the name Peaches.

When the twins were seven, their mother had planted a peach tree in the backyard. Three years later, when the twins were ten, the peach tree produced its first small crop of fruit. Their mother had planned to use the peaches to make a cobbler as soon as they were ripe. She was so excited about the cobbler that she checked the peaches every day, impatiently monitoring their progress. Annette knew this, but Howard didn't. One afternoon while playing in the backyard, Annette thought up a great scheme. She made a face at Howard, teasing him that he couldn't hit her with one of the peaches. Being a normal ten-year old, Howard refused to let his sister get away with that sort of challenge. Howard picked a peach and threw it at her. She dodged it and continued to taunt him. It was only a few minutes until every peach had been picked from the tree—and not one peach found its mark, thanks to Annette's agility. Their mother was furious. Howard ended up on restriction for a month. And worse, he ended up with the nickname, Peaches. It was humiliating, but the more he complained the harder the name stuck.

Howard brushed a hand nervously through his hair. "What right do you have calling me a jerk?" he mildly protested. "I think I did quite well for myself. Up until the time that smug lady angel and her friends tampered in my affairs, at least." Howard knew his sister was referring to his actions with Lori, not his professional dealings. But he thought it wouldn't hurt to bring up his success. And it might soften the blow of the real issue.

Annette didn't take the bait. "You did quite well for yourself, Peaches? Is that what you think? Oh, sure, you made a lot of money along the way, but what happened to your character? You thought nothing about who you stepped on to get one more rung up the ladder. And this thing of your going after another man's wife . . ." She made a clicking sound with her tongue. "That's worse than being a jerk, big brother. That's just plain despicable."

Howard threw up his hands. "All right, little sister! Angel or no angel—you don't know what you're talking about. I happen to be in love with the lady, and I happen to know I'm the one who can make her happy. Not that loser, Brad Douglas, she's married to now."

Annette shook her head. "I can see I have my work cut out for me, Peaches. Without me there to keep you in line, you've really gone off the deep end. But I'm back now and I'll have you whipped into shape in no time at all."

Howard did a double take. "What are you talking about, Annette?"

"I'm talking about the reason I'm here, big brother. To get your head back on straight and to set your feet back on their destined path. I was offered the chance to take you on as my assignment, and I accepted."

"My head is on straight, Annette Placard. And there's nothing either of us can do about my destiny until such time as those angels you run around with give me back my life."

"There's no sense arguing with me," she said. "I know my job, and there's nothing you can do to stop me. We're going to embark on a little project, Peaches, but not before you shave off that gross-looking beard. Tell you what—you grab a quick shower, shave off the beard while you're at it, and I'll get you some new clothes to wear on our trip."

"I swear, little sister, I think you've lost your mind. There's a downpour outside, remember? Where am I going to get dry wood to build a fire? And how am I going to build a fire, anyway, with the deluge of water out there to extinguish it? Shave and shower, indeed. Maybe as a angel, you still have all those wonderful conveniences, but as a mortal held prisoner on this island—I don't."

"You're forgetting, big brother, I'm a second-level angel. You want your storm stopped? So, let's stop it." She snapped her fingers, and instantly all sounds of wind, rain, and thunder vanished. Then before he could recover from the shock of this surprising display, she hit him with another little tidbit. "I'll put Brad's old shower back in service for you, Peaches. You'll have all the hot water you want. You'll find your new clothes lying on the bed when you finish."

Howard's head was spinning. There was just too much coming at him and it was coming much too fast. He wanted to ask her more about the storm, and about the shower she spoke of. But she didn't give him the chance. "I'll give you an hour, Peaches," she said. "That should be long enough for you to get ready. When I get back, we have a lot of ground to cover. So don't dilly-dally, okay?"

Howard slapped a hand to his forehead. "What are you talking about, Annette?!" he snapped. "You're confusing the life out of me."

"I'm talking about your destiny, Peaches. Enjoy your shower, but don't take too long at it."

As Howard looked on completely astounded, his sister simply vanished from before his eyes. "Annette!!!" he cried after her. "Where are you going?!" It was useless. She was gone and that was that. Call after her as he might, it wasn't going to bring her back. Feeling his knees weaken, Howard slumped down in the wooden chair. There he sat for several minutes, trying to sort out everything that had happened since he had awakened to the sound of thunder less than half an hour earlier. Dealing with angels over the past year and a half was a strange experience, but seeing his sister like this overshadowed it all.

At last, he stood and walked to the back door. Opening it, he looked outside. Everything was wet from where the rain had been, but there wasn't the slightest sign of any storm remaining. A glance at the sky revealed a myriad of sparkling stars. There was even the sliver of a new moon.

Howard closed the door and made his way back to the bedroom. He checked the bed. It was completely dry, with not one trace of the water that had left it soaked such a short time before. He glanced at the door to Brad's old bathroom. Dare he check it out?

Walking to the door, he took hold of the knob and slowly twisted it. Shoving it open, he peered inside. What he saw took his breath away. There was soap, shampoo, shaving cream, a clean washcloth and towel, a brand new razor, a comb and hair brush, and a pair of scissors. Even the old mirror that had previously been shattered was restored better than new. He reached for the water handle in the sink and gave it a twist. Not only did he discover it produced running water, it was actually hot. His sister had apparently thought of everything. Howard closed his eyes and let it sink in. How long had it been since he had enjoyed a real shower?

He shook his head in wonder. What level had he sunk to that something as simple as a hot shower was enough to make him want to shout for joy? Two years ago he had lived in a world of unlimited luxury, but he had descended from the brightest of day into the darkest of night.

And all because of those meddling angels, he muttered to himself.

Forcing that unpleasant thought out of his mind, he turned on the water and soon had it adjusted to an inviting temperature. Removing his clothes, he neatly folded them and laid them on the counter. Then he stepped into the shower and pulled the curtain closed—and enjoyed the closest thing to heaven he had known in over a year and a half.

CHAPTER 4

Lori had read only a page or so when she looked up to see Brad entering the room. "Hi, babe," he said. "Bet you didn't expect to see me home this time of day, did you?"

Lori stood and greeted him with a kiss. "Bet you're wrong," she responded with a grin. "I was told you were on your way home by a certain visitor who showed up to see me this morning."

"You what?" Brad gasped, laughing. "What visitor? Wait, don't tell me—it was Captain Blake, right?"

"No, it wasn't Captain Blake, silly. Why would you think that?"

"Because I saw the captain myself today, that's why."

Lori couldn't believe it. "You saw the captain?" she asked excitedly. "Are you kidding me?"

"Not at all. He showed up at the studio informing me I was needed at home." Brad looked at her. "So who was your visitor if not the captain? Who else would know I was coming home early?"

"I saw an angel, too," she replied gleefully. "My angel was Jason Hackett. Showed up right in my kitchen, he did. I served him a ginger ale and he even complimented me on being a good hostess."

Brad raised an eyebrow. "Jason was here? What's going on, babe? It must be something big if we both had angels talking to us this morning. What did Jason have to say?"

"He told me you were on your way home, among other things, and that you had a visitor who would send you home. I had no idea your visitor was the captain. I'll bet you were glad to see him again, weren't you?"

"I sure was. I do miss him, you know. After spending ten years with him on the Caribbean island, he did get to be a habit."

"So tell me about his visit."

Brad smiled remembering. "I'd just stepped into my office to make a phone call when there he was. *'Would ye be lookin' at yerself, Bradley Douglas,'* he said. *'Shipshape as a four-mast cutter, says I. Aye, and the lovely lady Lori be good for ye in my estimation. Speakin' of which, I be here to send ye home to the lady. There be an item of importance the two of ye need to be lookin' into.'"*

Lori laughed at Brad's interpretation of the captain. Brad was good at any voice impression, but he was especially good at doing the captain.

"He was adamant about my getting home as soon as possible," Brad went on. "Said something about a manuscript that you'd have by the time I got here. I hope you know what he meant, because I certainly don't."

Lori held up the manuscript she had been reading. "Here," she said. "This is what he meant. Jason left it with me with instructions that the two of us should read it together." She handed the manuscript to him. "Look. It's called *An Angel in Time,* and it was written by Loraine Parker. She's the distant aunt I was named after, but you already know that. I've told you a dozen times or more."

Brad examined the papers. Being a motion picture director, he was used to handling all sorts of manuscripts. "Do you know what you have here?" he asked. "This is priceless. Look at the date on the title page. It was written in 1885. You say Jason gave this to you? Where did he get it?"

Lori reached out and lightly touched the manuscript. "All Jason said was it's been hidden from the eyes of the world ever since it was written, and he wants us to read it. He tells me we're going to find some very interesting things between its covers." Moving her hand to Brad's arm, she gave a gentle squeeze. "He hinted at something else, too. I'm not absolutely positive, but I suspect this manuscript has something to do with Howard Placard."

"Howard Placard?" Brad cut in. "This manuscript was written more than a century ago. How could it possibly have anything to do with Howard?"

"I don't know. I'm only repeating what Jason told me."

"Loraine Parker," Brad said, reading the name of the author again. "Hey, wait a minute!" he said, snapping his fingers. "You have a photograph someplace. You know, the one you tried to convince me was a picture of Loraine Parker."

"That's right!" Lori exclaimed. "I forgot about that." She stepped over to the bookcase on the far wall and pulled down an old photo album given to her by her father several years earlier. "Here it is," she said, thumbing through the pages until she spotted the picture of Loraine. She returned to Brad's side and held out the album for him to see.

Setting the manuscript down for a moment, Brad took the album and removed the picture to get a better look at it. "But this can't be a picture of Loraine Parker; this is a Polaroid photo. The first Polaroid camera wasn't invented until 1947, and it was well into the sixties before color came along."

"I have no idea of how this photo came to be, Brad. But my father assured me it is Loraine Parker, and he wouldn't lie, you know that. And, no, it's not a picture of me either. That is what you were going to hint at next, isn't it?"

"It does look like you, babe." Brad shrugged and his lips curled into a silly grin. "It was just a thought."

"Well, it wasn't a good thought. I've never worn a costume like the one she's wearing in my life."

"Hey, I'm not trying to dispute your word or your father's. If the two of you are convinced this is Loraine Parker, then it's Loraine Parker. I suppose it could be a Polaroid copy from an old print— although the quality is better than what I'd expect with that possibility." He considered it a moment longer. "Could be there's something in Loraine's manuscript to clear up the mystery. From what I've seen so far, the manuscript seems to be a story about her. A photograph was a big thing in her day, maybe just big enough that she would mention it."

"I only know one way to find out," Lori stated.

"It looks like this is what the captain sent me home for. What do you say we see what your Aunt Loraine has written here?"

"All right," Lori said, taking the manuscript from Brad. "We can take turns reading, and since she's my aunt, I'll lead off. Any objections, big guy?"

CHAPTER 5

When Howard stepped from the bathroom, he discovered his sister had been true to her word. The clothes were there on his bed, just as she had said they would be. He had to grin at what she had picked out for him. There was a light blue cotton shirt, a pair of denim trousers, a pair of western style brown leather boots, and a genuine black Stetson hat. In a way, these were the natural clothes Annette would pick for Howard, since they were things he would have worn when the two of them lived together on their father's Arizona ranch, before the tragic accident that took her life.

Howard put on his new clothes, and stepping to the mirror, he took a good look at himself. It was the first time in a year and a half he had seen himself clean shaven. It not only looked good, it felt good, too. He tried on the hat. What memories this brought back. Except for the length of his hair, and a look of maturity the years had added to his face, he reminded himself of the young man he had been before beginning his climb up the ladder of worldly success. Strangely, he found himself missing those days. Life had been so much simpler back then. Those were happy times, too. Not that he hadn't enjoyed the years since, because he had. But the later years were anything but simple. Life in the motion picture world was like a battlefield. Every day was a war. And Howard's pleasure came from winning the war one battle at a time. The more powerful he had become, the more weapons he had to wage his battles—and the more he was able to control his rivals.

In thinking about it now, he could see a definite dividing line between what could almost be described as two separate lives. Taking it one step further, it was as if there were two different Howards. There was the simple Howard, who in his youth had found joy and pleasure in the peaceful setting of his father's ranch. Then had come the more complex Howard, whose claim to happiness was his ruthless climb to the pinnacle of success.

Howard's thoughts were suddenly interrupted by a whiff of something more heavenly than he had smelled in a very long time. It smelled like—but no—that was impossible. It couldn't be. And yet . . . Howard left the bedroom and made a beeline for the kitchen. As he stepped into the room, he was amazed at what he saw. The table, which had been empty when he was in the kitchen a short time back, now held a scrumptious breakfast. He saw a plate of eggs, bacon, and hash browns with some toast and a small jar of what appeared to be grape jelly. And there was a large goblet of milk. All the things Howard used to love for breakfast when he was still on the ranch.

"Would you look at this?" he remarked out loud. "I not only get a hot shower and new clothes—I get a breakfast like this to top it off. I have no idea what that sister of mine is up to, but so far she gets my vote."

Howard wasted no time in taking advantage of this unexpected gift. And to his pleasure, it tasted every bit as good as it smelled.

The light of the morning sun was just penetrating through the kitchen window as Howard washed down the last piece of toast and jam with a swish of milk. Placing the glass back on the table, he wiped his mouth with his napkin. "Now that's what I'd call a meal," he said.

"I thought you'd appreciate it," came Annette's unexpected response. Howard glanced up to see that she had reappeared as suddenly as she had vanished earlier. "Little sister takes pretty good care of big brother, wouldn't you say, Peaches?"

"Annette! Can't we drop the Peaches thing? I'm not a kid anymore. I'm a highly respected motion picture producer." He chuckled lightly. "Or I was before your angel friends got a hold of me."

"Don't go blaming my friends for what happened to you, big brother. You brought it all down on your own head. And what's more, you deserved it."

Howard ignored her chastisement. "When did you learn to cook like this, Annette? Back on the ranch you couldn't make toast without burning it."

"Maybe I wasn't the best cook, but neither were you, Peaches," she defended herself. "And I was every bit as good a ranch hand as you . . . Maybe even better. Name one thing you could do that I couldn't do just as well."

"I didn't say anything about me being a better cook than you, Annette. I just asked where you learned to cook like this. Do they teach these things in angel school, or what?"

"Well, I didn't exactly cook it," she admitted. "I had a little help."

Howard's eyes lit up. "Jason Hackett cooked this breakfast, didn't he?"

Annette looked a little surprised. "How did you know?"

"The only other decent meal I've had since living on this island is one Jason cooked up for me as a favor to a lady who promised me a special meal earlier."

"Oh yes, you mean Jenice Anderson," Annette remarked.

Howard stroked his brow. "You know about Miss Anderson being here on the island?" he asked.

"I told you, big brother, I know everything about you. I've done my homework. And homework is easy with the records we have on my side of the line. Here, let me show you."

Annette pointed to one end of the room, and when Howard turned to look, he was astonished to see another one of her angel tricks, one that instantly caught Howard's interest. As a movie producer, he had seen state of the art technology in every aspect of the industry. But he had never seen anything to compare with this. Right there, in his kitchen, a highly technical motion picture screen had opened up. The quality of what he was seeing was unbelievable. Not only was it three-dimensional, it was so lifelike he felt he was actually a part of the picture.

"This is what we loosely refer to as a holographically enhanced playback," Annette explained. Howard's only answer came as a stunned nod. "Do you know what you're watching here, big brother?"

"Yeah," he answered, still mesmerized by what he was seeing. On the screen before him stood three people—a slightly younger version of himself and a man and woman who had come to his island some months earlier, trying to escape a gang of drug runners. "That's Roy Jenkins and Jenice Anderson," he said to Annette. "They're the ones I helped out by giving them that boat I found on the island a few days before they showed up."

"I know," Annette said, smiling.

Howard looked back at Annette. "I took the boat out a couple of times myself," he calmly admitted. "I could have escaped from the island in it." He paused for a breath. "I'm sure you know why I didn't make my escape, little sister."

"Sam would have sent you straight to prison," Annette said dryly.

Howard shrugged. "Like I said, this island is a whole lot better than prison. So I had no use for a boat." Although Howard remembered every detail of his visitors' brief, hurried visit to his island, his eyes turned toward the movie screen as if he'd never seen a movie before.

* * *

"How can we ever repay your kindness, Mr. Placard?" Jenice was asking as Roy pulled in the anchor.

"I'll tell you how," Howard answered. "When this is over, you can send me a care package. I haven't had a good meal in so long I've forgotten what it's like. Make it a Porterhouse or a New York cut. A big one. A baked potato, lots of butter and sour cream—throw in the makings for a fresh garden salad—and a coconut cream pie. That's the way you can repay me. Right about now I'd give everything I own in this world for a meal like that."

Jenice smiled and answered him, "I'll go you one better, Mr. Placard. When this is all over, I'll personally hunt out the best chef in these parts and send him here to fix the meal for you."

Howard smiled gratefully. "I'll be looking forward to it, Miss Anderson. And Godspeed to both of you."

Roy eased the throttle forward. The stern lowered into the water as the propeller caught hold. Slowly, the boat inched forward toward the open sea.

* * *

As the holograph faded away, Howard turned back to his sister. "They were good people," he said. "Do you happen to know if everything worked out for them?"

"Oh yes, it all worked out perfectly. The drug runners were apprehended, leaving Jenice and Roy to get on with their lives. And as you know, Jenice kept her word and sent Jason Hackett back with the meal she promised."

"Yes, she did," Howard affirmed. "And what a meal it was." He glanced back at the empty plate on the kitchen table. "And what a meal this one was. Thanks, sis. Even if you didn't cook it, I know it was you who managed to get it to me."

"You're welcome, Peaches. Now what do you say? Shall we get started on our little project?"

"What is this project you keep bringing up, Annette?"

"It's our project to straighten out your destiny, my dear brother."

"Straighten out my destiny? Why do I suspect that your motives in 'straightening out my destiny' have something to do with Lori Parker?"

Annette pointed a finger at Howard. "Her name isn't Lori Parker. Her name is Lori Douglas. You know, I'm really disgusted with the way you've been acting, Peaches my brother. Before I'm finished with you, you're going to be disgusted with yourself, too. Disgusted enough to apologize to both Lori and to Brad."

Howard stiffened. "I won't apologize because I'm not wrong about this. Lori Parker is the one for me, and I know I can make her love me if I'm only given the chance. That's where my destiny lies, little sister. With Lori Parker."

"No, Peaches, you're wrong. Your destiny lies with another lady. One you've yet to meet. But that's a little problem I'm about to rectify. If you're ready for the first step in our project, take my hand."

Howard glanced at Annette's outstretched hand. He had no idea what she had in mind, but angel or no angel, his little sister commanded his trust as no other ever could. Even when she disagreed with him over someone as important in his life as Lori Parker, he still trusted her. He took a breath and slowly placed his hand in hers.

No sooner did Howard's hand touch Annette's than the whole scene around them changed. Howard caught his breath as he realized they were no longer on the island. Even more amazing than finding himself in a new setting was what he found the new setting to be. The familiar smell of his mother's rose garden filled his nostrils as he looked again at the old backyard just as it had been when they were a family at home on the Arizona ranch. It took only seconds for him to realize this was another of his sister's holographs, like the one he'd just seen. And in the time it took him to realize this, he realized something else, too. Annette had not only brought him to the backyard of the old ranch, she had chosen a particular moment in time past to bring him here. He instantly recognized the young man in the holograph as himself, and the young woman as Annette. The younger Howard was picking peaches off a young peach tree and throwing them one at a time at the younger Annette, who was managing to dodge them all.

Still holding her hand, Howard turned to face Annette. "Is this your idea of working on my destiny?" he asked. "Bringing me here to watch this? You know, if there was one thing I ever did in my life that I'd like to forget, it's the peach tree incident."

Annette grinned. "Pay attention, Peaches," she said. "Here comes Mom out the back door with her mop. You're just darn lucky you were able to outrun her. I think she'd have killed you on the spot."

"If this is all you had in mind for your project, little sister, you can scoot me right back to the island. I don't find this the least bit amusing," Howard grumbled.

"All right," she laughed. "I'll change the scene. But I fail to see why you don't find this amusing. I find it hilariously funny myself."

The scene shifted, and Howard felt his pulse quicken at what he was witnessing this time. Both he and Annette were in this scene, too, but they were older now, somewhere around eighteen or nineteen, he would guess. Howard was riding the black stallion, and Annette was on the spotted mare as they raced for the cottonwood tree at the far end of the pasture.

"I can't believe this!" Howard shouted. "You have this race on one of your recordings. I hope you have a good angle on the finish line. That ought to prove once and for all it was me who won this race."

"I won this race and you know it, Peaches. I always beat you."

"In your dreams," Howard laughed, suddenly very much enjoying himself. "Can't you move us in closer to the finish line so we can get a good look at it?"

Annette's face grew solemn. "I could if I wanted to," she said, her voice lowering a level.

Howard turned to stare her straight in the face. "What do you mean you could if you wanted to?" he snapped. "This is my chance to prove I won the race."

"Or it could show that I won the race, big brother. But what would that prove, really?"

"It would prove I beat you, Annette!" His eyes widened. "Wait a minute! You've already seen the finish of this race, haven't you? That's why you don't want us to see it now! You don't want me to prove I beat you!"

She gave a slight smile. "You're wrong, Peaches. I haven't seen the end of the race, and I never want to. I'm pretty sure my horse was a nose ahead of yours at the finish, but it's not all that important to know for sure. You and I had a lot of wonderful times together, big brother. We built memories that will last us both forever. Why go spoiling a memory with a cold hard fact? You think you won the race; I think I won the race. Let's just leave it that way—what do you say?"

At first, Howard wanted to protest—but as he looked deeper into her eyes, he knew what she was saying was true. Half the fun of this memory was not knowing for sure. He looked back at the young riders rapidly approaching the cottonwood tree. "Shut it down, little sister," he said. "There's no sense embarrassing you by proving my point."

As he watched, the young riders both faded away into oblivion, but he and Annette still remained at the edge of the pasture. Howard glanced up at the midday sun in the overhead sky. Its warmth felt good against his skin. And the smell of the pasture teased his senses with tantalizing familiarity. "You and I had some great times in this pasture, didn't we, sis?" he reminisced.

"Yeah, we did," she quickly agreed. "My memories in this pasture are some of the best from my short stay in this world."

Howard looked at her again. "I missed you, you know. When you left me, it was like losing half of everything I was."

She nodded. "This might sound strange to you, big brother, but I missed you, too. Being on the far side of forever is a wonderful experience, but leaving you behind was one of the hardest things I ever had to do."

Howard swallowed away the lump that formed in his throat. "The plane crash," he said. "I imagined a thousand things about how you must have felt when it happened. "Was it . . . ?"

"Something mechanical went wrong with the plane. I never did learn what it was. I was never really interested in knowing. We knew we were going down, and those last seconds were pretty frightening. But they passed in a hurry. I died thinking of you, Peaches. The last thing I saw in my mind's eye was a picture of your face. You and I raced to a lot of finish lines in our time together. But at that instant I knew we wouldn't be together again until the last finish line was crossed."

Howard had to look away for a time. Over the years he had built up a defense against the pain that returned to fill his heart now. "The moment of impact was easy," he heard her say. "It happened so fast, there really wasn't any pain. All I knew was there was a bright light against the edge of the sky. And when I looked, Grandfather Placard was there waiting for me with outstretched arms and the warmest smile I've ever seen."

"Grandfather Placard came for you?" Howard asked, not looking back.

"Yes, he was there to escort Dad and me home. Chris Schroeder's sister was there for him."

Chris Schroeder had been the ranch foreman and had been in the plane with Annette and their father when it crashed. None of them survived.

"How's Dad?" Howard asked. "Or is that something you're not allowed to tell me?"

"Dad's fine. He misses Mom, but other than that he's happy as a lark. He's a first-level angel working in the Universal Guidance Training Department. Dad's responsible for training newly recruited guardian angels. Those angels have a three-week orientation before being assigned to a senior guardian angel, where they start their on-the-job training. Since guardian angels have such a heavy load and such immense responsibilities in the mortal world, it's imperative they receive adequate training before being sent out on their own."

"Then there really are guardian angels among us?" Howard observed. "I always wondered."

"There's an army of angels on the job all around you, Peaches. For the most part they remain unseen, but they're there, nevertheless. And Dad is one of their teachers."

"Dad would be good at that," Howard said.

"They gave Dad the choice of stepping up to a second-level angel, but he declined. He wanted to wait for Mom. Most people on our side make that choice, if there's someone they're waiting for."

Howard turned to face her again. "Since you're a second-level angel, I guess that means—"

"Now don't go getting the idea I don't have someone, because I do. I'm dying to tell you about him, but I want to hold out for the right moment. So, you'll just have to wait."

Howard's jaw dropped. "You've found someone over on your side? I hope you know how strange this all sounds to your mortal brother. I had no idea people could find someone anyplace but right here."

"You'd be surprised at the ways people meet each other, Peaches. There's no hard and fast rule about two people having to spend their time in mortality together before they can share a forever contract."

"Well, little sister, I hope you have better luck with the one you've found than I've had with the one I've found."

Annette shook her head. "You never give up, do you?"

"Don't know what the word 'quit' means when it's standing in the way of something I want," Howard huffed. "And you can bet those little pink booties they brought you home from the hospital in, Lori is the one for me."

"And you can bet your little blue booties I'll prove you wrong about that before my project's finished, Peaches." Without giving him the chance to respond, Annette pointed to the split-rail fence about fifty feet away at the edge of the pasture. "See those cans on the fence, Peaches?" she asked. "Remember when I used to outdraw you and clean the cans off the fence before you could get your gun out of the holster?"

"I swear," Howard shot back, "you do have a way of remembering things to suit yourself, don't you, sis? There wasn't one day of our lives I couldn't outdraw and outshoot you."

"Care to put your shooting finger where your mouth is?" she countered.

He laughed. "I'd be glad to, little sister. But in case you haven't noticed, neither of us brought a gun along."

Annette returned his laugh. "You keep forgetting, Peaches, you're dealing with a second-level angel now. You want guns, I can fix that."

She snapped her fingers, and Howard was shocked to find a holster around his waist. Glancing down, he discovered his old target revolver seated in the holster. He looked at Annette. She was wearing her revolver, too.

Howard shook his head slowly. "I'm telling you, sis. Seeing you again is the greatest thing that's ever happened to me. But dealing with the idea of you being an angel—that takes some getting used to," he admitted.

She reached down and picked up a stick. "Just like always," she said. "I give this stick a toss, and we draw when it hits the ground."

"Ha!" Howard grunted. "Do you think I'm crazy? This can't be a fair contest. How am I supposed to keep up with your angel antics?"

"I won't use my angel antics, as you call them, Peaches. It's you against me. Just like old times."

Howard pulled the revolver from his holster and spun the cylinder. Then, holding it in his open hand, he checked the balance. "Do I have your word on it?" he asked.

"No angel antics," she responded.

Howard shoved the revolver back in the holster and looked over at her. "Throw the stick," he said.

She smiled and gave it a hefty toss. About ten feet up, the stick arched and began its descent toward the ground. No sooner had it touched, than both revolvers had cleared leather and were blazing away at the six cans on the fence. In less than a second, all six cans were sent flying, and both revolvers were back in the holster. Howard and Annette looked at each other for one quiet moment, then Howard thrust his fist high into the air. "Yaa-hoooo!" he screamed. "That was more fun than I've had in I can't remember how long. Just like always, I got three cans and you got two, little sister."

"I think if you'll check the center can, Peaches, you'll find it was hit twice. Just like always."

He grinned. "All right, little sister. Let's check the can." Together they walked through the gate and over to where the center can had ended up. Howard picked it up. "Two holes," he laughingly admitted.

"Just like always," she said again.

"Just like always," he agreed. "You're the only one I could never beat, little sister." His smile faded. "After you were gone, it wasn't much fun anymore. I still belong to a shooters' club—or did before I was banned to the island—but the sport wasn't much fun without you."

"You did good, though. To this day, no one's ever beaten you. I know, I've been watching."

Howard reached for the revolver again, only to discover it was gone. "Sorry," Annette said, noticing. "The guns were just part of the holograph. Since we won't be needing them anymore, I disposed of them."

"Yeah, that's what I figured. I guess this whole time we're spending together is just a holograph that will have to come to an abrupt end, right?"

"That's pretty much how it has to be, big brother. Nothing in this world lasts forever."

Howard looked at the can he was still holding. He ran a finger over the smooth side of one bullet hole. "Well, anyway, thanks for working it so we could have one last contest together. It was a kick, sis." He glanced up. "And thanks for what time we do have. That's a kick, too."

Annette reached out and took the can from him. "I'd dearly love to stay here in this pasture playing memory games with you—" she gave the can a toss, "—but we have a project waiting. It's time to move on."

Howard sighed and took one last look around at the pasture. "All right," he reluctantly conceded. "Where to from here?"

CHAPTER 6

Lori and Brad sat down on the sofa, where Lori began reading aloud from the old manuscript. As she read, the words seemed to come to life. They nearly leaped from the pages, playing out a series of vivid scenes as the story unfolded. It was almost like watching a movie with the screen inside their mind's eye.

* * *

Loraine Parker glanced through the stagecoach window at the desolate desert scene stretching out as far as the eye could see. She hated every inch of it. Having grown up in the magnificent city of Boston, she was used to a much different setting—the feel and smell of the ocean breeze, the majestic sight of white sails atop merchant ships continually moving in and out of the scenic bay, shops lining both sides of quaint little streets with wares of every sort imaginable on display. To Loraine's way of thinking, the worst day Boston ever offered up was heaven compared to this loathsome Arizona desert. At least in Boston, all the conveniences available in 1885 were at one's fingertips. Here, on the desert, who would ever know it wasn't still 1865—or even earlier?

The heavy sound of horses' hooves digging into the dry buggy trail pounded her ears like drums from some Indian war ritual. Dust from the surface of the road floated upward into the open compartment, making breathing difficult at best. Having poured a small amount of water onto her kerchief, she used it to cover her nose and mouth in an effort to filter out at least some of the choking dust. Turning her attention to the only other passenger in the stagecoach, she discovered her brother, Amos, was fast asleep. She envied him. Sleeping on a bouncing stagecoach was something that would come naturally to a fourteen-year-old boy. A smile crossed Loraine's lips as she looked at Amos' face. Amos was her only brother. She had no sisters. She had been eleven when Amos was born and had been his number one defender from all ills and provocations since that day. Oh, it was all right for her to pick on him, but no one else had better try it!

With their mother, Anelladee, sick so much of the time, Amos had come to think of Loraine more as a second mother than as a sister. But that was okay, Loraine didn't mind. Nor did she mind being asked to remain behind in Boston to look after young Amos while her parents made the dreaded but necessary trip to the city of Mesa, way out west in the Arizona Territory. That was nearly six months ago.

James Parker would never have traded Boston for the Arizona Territory if it hadn't been for his wife's failing health. For years Anelladee had suffered from consumption, and the foggy air of Boston had taken its toll. With each passing year she had grown a little worse. At last the time came when the doctors declared she would need to either move to a drier climate or give up all hope of living long enough to see her grandchildren.

Fortunately, James had long ago made his fortune as a tradesman, a fortune of sufficient means to maintain his family quite comfortably without working another day of his life. And so, when given the ultimatum by Anelladee's doctors, his choice was a simple one. He would find a suitable climate, and he would take her there. After an extensive study of several possible locations, James reluctantly settled on the city of Mesa, which was more than a little frightening since the Arizona Territory was outside the boundaries of the United States. Everyone figured it would become a state someday, but no one knew when that might be. Under the circumstances, both James and Anelladee felt it would be better to leave Amos behind with Loraine until it was determined whether or not the move would be permanent.

The drier air of the Arizona Territory had brought an instant and remarkable change to Anelladee. She found herself breathing better than she had since she was a small child. The color returning to her cheeks was equally matched by the cheeriness returning to her smile, and the vigor returning to her step. Without question, the move proved to be a good one. And so, Loraine and Amos were summoned to join them in their new home.

Loraine drew a breath through her moistened kerchief and looked again at the passing desert. How brown everything looked. She hated it. At least, it was October now and the blistering heat of summer had subsided into the somewhat milder days of early autumn. Granted, it was still hot by Boston's standards, but at least it was a dry heat, and for this, she was very grateful. The trip from Boston had been long and draining, but if all went well they should be in Mesa by nightfall. The first thing she wanted was a real bath, followed by a pleasant night's sleep in a real bed. After that, there would be plenty of time to become acquainted with her new home.

Suddenly, her thoughts were interrupted by what sounded like gunshots. A quick glance across at Amos found him wide awake. "Did you hear that, Amos?" she asked.

"I heard it," he exclaimed. "It sounded like gunshots. You don't suppose the stage is being held up, do you, sis?"

"Of course the stage isn't being held up," Loraine laughed nervously, wishing she could be as convincing to herself as she was trying to be with Amos. But the loud cry of "Heee-yah!" from the driver and the feel of the stagecoach lurching forward at greater speed made her doubt her words.

"Look!" Amos shouted, pointing out the stagecoach window, a frightened look crossing his face. "The stage *is* being held up. Here come the outlaws now!"

From where he was seated, Amos could see out the back of the stagecoach but Loraine had to twist around to see where her brother was pointing. "Oh my," she gasped at the sight of two men on horseback in hot pursuit of the stagecoach. "It looks like you may be right, Amos." Why hadn't she carried her revolver in her handbag, she asked herself now, instead of packing it away in one of the suitcases? Having access to her revolver now would make her feel much more at ease. "Quick, Amos!" she shouted. "Get to the floor!" With this, she reached across and shoved the boy to the floorboards of the coach. Then she leaned over him, crouching as low as she could herself.

* * *

"This is incredible," Lori exclaimed. "I've heard this story dozens of times, both from my father and my grandfather before him. But hearing Loraine's words firsthand is a new experience. It's like hearing the story for the first time."

"Here," Brad said, taking the manuscript from her. "Let me read a while."

CHAPTER 7

Howard stared at the holographical scene of himself dancing cheek to cheek with a lovely young woman. He recognized the occasion as the senior prom at his old high school. The young woman was Christina Wilson. "Why have you brought me here, Annette?" he asked. "I haven't thought about Christina Wilson in years."

"She was a beautiful young woman, Peaches. You really never gave her the credit she deserved."

"Yes, she was a beautiful young woman," Howard agreed "I can't deny that." Seeing Christina again triggered many old memories for Howard.

* * *

Howard and his sister had been the youngest of four children in the Placard family; the other two children were their older brothers, Charles and Osborne. Their father, Ryan Placard, met their mother, Patricia Simmons, while both young people were attending Harvard, their sights set on law degrees. They fell in love and were married within a month of the day they met. It was shortly after that when tragedy struck the Placard family. Ryan's father, Gregory Placard, took pneumonia and died. Ryan was called home to Arizona to take over the ranch. While this had never been his intended career, it just worked out that way.

Although the ranch left the Placards modestly wealthy, Patricia hated the life it offered her. As the twins approached young adulthood, Patricia carefully laid out plans for their future, plans very similar to those previously made for their older brothers. As a loving mother, she simply wanted something better for her children than the life she had so hated—the life of a rancher.

She wanted all four of her children to attend Harvard, as she and Ryan had done before them. And in what she felt was the duty of a loving mother, Patricia set out to find the perfect mates for each of her children. For Howard, that meant the prominent Miss Christina Wilson, daughter of newspaper tycoon Lloyd Wilson. The same Christina Wilson at whom Howard was gazing now, thanks to his sister's holographs.

* * *

"I do agree, she's beautiful," Howard said again. "But I didn't love her, you know."

"I know," Annette smiled. "Any more than I loved Roger Zimmerman, the fellow Mom had picked out for me. But not loving them didn't matter much back then, did it?"

"Not with our mother," Howard laughed. "I never saw a more strong-willed person in my life than Mom. I always thought I was more like Dad, but I guess in the end I turned out to be more like her. She ruled our family with an iron fist; I later ruled my empire the same way." Howard paused in thought for a moment, then added, "If you had lived, little sister, I probably would have married Christina, and you probably would have married Roger."

Annette walked around until she stood directly in front of Howard. She reached out and smoothed his shirt collar. "You're right, Howard. That's exactly how it would have turned out." Laying a hand on Howard's arm, she asked a question that struck him rather strangely. "Have Sam or Jason ever mentioned the higher authorities to you?"

He nodded yes. "I get the idea that the higher authorities are the ones in charge on your side of the line, is that how it goes?"

"That's right," Annette nodded. "The higher authorities are in charge of everything. There's nothing they're not aware of and no problem they haven't provided a possible solution for. They don't take away our agency, but they do provide situations that open doors into our prospective destinies. It's up to us to walk through the door before us or turn our back on it. They won't make that choice for us. They only provide the door."

"I can see this is leading up to a lecture of some sort," Howard said. "I know you well enough to be sure of that."

Stepping back, Annette glared at him. "Not a lecture, Peaches. I'm trying to teach you something here. Now are you going to keep interrupting, or will you be still and listen?"

"You have my complete attention," Howard promised. "Hit me with your best shot."

"The key word is *destiny,*" she explained. "And the bottom line is this: Christina Wilson was never a part of your destiny. And just in case you can't guess, Roger Zimmerman was never a part of my destiny. To the contrary, my dear brother, you are destined to share a forever contract with a very special lady, just as I'm contracted to a very special man. I've already met my guy, and you'll be meeting your lady very shortly now. And before you say it—no, your lady is not Lori Douglas. Lori belongs with Brad, pure and simple."

Howard stiffened and a jolt of anger rippled through him like an electric shock, but he forced himself to hold his tongue. However, her next words shocked him so completely, all thoughts of Lori Parker fled his mind. "That's why I was allowed to be taken in the plane crash, big brother. By crossing the line, I was spared being pressured into marrying Roger Zimmerman. And you were spared the same fate with Christina Wilson."

"What?" Howard's face went hot. "Are you telling me your higher authorities took your life to prevent us from marrying the wrong people?"

"I'm not saying they took my life," Annette clarified. "They simply chose not to prevent the plane from crashing when it developed a problem. If they had chosen to step in, I could have lived many more years. But they knew that if I were taken in the crash—it would help straighten out the mistake that had been made in our destinies."

Hearing her words, Howard couldn't remember ever being more confused than now. "I don't understand," he responded. "How did your higher authorities figure that your dying in the crash would keep me from marrying Christina Wilson?"

"I told you, the higher authorities know everything. They knew about the mistake that would be made in our destinies before we were born, and they knew how you would react to my death. They knew it before either of us was born. So, they chose not to spare my life when the time came. The plan was put in motion long before we drew our first mortal breaths. Think about it, Peaches. What did you do when I was no longer there to keep you in line?"

Howard considered it. Annette was right. Nothing had ever happened to him that could compare to losing his sister. Losing his father was bad enough, but Annette had been part of him. When she was taken, it had felt to Howard as if he were being split down the middle and one half was being taken away. As he saw her placed in that cold hard ground, part of him was buried with her.

Howard had never really wanted to go to Harvard in the first place; he was only going to satisfy his mother. Howard's real love was the land and the animals. He often felt as if destiny had made a mistake by sending him to this life a century too late. The ranch would have been his personal choice for a career. But with Annette gone, even the ranch took on an emptiness that couldn't be filled. When his mother decided to put the ranch up for sale, he didn't have the heart to protest. Nor did Charles nor Osborne have any desire to save the ranch. They had followed their mother's wishes to the letter and were partners in a law firm that she had personally financed. The two older sons had also married according to their mother's wishes.

Although Patricia Placard had loved her husband deeply, the ranch meant nothing to her now, which was why she decided to sell it. It was less than a month after the funeral when she found the right buyer. The same day the papers were signed, she approached Howard about his enrolling at Harvard. No one was more surprised than Howard himself at the way he had handled this unpleasant situation.

"No, Mother," he said bluntly. "I won't be going to Harvard." Howard would never forget the look in her eyes at his words. Looking back now, Howard knew he couldn't have handled it any other way. When Annette died, a huge part of Howard's world had died with her. He had never embraced the thought of attending Harvard, but he had resigned himself to the idea. It could have been bearable as long as Annette was there with him. But thoughts of going to

Harvard without her were anything but bearable.

When Howard opposed his mother that day, it was a first. Never before had he challenged her slightest wish. This incident marked the birth of a new Howard. Once he learned he could stand on his own feet, he never stepped backward again. If refusing to attend Harvard wasn't enough to send Patricia Placard into shock, his refusal to marry Christina Wilson provided the final push. "You have to marry Christina Wilson," she argued. "If you let that young lady slip through your fingers, you'll ruin two lives. Yours and hers."

"I'm sorry, Mother," Howard had told her. "I can't face Christina Wilson, or anything else I had planned for my future. I've got to find a new life for myself. A life that will take me away from everything that might have been if Annette had lived."

As these thoughts passed through Howard's mind, he looked again at the holograph of his senior prom. He and Christina had now moved to the punch bowl and were talking to some of their friends. "You're telling me the higher authorities knew I'd stand up to Mom with you out of the picture?" he asked Annette.

"They knew exactly what you'd do. They even knew you'd choose a career in the motion picture industry."

Howard considered this. He wondered if Annette's higher authorities hadn't begun inspiring him in this direction all the way back in his high school years. It was there that he had first begun dabbling in filmmaking. Even then, Howard had shown promise in this direction, and one of his teachers, Mr. Carson Finch, picked up on it. Carson was an English teacher who took his job quite seriously. Time and again, Carson went the extra mile in helping one of his students, if he deemed the student worthy of his help.

Howard was just one such student. Carson Finch recognized Howard's ability at filmmaking, and took the necessary steps to provide Howard with an opportunity to use his talents. Howard's first project was filming a school play presented by the drama class. That went so well, he quickly got the chance for a follow-up project. This time, he did a documentary for the American History class. From that point on, requests for his services never let up until after graduation. And by graduation, Howard had amassed a very impressive resume.

After Annette's death, Howard made the decision that this was what he wanted to do for his life's work. It took some effort to convince his mother, but at last she gave in. Her own father had some connections in the motion picture industry through the bank he ran, so she went to him for help. The door was opened, and Howard stepped into the glamorous world of lights, cameras, and bronze statuettes.

He buried himself in his work with a passion, and it soon became evident that Howard had a certain knack for picking winners at the box office. His reputation skyrocketed, as did his enterprise. A few short years into his profession, he had already amassed a greater fortune than his father had in a lifetime on the ranch. Howard also gained a reputation as an industry shark. No one dared to cross him. He reveled in this feeling of power and vowed never to bend his will to another again as he had done with his mother in his younger years.

Howard was so lost in his memories that he hardly noticed when Annette reached out and took hold of his hand. "This may come as a surprise to you, Peaches. But the higher authorities not only knew you'd become a movie producer, they actually helped you succeed in your career."

This statement immediately pulled Howard back to the present. "What?" he asked, irritated and shocked at the suggestion. Never had he considered that there was any other reason for his success than his own drive and ability.

"Peaches," Annette explained, "every person who ever lives is unique, and because of this, the higher authorities plan a set of unique circumstances to accommodate every individual. You need one set of experience and learning opportunities while I need another. Since the higher authorities know in advance what each of us needs, they devise a road map just to fit those needs. In your case, you needed to be placed in a position of power to test how you would handle that power. The higher authorities wanted to prove what you're made of. One way or the other."

What his sister was saying went against everything Howard had ever believed about himself. Without question, he had enjoyed his feeling of power. And he had enjoyed the act of being in control at all times. Now, his sister was telling him he never really was in control.

According to her story, it was these higher authorities who were in control. If this was true, it was a humbling revelation, to say the least. "And taking my power away?" he asked, soberly. "Was this part of the plan to test what I was made of?"

"Yes, Peaches, it was."

"Okay, I give up. Did I pass the test? Was I made of the right stuff?"

"I don't know yet. You're right in the middle of your final exam. That's why I'm here. So get ready, Peaches. It's time for our next stop along the journey. And this one could be a little tough to handle."

"Hold on a sec," Howard said, raising his hands. "Can we slow things down just a little? I know this time we're sharing together has to be limited, and I want it to last as long as possible. It's obvious that you know all about me. Can we talk about you for a while?"

"Sure," Annette agreed easily, "but there are some things I can't tell you because I'm bound by certain rules. So if you ask the wrong question, I won't be able to answer."

Howard nodded. "You mentioned working in a records department your first years on the other side. I assume you have other duties now. Are you a guardian angel?"

"No," Annette shook her head. "I'm not a guardian angel. Guardian angels are first-level angels. I have a great job. I work in the Family Origin Department, and I match angels who are on their way to their mortal life with the family they'll report to down here. I tell you, it's a blast. And while we're on the subject, I learned something very interesting about you and me, brother dear. When it came our turn to be born, I was scheduled to make my appearance three minutes before you. But it seems like you put one over on me. You went to my counterpart in the job back then, and you talked him into sending you down before me! In the original plan, I was to have been your BIG sister."

Howard started to laugh. "No kidding? I did that to you before we were even born?"

"Sort of makes up for the peach tree incident, doesn't it?" she said, not even trying to hide her sarcasm.

For the first time, Howard didn't even flinch at the reminder of that day. "All right, little sister! You've made my day! I was getting the best of you before I even knew I was doing it. Hot dog! This is great!"

Annette let him have his laugh, then she said sharply, "That's it. No more questions about me. Hold onto your hat, Peaches. Here we go!"

It didn't take Howard long to realize where Annette had taken him this time. They were back on the ranch, on a particular day that was etched so deeply into Howard's memory that he knew he could never forget it. It was the day he first saw Lori Parker.

* * *

Lori had come to the ranch with a group of high school girls on an extended field trip. Howard's father provided the horses, and Chris Schroeder, the ranch foreman, was their guide. After one look at Lori Parker, Howard had quickly volunteered his assistance on the excursion. The group had spent the afternoon on horseback touring the foothills behind the ranch, and Howard had been unable to keep his eyes off Lori that whole day.

He stared at the holograph, then turned to Annette. "Why did you bring me here? What's it supposed to prove?"

"It's all part of your final exam, Peaches," she explained. "The higher authorities want you to have the events of this day fresh in your mind before we move on."

Howard's face was pained as he watched the scene play out. "I fell in love with her right there on the spot. If only I'd had the courage to stand up for what I really wanted that day . . . Instead, I bent like a twig in the wind to our mother's will, and Lori slipped through my fingers. The next time our paths crossed, she was married to Mr. Brad Douglas. Do you know what I'd give for the chance to relive that day, Annette? Everything I own. If I'd only followed my heart instead of my head, I could have won Lori's heart, and Brad would have been the third man out." Howard gave a dejected laugh. "Who knows? Maybe Brad would have married Christina Wilson."

Turning his back on the holograph, he shook his head remorsefully. "But I didn't follow my heart. And I've been the third man out ever since. I suppose you're going to tell me your higher authorities knew I'd make that mistake . . . Am I right?"

"The higher authorities knew what you'd do, Peaches. But that doesn't make what you did a mistake. I take it you've seen enough of this segment. Shall we move on?"

"I have," Howard agreed. "Memories of this day are too painful to dredge up any further."

"I doubt the next scene will be any too thrilling either," she warned him. "But the higher authorities want you to see it."

Howard cringed as he anticipated her meaning. The holograph changed and his worse fears were confirmed. She had brought him to a day a few years down the road from the one he just witnessed. What he was looking at now was the day his and Lori's paths crossed for the second time. It was on a sound stage at the motion picture studio, where Howard was overseeing the final few scenes of a movie he was producing. "That's you over there," Annette said, pointing to the figure of a man standing just offstage.

Howard watched the younger version of himself and nodded. "Yes, that's me. I had a habit of dropping in unannounced on my filming crews. Kept them on their toes, never knowing when I might show up."

"The Howard we're looking at here is much different from the young Howard we just saw back on the ranch, wouldn't you say, Peaches?"

"You got that right. I may have been a twig in the wind as a kid, but I was a man in control by the time this day rolled around."

"And after all these years you'd never forgotten the face of the young girl you saw back on the ranch, had you?"

"I never thought I'd see her again," Howard admitted. "And suddenly, here she was. Right in the middle of my own sound stage. I couldn't believe my good fortune. And you can bet, it didn't take long to realize I'd been given a second chance. There was no way she going to slip through my fingers again. I walked right up and introduced myself as the man in charge of filming the picture." He sighed. "I guess I thought that would blow her off her feet."

"Uh huh," Annette said as she watched it all take place in the holograph. "But the wind left your sails when she introduced herself as Mrs. Brad Douglas."

Howard scowled. "I couldn't believe it. Brad Douglas was one of the best directors I'd ever hired. And here I learn he was married to the woman I'd dreamed of every night for who knows how many years. How could fate have been so cruel?"

Annette gave him a long, steady look. "Did you ever think what course your life might have taken if you had accepted the fact that she belonged with another man right then and there?"

"I tried to put aside my feelings for Lori," he said, "but I couldn't get her out of my mind. I felt drawn to her, like a nail to a magnet. And yes, I did feel powerful enough to take her away from Brad. All I needed was the chance to show her what kind of a man I was. And what kind of life I could offer her."

"Brad Douglas was just one of your employees, and you were a powerful man in the industry. Brad had something you wanted, and you were powerful enough to take what you wanted from him. So you hit on the plan to send Brad to Acapulco, Mexico, on the pretext that he was the only one you trusted to do a film there," Annette said with a tone of wonder in her voice, as if she could hardly believe her brother was capable of such a scheme.

Howard flushed miserably. "I was obsessed with winning her affection—regardless of the fact that she was the wife of my director." He couldn't believe how uncomfortable he was discussing this subject with his sister. He had made a choice, and over the years he had managed to justify that choice in his own mind. But with the realization that Annette had observed the whole thing came a pain that stung like the bite of a sidewinder. There was no use denying any of it or trying to hide the smallest part of his actions. Annette knew it all. She had seen it in these blasted holographs.

"I, uh, did send Brad away to Acapulco," Howard reluctantly admitted. "On the day his flight left, I went to the airport and faked a chance meeting with Lori. I invited her to lunch, and that opened the door for me to make my move. Brad was gone for the next three months, and I took advantage of every minute of his absence." He shrugged. "The rest is history. I never did win Lori away from Brad, even though Brad saw us together and left for nearly ten years." He gave a humorless chuckle. "I had no idea at the time, but those ten years were spent on the very island I've been banned to now. Sam called it 'retribution.'"

"And you should have learned your lesson by now," Annette scolded him. "But you still have this thing about going after Lori again—if and when you ever leave the island."

Howard narrowed his eyes as he looked at his sister. "Oh, I will go after her again, make no mistake." Howard's lip curled into a bitter sneer. "Brad Douglas doesn't deserve a woman like Lori. I'm the man for Lori. Always have been. Always will be."

"No, Howard," Annette said firmly. "You're *not* the man for Lori. And Lori's not the woman for you. But—there is a reason why you *think* she's the right one for you. And when I show you that reason, it's going to knock your socks off."

Howard hardly seemed to hear her as he looked at the scene still before him. "Oh, I've made my share of mistakes over the years," he muttered. "That's the only reason she's still with Brad now. And you can bet—"

Annette cut him off. "What's done is done, Peaches," she said. "It's time to look forward, not backward." She paused a moment, thinking about what she had just said. "On the other hand, I could be wrong," she corrected herself. "Maybe this is the time to look backward." Reaching into her pocket, she removed a small, round metal object and held it up so Howard could see it. "Take a look at this, Peaches. Tell me if you recognize it."

At first, Howard looked nonchalantly at the object, but no sooner had he recognized what it was than his interest perked up. In her hand was a medallion, and if it wasn't the same medallion he had carried in his pocket for more than ten years, it was strikingly similar to it. "Where'd you get that?" he asked, suddenly excited.

Annette smiled mysteriously. "Where I got it is of little importance. The question is, have you seen it before?"

Howard took the medallion from her and looked it over closely. "I—I'm not sure," he responded. "I've seen one like it, only . . ." He studied it a moment longer, then raised his eyes to meet hers. "With everything else you know about me, I'm sure you know about the medallion, too."

"You're catching on, Peaches," Annette chuckled. "And you're right, I do know about the medallion—although the one you're looking at now has a major difference from the one you had before, doesn't it?" She paused for dramatic effect before continuing, "Specifically, the bullet mark is missing from this one."

Howard's forehead wrinkled in confusion. "I don't get it, sis. If this is the same medallion, what happened to the marks on it?"

Annette grinned. "Sort of blows your mind, eh, Peaches? You should know by now what to expect from a second-level angel. This is the same medallion you carried around all those years—with one exception. I'm handing you the medallion in perfect condition. It hasn't stopped the bullet yet."

"What?" Howard looked dumbfounded. "The medallion I used to have stopped a bullet a long time ago. This can't possibly be the same medallion—unless you've used your angel antics to modify it," he added suspiciously.

Annette took the medallion from him and shoved it into his shirt pocket. "Don't worry about the medallion now," she said. "You'll understand it all a little later on. Right now we're going to make a trip to the airport."

The holograph changed again, leaving Howard very nervous about what he was watching with his sister. After Brad Douglas had boarded his flight bound for Acapulco, Mexico, Howard had shown up on the pretext of seeing Brad off—having made certain that Brad was safely on the plane before he arrived. Striking up a conversation with Lori, he soon had her convinced to join him for lunch. Since she didn't want to leave her car at the airport, they took her car.

The scene in the holograph now showed them walking through the parking lot. "Just relax and watch this part of the show, Peaches," Annette directed him. "This is where Lori tells you about the medallion."

Watching and waiting for the scene to unfold before him, Howard drew a deep breath. What memories this scene stirred in his mind, bittersweet memories of the time he had almost stolen Lori away from Brad.

* * *

"This is Brad's car?" Howard asked Lori as they approached a two-tone brown Pontiac Grand Prix. "I'm surprised. Most film directors drive something a little wilder. I somehow pictured Brad in a racy sports car."

Lori laughed. "Like a candy-apple red Porsche 911," she asked.

"Yeah, a Porsche—or something of that nature. Certainly not an old man's car like this Pontiac."

Lori sighed. *"Believe me, Mr. Placard. I've tried to talk Brad into buying a Porsche. Oh how I've tried, but you have to understand the way Brad thinks. To him, everything has to be practical. That's the biggest rule in his life: if it's not practical, we don't do it."*

Lori stepped to the passenger side door and took her keys from her purse with the intention of unlocking the door. To her surprise, Howard reached out and took the keys from her. "Here," he said. "Let me do that. Where I come from, it's the man's place to open doors for the lady, not the other way around."

Lori stood out of the way while Howard opened the door and motioned her inside. "You might as well let me drive while we're at it," he smiled. "I know where we're going, and it would be easier for me to drive than try to give you instructions." With a shrug, Lori slid into the passenger seat. Howard closed the door, then rounded the car to the driver's side.

As he settled himself in his seat, he looked at the key ring she had handed him. A curious medallion was fastened to the ring; it was about an inch and a half in diameter and engraved with what appeared to be a family crest of some sort. In the middle of the medallion was a large dent. "This is an interesting charm," he observed. "It almost looks as if it stopped a bullet at some time. Is there a story behind it?"

Lori glanced at the medallion. "Yes," she responded with a soft smile. "It does have a story behind it. My father gave it to me, and it was passed down from generation to generation. It belonged to my great-grandfather, Amos William Parker. Amos was only fourteen years old when he and his older sister were victims of a stage holdup. They probably would have been killed if it hadn't been for a mysterious stranger who happened along just then."

"A mysterious stranger who happened onto a stage holdup?" Howard remarked with keen interest. "I'd like to hear the whole story sometime. Being a motion picture producer, I'm always on the lookout for an interesting story. So how did this stranger save their lives?"

Lori shook her head. "I'm sort of sketchy on all the details, Mr. Placard. But apparently one of the stage robbers shot at the stranger. The medallion you're looking at stopped the bullet and saved his life. He was able to apprehend the robbers, and later gave the medallion to my great-grandfather. That's about all I know."

"That's quite a story," Howard said as he slid the key into the ignition and started the engine. *"Now, how about if we drop the Mr. Placard thing? I keep thinking you're talking to my father. Call me Howard, please."*

* * *

"You were a real jerk, you know that, Peaches," Annette remarked, pulling Howard's attention away from the holograph. "A real jerk! I'm ashamed to call the Howard in this holograph my brother. If I'd been around when you were pulling this little stunt, you can bet I'd have been in the middle of your case faster than an angry bee after a honey thief."

Howard was too embarrassed to answer. All he could do was listen as she expounded on what they had seen in the holograph. "When you got home that night, Peaches, you discovered the medallion had come loose from Lori's key ring and had remained in your pocket. It wasn't that you didn't intend to give it back to her at the time, but when she never mentioned it—you just let the subject slip."

"For crying out loud," Howard complained. "Is there anything about me you don't know? I swear, if my life was a meal, you'd have it scrutinized right down to the last crumb. I feel like a kid caught on surveillance tape in the act of stealing watermelons, only to have the tape broadcast on the five o'clock news."

"Good analogy," Annette answered with a shrug. "Except in your case it wasn't watermelons; it was another man's wife."

Howard shifted his weight nervously from one leg to the other. He let Annette's cutting remark pass unchallenged this time. "The medallion was something to remind me of her," he said quietly. "I just hung onto it."

"For more than ten years?! You didn't give it back until that day on your yacht, the day Lori finally broke free from you, when the medallion accidently fell from your pocket. And that was only because Lori noticed it and took it back from you. You do remember that day, don't you, Peaches? The day Sam condemned you to the island?"

"It was the worst day of my life," Howard grumbled. "And don't you dare do a holograph of that nightmare. That's a day I'd just as soon forget."

"I won't put you through the pain of seeing it again, Peaches. But I just wanted to remind you it was the day when Lori got the medallion back from you. It's important for you to remember that for when you get a little further along in our project. And by the way, it's just about time I toss you right in middle of the action. There's only one thing left to do first. And that's get you a haircut. You look terrible. I won't have the lady you're about to meet seeing you like this. We'll make a stop by the celestial beauty salon where I have my hair done. My friend Sally works there. She's just the one to give you the perfect cut. Come on, Peaches. Let's go."

CHAPTER 8

Brad opened the manuscript and let his eyes run down the page until he found the spot where Lori had left off reading. "It's evident this book is authentic, babe," he said. "Loraine's writing style and phrasing are consistent with the time period. This is probably the most valuable manuscript I've ever had the privilege of reading."

"You really think so?" Lori asked.

"Yeah, I do. Looking ahead a few lines I see Loraine's about to introduce us to the stage driver. Hmmm, and it looks like there really were robbers . . ."

"So don't leave me hanging. Just read it, okay?"

After a playful glance at his wife, Brad obliged. And just as he had supposed, the story did begin to pick up pace.

* * *

Jeremiah Samuels glanced over his shoulder at the two horsemen half hidden behind the dust cloud kicked up from the speeding stagecoach. Anger boiled in his veins as he contemplated what was happening here. In the ten years Jeremiah had been driving for this stage line, he had never been robbed. No—not even once. Not that there hadn't been robbery attempts, because there had. Four of them, as a matter of fact. But in all four cases, he, Jeremiah Samuels, had managed to foil the attempts.

What rotten luck that Benson had been sick and unable to accompany Jeremiah on this run. Benson had been Jeremiah's shotgun on nearly every run for the past six years. Jeremiah trusted Benson, who had proved his worth on more than one occasion. But none of that mattered now. Jeremiah was alone on this run, and without Benson's shotgun at his side, there wouldn't be much hope of outrunning this pair of cutthroats. With a snap of his wrists, Jeremiah cracked the reins hard over the backs of the team. "Heee-yah!" his voice boomed, as he cracked the reins again. With an abrupt lurch, the stagecoach shot forward at greater speed.

Jeremiah glanced at the saddlebags on the seat next to him. He knew that was what the culprits were after. They contained the payroll for a construction company engaged in building irrigation canals along the borders of the Salt River. The money was destined for a Mesa bank. Jeremiah wasn't sure exactly how much money was in the saddlebags, but he was sure it was a substantial amount. Common sense told him there was no way he could outrun these men, and he knew there would be no way he could protect the saddlebags once they caught up with the stage. He made a quick decision.

Glancing over his shoulder again, he satisfied himself there was sufficient dust between the stage and the pursuing riders to block their view of his intended action. Turning his attention to the trail in front of him, he spotted a large clump of rocks off to the side. Grabbing the saddlebags, he hurled them as far into the clump of rocks as his arm would allow. A slight smile of satisfaction crossed his lips as he watched the saddlebags vanish from sight. Again, he cracked the reins. "ROLL-'EM-OUT!" he barked to the horses. "Let's get all the distance we can between us and those saddlebags!"

Back inside the stagecoach, Loraine pressed Amos all the harder to the floor. More shots rang out, and the sound of the approaching horses grew louder. "Hold up, there!" someone yelled. "Afore we put a bullet clean through yer ornery hide!" Loraine's heart was in her throat as she felt the stage grind slowly to a stop. In an instant, the riders had pulled up alongside. She glanced up just enough to ascertain there were two of them. Each had his hat pulled low with a bandana covering his face from the eyes down. Loraine felt a shudder of fear. Instinctively she buried her face hard against Amos' back.

* * *

"This story gives me goose bumps," Lori exclaimed. "I feel as though I'm right there in the stagecoach with Loraine and Amos."

"It's a cliffhanger, all right," Brad agreed.

CHAPTER 9

Howard and Annette were back on the island now, in the bedroom of Brad's old house. Howard was admiring his new haircut in the vanity mirror. "That was some beauty salon, little sister," he remarked. "I've never seen anything like it. How do they cut hair using nothing but light beams?"

"It's all part of the territory on my side of the line," Annette smiled. "I've been there twenty years and I still can't get over it. Believe me, laser hair clippers aren't the only thing that would blow your mind if you spent a day in my world."

Howard brushed back his hair and replaced his hat. "I'll take your word for it, sis. So who's the lady you had in mind for me to impress with this haircut?"

"The lady of your destiny," Annette announced dramatically. "And believe me, she'll be positively dazzled when she sees how handsome you are with your new haircut and the clothes I've picked out for you. I guarantee it."

"I'm not interested in meeting this woman or any other woman for reasons of the heart," Howard grumbled. "We might as well get this settled first thing out of the gate. There's only one woman who can hold my interest in that direction, and we both know who she is."

Annette just smiled. "Don't thank me now, Peaches. There'll be time enough for that once you're smitten by this lady. Okay," she said briskly, "we have some ground rules we need to cover before taking you to meet her. Here's the deal. Basically, you're on your own. I'll be with you most of the time, but the higher authorities have made it clear that I'm not to overstep my bounds. The object of this whole thing is to help you find yourself and to prove who you really are."

Howard stared at her. "Annette, you're doing it again. Slow down and tell me what it is you're raving on about."

"I am not raving." Annette glared at him. "I am trying to explain some things to you. Now stop interrupting and listen to me. The higher authorities are putting you through a test, and you have to take the test on your own. If I do it for you, it won't count."

Howard just shook his head. He hadn't the slightest idea what Annette was going on about, but he realized there was no use in asking any more questions. He'd just have to wait and see where all this led. What she did next caught him completely by surprise. She stepped to the dresser and picked up a pair of saddlebags that he hadn't even noticed being there.

"Here," she said, handing him the bags. "Here are some things I've thrown together for your trip. Take a peek."

Howard took the bags still staring at her. "You keep talking about a trip! What trip?"

Annette shrugged off his questions. "We'll get to the trip in a minute. Do as I asked and check out the contents of the saddlebags. You need to know what's in them."

"I liked you better when you were a flesh-and-blood sister," Howard grumbled. "I think you've let this angel thing go to your head." He opened one flap on the saddlebags and took a peek inside. "Pepper spray," he quizzed. "You're sending me on a trip where I'll be needing pepper spray. That's a comforting thought."

"I never said I was sending you on dream vacation, Peaches. Take my word for it—the pepper spray will come in very handy," Annette promised.

"Humph," Howard grumped, looking deeper in the bags. The next thing he spotted were three pairs of Nike sport shoes. He didn't even bother asking. Under the shoes, he found two canteens, a six-cell flashlight, a pair of handcuffs, and several other odds and ends. If that wasn't strange enough, there was a plastic first-aid kit with a hypodermic needle inside. This one he did question. "A hypodermic needle? Come on, Annette. You can't seriously want me to be in a situation where I need this."

"Oh yes I can," she corrected him. "The needle contains a combination of an antibiotic and a tetanus shot. You'll be needing them. You can bet on it."

Next Howard checked the opposite side of the saddlebags, where he found a Polaroid camera and a couple of electronic devices of some sort. "What are these?" he asked, pointing to the electronic devices.

Annette laughed. "All the spy movies you've produced and you don't recognize tracking devices when you see them? One half sends out a signal; the other half is the locator."

"Tracking device?" Howard repeated. "Like we use in the movies? I can't wait to see why I'll need these little items."

"What you're looking at is state-of-the-art tracking, Peaches. At least as far as your mortal world is concerned. The range of this little thing is twenty-five miles or more."

Howard shrugged. "All right, Annette. Don't you think it's time to tell me about this trip you're sending me on where I'll be needing all this stuff?"

Annette took the saddlebags from him and secured the straps on both sides. "Let's put it this way," she told him. "In this case, the word WHERE is not as important as the word WHEN. You're about to become a time traveler, Peaches. I'm sending you back to the year 1885. Sort of gets you in the pit of the old stomach, doesn't it?"

"Eighteen-eighty-five?!" Howard gasped. "You can't do that—can you?"

"Sure," she grinned. "The higher authorities can do anything."

"Time travel, huh? Who do you take me for, little sister? Michael J. Fox, or Christopher Lloyd?"

CHAPTER 10

Brad picked up again where he had left off reading the manuscript.

* * *

"You'll never get away with this, you cursed varmints!" Jeremiah barked loudly.

"Get down from there!" one of the robbers shouted back, paying no heed to the warning. "We know about the payroll you're haulin' and we aim to take it for ourselves. We got nothin' personal against you, driver. Just do what we say, and you won't get hurt. All we want is the payroll."

"There ain't no payroll!" Jeremiah shot back. "You've been misled. Now get on about your business and let me get this stage back on the road to Mesa. I give you my word, if you back away now—I'll never mention this little incident to a living soul."

"You're a liar!" the outlaw growled. "Get down off that stage now!"

Jeremiah glanced at the shotgun holstered next to his seat. He toyed with the idea of using it, but was wise enough to realize he'd never have time to get off a shot. He wouldn't be good to anyone dead. He drew a deep breath. He could only hope these men were so interested in the payroll money that they wouldn't notice he was carrying passengers. Knowing their kind as he did, he realized any passenger would be in danger of being robbed; but he wasn't hauling just any passenger. The lovely young woman inside might lead these culprits to think of more than just robbery.

"I'm coming down," he said, trying to keep their attention on him and not on the inside of the coach.

As his feet touched the ground, he shot a quick glance through the open window of the stage. To his relief, both passengers were out of sight. He quickly moved to a point where the robbers would be looking away from the stage as they spoke with him.

"The money!" one of the men snapped. "Where is it?!"

Jeremiah rubbed the back of his neck. "I told ya, there ain't no money. Other than a hundred or so dollars in my own wallet, and you can bet the two of you ain't getting yer hands on that." In reality, Jeremiah would have been lucky to have fifty cents in his pocket, let alone a hundred dollars. But he wanted to tempt them, and fifty cents just wouldn't do the trick.

"A hundred bucks?" one of the men mused, his eyes lighting up as he took the bait. "Well now, I think the payroll money can wait just a bit while I get a look at that wallet of yours. Don't try to be no hero, friend. Just hand it over."

Jeremiah pulled out his wallet and held it up. "You want this, pal," he smiled teasingly. "Well then, come and get it."

The robber's expression hardened. He cocked the hammer on his pistol and held it out in front of him. Cautiously, he stepped forward until the barrel of the gun rested inches from Jeremiah's nose. This was exactly what Jeremiah wanted. With a violent swoop of his left hand, the gun was brushed aside even as the sound of a discharging bullet whizzed past his ear. Next, Jeremiah's right hand delivered a crashing blow to the robber's lower jaw. The man went down hard.

With lightning speed, Jeremiah body-slammed the second man, forcing him backward into the side of the stagecoach. However, to Jeremiah's misfortune, this fellow managed to get off a shot that didn't completely miss the mark. Grimacing in pain, Jeremiah gripped his leg, already red with his own blood, and slumped to the ground.

Startled by all the commotion and the sound of the gun shots, the team of horses bolted. Confused, they turned themselves around and headed back in the direction they had come from. Jeremiah, helpless to do anything to stop the animals, could only watch with great alarm as the unmanned coach hurtled down the trail, taking with it the two hapless passengers still inside.

"Quick!" the robber nearest Jeremiah shouted. "After that stage. The money's getting away."

In a feeble effort to stop the men, Jeremiah reached out and grabbed a handful of the robber's shirt, but a backhand from the man sent him sprawling to the ground. Looking up, he saw the fellow rummaging through his wallet looking for the money Jeremiah had led him to believe was in there. When he realized he had been tricked, the man slammed the wallet to the ground and joined his partner in trying to corral their own horses, which had also been spooked by the gunshot.

Jeremiah gripped his wounded leg and chided himself for not staying out of the way of the bullet. He was duty-bound to protect those two young folks on that stage, and he had let them down. All he could do now was pray. And that's what he did as he watched the robbers take off in hot pursuit of their quarry. At least they were a few minutes behind, thanks to having to round up their horses.

* * *

At this point, Brad paused to ask a question. "This Jeremiah Samuels? Isn't he part of your family tree, too, Lori?"

"Jeremiah's my great-great-grandfather," she said thoughtfully. "That's one thing that makes this story so neat. Jeremiah Samuels didn't even know his passengers on this run, but he would one day become Amos Parker's father-in-law."

"Ah, that's how it fits in. Amos Parker married Jeremiah's daughter. I hope they waited until they were a little older than they were when this was written."

Lori bumped her shoulder against Brad's in disgust. "No, people married a lot younger back then," she laughed. "Of course they waited until they were older, smarty."

"So what was Amos' future wife's name?"

"Jeremiah's wife was Stephanie, and they named their only daughter Brittany Ann. Brittany Ann and Amos were married—"

Lori's sentence was cut short by the sudden appearance of a visitor. "I see you two are well into Loraine's story," she observed. "That's good, but let me tell you—the best part is still to come."

CHAPTER 11

The thrill of seeing his long lost sister again, after all these years, filled Howard's emotions to the overflowing. Nevertheless, the experience left him a very confused man. The holographs she had shown him, the things she had told him, all of it combined had left Howard's head whirling like an autumn dust devil on the desert floor. What was all this talk about meeting the woman of his destiny, and of taking a trip backward in time? None of it made any sense. Or did it?

Howard knew his sister well enough to know she wouldn't lie to him, but he also knew when it came to pranks—Annette was a blue-ribbon champion. *YES!!* he cried out in his mind. *That's what she's up to. This whole thing is a prank.*

Howard felt a sudden letdown. If it was a prank, what chance did he have to thwart her efforts? She was a second-level angel, and he was a mere mortal. He released a long, lingering sigh. *Oh well,* he concluded. *Whatever it is she has in mind, it's worth it just for the chance to see her again.*

Gathering his courage, he spoke his mind. "All right, Annette. I'm onto your little game," he said, proud of himself for figuring it out before she sprang the trap. "I know there's a peach tree here someplace, and I know you're fixing to torment me into throwing the peaches at you. So why not just get it over with instead of beating around the bush like you're doing?"

"What are you talking about?" she spluttered. "How in the world did you get on the subject of peaches? Did I miss something?"

"I know you're up to some prank, little sister. And I'm sure with all the experience you have now, whatever it is will put the peach tree incident to shame. Why not just 'fess up and get on with it?"

Annette broke out laughing. "You think this is a prank, Peaches? I leave you alone for twenty years and you go to pot. On top of everything else, now you're paranoid? Give me strength, please."

Annette tossed the saddlebags to Howard, and he caught them in one hand. "Before I take you back in time, I'd like you to understand why I'm doing it," she said. "You've been working with Sam and Jason Hackett . . . Did you ever hear the story of how they got together?"

Howard still wasn't sure this whole thing wasn't a prank, but he went along with it for now. He tossed the saddlebags over his shoulder. "You mean the part about Jason being born thirty years before his time?" he asked.

"Yes that's the part I mean. How would you feel if I told you the same thing happened in your case, Peaches? Only with you, it was the other way around. You were born a century too late."

"I was born . . . ?" Howard's head jerked back. "Annette! You're playing games with me here."

"No, big brother, I'm not playing games. You were born a century later than you should have been. So was I. It was a simple mistake in our records, much like what happened to Jason. The only thing they got right was that we were meant to be twins."

"This is a prank! I knew it!" Howard said gleefully, convinced that he was right. "You're just trying to convince me that I should have lived in 1885 and you're taking me back there to meet some lady I should have known."

"You think it's a joke, but it's true," Annette said seriously. "The lady you were destined to meet was born when she should have been, in 1864. But you weren't there to meet her because you were born more than a century later—that is to say, *we* were born."

Howard was rapidly losing patience. "This is all nonsense, Annette. Admit it."

"It's not nonsense," Annette insisted. "When Jason was born thirty years too soon, the higher authorities approved a plan to correct the problem. In our case, Peaches, they approved two plans: one plan to correct the mistake that kept you from meeting the lady of your destiny, and a second plan to correct the mistake of me not meeting the guy I was destined for."

"Oh, I see," Howard said sarcastically. "Not only was the lady I was supposed to meet born in 1864, the guy you were supposed to meet was born then, too." He grinned and added, "Were they twins, too—like us?"

Annette ignored the tone of his voice and tried to answer calmly. "Actually no, they weren't related at all. And my guy was born in 1861."

Howard rolled his eyes. "Excuse me, at least it was an honest mistake. What the heck, I was only off by three years."

Annette waved her finger a him. "I can see I'm not getting through to you, Howard. Let me approach this from another direction. You seem to feel your power and wealth were taken from you unjustly. How would you like to have it all back? Your position at the studio, your private beach, your houses and yachts . . . ? What about it, Peaches? Would that make you happy, having it all back?"

Howard straightened as he studied his sister's face. No question about it, she had his attention now. "Don't dangle a carrot in front of me that I can't ever have," he said, "unless you're serious. Are you really saying there's a way I can have my wealth and power back? Or are you just teasing?"

"Short and sweet, Peaches—you can have it all back. But not without a price."

"Oh, I see. Now we're getting down to the fine print. So what's it going to cost me, little sister? Let me venture a guess. I have to swear before this world, your world, and your higher authorities that I'll never interfere with Lori's marriage again. That's what it'll cost to get my empire back right?"

"Sorry, Peaches. You missed the mark this time. It has nothing to do with giving up Lori Douglas. It has to do with giving up the lady you're about to meet."

Howard struggled to understand what Annette was saying. He knew there had to be a catch; there was always a catch when dealing with angels. But he was having trouble pinpointing what that catch was in this case. "Let me get this straight," he pressed. "I can have my empire back and don't even have to give up Lori. Tell you what, little sister. We can just forget about 1885 and the lady who's supposedly waiting for me there. Just send me back to my wealth and power right now, and be done with it."

She shook her head. "Can't do that, Peaches. The only way the higher authorities will give you the choice of having your empire back is for you to meet the lady in 1885 first."

Howard rubbed the back of his neck with a sigh. "It's always something, isn't it?" He adjusted the saddlebags to a more comfortable position on his shoulder. "What are we waiting for? If I have to make a detour through 1885 to get back to my empire—then let's do it."

"Let's!" Annette quickly responded, her face alive with a smile. "Get ready, Peaches. You're about to get your first glimpse of the world the way it was when you and I should have lived in it."

* * *

Lori caught her breath at the sight of Samantha, who had popped in just as Jason had hinted she would, just a little sooner than Lori had expected. "You sure know how to startle people, don't you, Sam?" she said. "I don't suppose you ever considered ringing the doorbell."

"Hey," Samantha shrugged. "It's common knowledge that angels don't knock. Why would you expect one of us to use a doorbell? And think of the steps I saved you by your not having to answer the door."

"Good to see you again, Sam," Brad greeted her. "Lori mentioned that Jason was here earlier. We've been going over the manuscript he left. It's very interesting."

"I thought you'd like it. But the best part is yet to come, and guess what? I'm going to add some excitement by showing you the rest of the story as a holograph. Much more realistic that way than simply reading the account."

Lori and Brad weren't strangers to Samantha's holographs. They had been treated to several when Samantha was trying to save their marriage. Just reading Loraine's manuscript was thrilling, but the thought of seeing her story through the eyes of a holograph sent chills through Lori. "What are we waiting for, Sam?" she asked eagerly.

"You really are interested in this manuscript, aren't you Lori?" Sam said with a laugh. "Just be patient, I'll get back to the manuscript as soon as I take care of one other little item that needs doing."

Lori winced. Unless she missed her guess, this was where Howard Placard was about to come in. Jason had hinted that Howard was somehow involved in Loraine Parker's story and that Samantha would be the one to explain the hows of his involvement. "This other little item you mentioned, Sam. Please tell me it has nothing to do with Howard Placard," she begged.

"Can't do that, Lori." Samantha shook her head. "The case Jason and I are working on concerns two people, Loraine Parker and you-know-who. It's the you-know-who I need to bring you up to the minute on before we go any further with Loraine."

Lori felt a shiver at Samantha's words. "Will I never be rid of that man?" she asked. "What possible reason could you have for bringing his name up in our house again, Sam?"

"It all boils down to this," Samantha explained. "The higher authorities want you to forgive him, Lori. And the same goes for you, Brad."

"Forgive Howard?" Brad responded. "Under the circumstances, that could be a tall order to fill, Sam. You know what that man put me through. And you know what he put Lori through."

"Believe me, Brad, I know it all. But forgiving him is for your own good. Resentment brings nothing but trouble, even when there's a good reason. That's the reason Jason was here this morning with the manuscript, and that's the reason I'm here now. The higher authorities are giving the two of you the chance to get that resentment out of your lives."

Brad started to say something, but Samantha held up her hand, cutting him off. "Hear me out, okay? I want to show you a holograph of what Howard's been up to since early this morning. After that, I want to show the holographs finishing Loraine's story. When I'm finished, if the two of you still don't feel you can forgive Howard, I'll simply walk away and the subject will never be brought up again. Is that fair?"

For a long moment, Lori and Brad stood looking at each other. It was Brad who spoke first. "What do you say? Do we give Sam a chance?"

"How could we do anything else? We owe her a debt we could never repay. Go ahead, Sam. Start the show."

"All right," Samantha agreed. "As I said, I want to bring you up to date on what Howard's been up to."

Samantha opened the holograph at the moment when Howard had been awakened by the thunder to discover the leak over his bed. From that point, the holograph depicted everything that happened to Howard that morning. These things weren't easy for Lori to watch, and an occasional glance in Brad's direction told her he wasn't finding it all that easy either.

* * *

The first thing Howard noticed as the scene shifted again were the saguaros. Of all the cacti Howard had ever seen, he loved the saguaro best, which was only natural, since he was raised on his father's Arizona ranch where saguaros have flourished for centuries. It took Howard only seconds to realize that this was where Annette had brought him—to Arizona. "Sort of looks like home, doesn't it, sis?" he said wistfully.

"It should, Peaches. You're sitting right in the back pocket of the old ranch. Over there, to the north, do you recognize those peaks?"

Howard looked at the range of jagged mountain peaks silhouetted against the horizon. "The majestic Superstitions," he said, almost reverently. "The most beautiful mountains in the world as far as I'm concerned, little sister. So tell me, are we back in the year 1885 yet?"

"We are."

"Not much different from the Superstitions of our day, are they?"

"Not much," she agreed. "But there's a whole lot of difference in that dirt road you're standing next to, Peaches. Care to guess what it's called in your day?"

Howard glanced to the left, then back to the right. He looked back at the Superstitions and did some calculations in his head. "Off hand," he ventured bravely, "I'd say this is just about where US Highway 60 should be."

"Good job, Peaches! You nailed it right on the yellow line that won't be here for a good many years to come."

Howard looked around again, just to satisfy himself what he was seeing was real. "It wasn't a prank, was it, little sister?" he meekly asked. "You really have moved me backward in time, haven't you?"

"I can't believe you doubted me, Peaches. Are you convinced now, or need I give you more proof?"

"I'm convinced," he conceded. "Thoroughly confused, mind you—but I am convinced."

"Good," she said with a sharp nod of her head. "Now for your next question. Take a look down the road at that dust cloud off in the distance." She pointed and he looked up to see the cloud. "What would you make that out to be?"

Howard shielded his eyes. "It appears to be a stagecoach, little sister. Looks like four—maybe six horses pulling it. What are we looking at, a Wells Fargo Bank commercial?"

"Wrong! Look again, Peaches."

"Humph," Howard grunted. "From the way it's moving on, I'd almost say it's a runaway. I've filmed a few stagecoach scenes in my time, you know."

"Bingo," she said. "It is a stagecoach. An authentic Concord, the Rolls Royce of stagecoaches."

"I know that, Annette. I cut my teeth on stories of the Old West, same as you." He narrowed his eyes, taking a closer look. "I don't see any driver. Are there people on board, sis?" he asked, concerned.

"A young woman from Boston and her fourteen-year-old brother."

Howard's face turned serious. "Someone's got to help them! That stage has to be stopped or they could be killed." Howard paused, then added, "You're a second-level angel. You can stop the thing."

"I could—if the higher authorities would let me. But they have other ideas, Peaches. *You're* going to stop the stage," Annette said pointedly.

"Me?!" Howard bellowed. "How, for crying out loud?! I don't have a horse, and even if I did, I'm not sure I could get aboard the thing. I'm a producer, not a stuntman."

"I can put you on that stagecoach," Samatha said, "but only if you give me permission to do it."

"Oh boy," Howard said, wiping his brow. "I hate to see anyone get hurt, but I'm not sure I could stop a runaway stage, even if I were on it. But what's going to happen to them, Annette, if I don't stop the stage?"

"They'll both die," she said coldly.

Howard was sweating profusely now. "Isn't there another way?" he groped.

"There's no other way. Either you save them—or they die."

Howard pulled a handkerchief from his pocket and mopped his brow. He swallowed away the lump that had formed in his throat. "All right, sis," he said, struggling to build up his courage. "Get me on that stage."

CHAPTER 12

Samantha's holograph ended with Howard saying the words, "All right, sis. Get me on that stage." Brad and Lori sat motionless, stunned almost beyond words at what they had just seen.

"So what about it?" Samantha asked. "Did you learn anything about Howard you didn't know?"

"Peaches?" Lori snorted. "Howard's nickname is Peaches? If that man ever bothers me again, I'll tell the world about it. And I had no idea he had a twin sister. I didn't even know he was raised on a ranch."

"Neither did I," Brad admitted. "What's this thing about Howard going back in time? How can that be, Sam?"

"You have to understand, Brad. The higher authorities have all power over the dimension of time. To them, everything is one big NOW. It's as easy for them to move through time as it is for us to move through space. Taking Howard back to the year 1885 is no more trouble for them than taking him from one room in a house to another. And since they've approved Annette to represent them in Howard's case, Annette has the authority to move him through time the same as if they did it themselves. Understand?"

"No," Brad answered without the slightest hesitation. "But I'll take your word for it."

Lori spoke up. "I'm impressed that Howard would want to save Loraine and Amos by stopping the stage. Will he be able to do it?"

"To answer that question, we have two choices, Lori. Either you can read ahead in the manuscript, or I can let you watch it happen in a holograph."

"What's this?" Lori demanded. "I thought we'd already decided to see the rest of the story in a holograph."

Samantha laughed. "I'm joking, okay? So, make yourselves comfortable, and I'll show you how Howard handles his problem with the stagecoach."

* * *

"Oooohh—boy!" Howard groaned as he realized Annette had successfully moved him onto the speeding stagecoach. "You weren't kidding, were you, sis?" The smell of dust filled his nostrils as the sound of horses' hooves and metal wheels grinding against the packed soil grated noisily on his ears. He felt as if he were sitting on top of a jackhammer.

As he regained his senses, he realized Annette was there on the stage with him. He couldn't help noticing how beautiful she looked— in a sisterly way, of course. Her lovely blond hair danced wildly in the wind, and her smile reminded him so much of the smile she often wore as a happy-go-lucky young woman growing up on the ranch. Even if she were an angel, Howard knew she was enjoying the thrill of the moment on this runaway stage. That was Annette. She was always one to live on the edge, and she enjoyed life to the fullest. Seeing her here, like this, made Howard realize just how much he had missed her all these years. And it made him realize just how wonderful it was seeing her again. His heart ached at the thought that this meeting might be so short lived.

He also saw that she had brought the saddlebags and his hat. The sight of these mortal things reminded him of the immediate problem. "You really aren't going to help me out here, are you, sis?" he hollered so she could hear him over the noise.

"I got you on the stage, Peaches," she yelled back. "That's all I can do."

"It figures," Howard grumbled. Crawling forward, he reached the driver's station and pulled himself upright in the seat. His first thought was to find the reins, but a quick look revealed them to be dragging uselessly on the ground under the stagecoach. His next thought was the brake handle. He spotted it just to the left of the driver's seat. Grabbing the handle, he pulled against it with all the force he could muster. A spray of sparks exploded as the metal brake pad met the metal rim of the front wheel, but clearly, the stage wasn't going to stop. The horses were much too strong for this primitive brake to do the job.

"How am I supposed to stop this thing without the reins?" he shouted back at Annette.

"Dusty Lockhart!" she countered. "What would Dusty Lockhart do if he were in your shoes?"

This caught Howard completely off guard. Annette knew about Dusty Lockhart? No one was supposed to know about Dusty Lockhart other than Sandra Rose and Howard himself. Sandra was an obscure author who had come to Howard a few years back with a series of stories about her fictional character, Dusty Lockhart. Howard had fallen in love with Dusty in the first few pages he read. He always thought of Dusty as "Rambo on a horse." Howard had bought the copyrights from Sandra at a premium cost, hoping that public interest might shift back to westerns, so he could produce a series on Dusty Lockhart. Howard loved Dusty so much, he actually wanted to play the part himself if he ever did produce the films, which was the only aspiration to acting Howard had ever had.

"You know about Dusty Lockhart?" he called back to Annette.

"Peaches, I know *everything* about you," she yelled back. "So, if this were a film staring Dusty Lockhart, what would he do about now?"

What would Dusty do? Howard asked himself. *He might jump to the horses and stop them that way.* But Howard quickly ruled this idea out. He was no stuntman, and he would only end up killing himself by trying that. He would be no good to those in the stagecoach if he managed to kill himself. What else would Dusty do to stop this stage? he wondered. Then it hit him. If Dusty couldn't stop the horses, he'd probably look for a way to detach them from the stagecoach. Howard glanced down at the single metal pin coupling the tongue from the harness to the stagecoach. If he could find a way to remove that pin, the tongue would pull loose, allowing the team to break free.

But, of all the cursed luck, the pin was too far for him to reach it. His thoughts raced. There had to be some way. Then he spotted it. A double-barreled, twelve-gauge, open-hammer shotgun holstered next to the driver's seat. Howard grabbed the gun, yanking it free from the holster. Breaking open the breach, he found both barrels loaded. He checked a shell and was glad to see it was double-ought buck. Howard knew that double-ought buck was a heavy enough load to do some real damage.

He glanced down again at the wooden tongue tying the horses to the stagecoach. "I have two shots," he said aloud to himself. "That should do it." He slammed the breach closed and pulled back one of the hammers. Placing the weapon firmly against his shoulder, he took aim and squeezed off a shot. For an instant he thought a ton of dynamite had exploded in his ear, and the spooked horses lurched forward with even greater speed. He checked the wooden tongue and smiled. The shot had ripped it nearly in half.

Suddenly, Howard realized something he hadn't before. It wasn't just Annette who was enjoying the thrill of the moment of this "on-the-edge" stagecoach ride. Howard was enjoying it, too. It spoke to something from deep within his soul that had been hiding for a very long time. Howard had once been very much like Annette. He, too, liked to live on the edge. Over the years, this part of what made him who he was had been lost in the shuffle of amassing an empire. It felt good, enjoying this kind of thrill again. It even made him feel young—something he hadn't felt in a very long time.

Cocking the second hammer, he fired off his last shot. This time the tongue was left holding together by little more than splinters. "Yeeeeaaaahooo!!!" he cried, dropping the shotgun and gripping the brake handle again. He threw his weight into it, and for what seemed an eternity the stage continued hurling forward on its perilous course. Then, with a noisy snap, the tongue severed and the horses pulled free. The hapless coach veered hard to the left—its wheels digging deeply into the hard-packed ground. The leading wheel snapped, as spokes splintered like so many matchsticks. With the wheel shattered, what was left of the axle dug a heavy trench along its path until the stagecoach finally ground to a violent stop.

Howard leapt from the stage at the last possible second and hit the ground with a thud, grateful to have picked a soft spot. Taking a second or so to clear his head, he sat up and brushed himself off.

Annette was standing next to him, still holding the saddlebags and his hat. She reached down and shoved the hat on his head. "Nice job, Peaches. Dusty Lockhart would have been proud."

He glanced up at her, and after the two of them had enjoyed a good laugh, he observed, "I assume this sort of thing is easier for an angel than for a mere mortal like me. So help me, you don't have so much as one hair out of place, sis."

"Being an angel does have its advantages," she agreed. "Now stand up so I can talk to you, Peaches. There are some ground rules here that I need to explain before you get in any deeper."

Howard stood and brushed himself off some more. "Are the woman and boy okay?" he asked.

"They're a little shook up at the moment, but they'll be fine, thanks to you. Now listen up while I explain some things to you. I plan on sticking pretty close most of the time. I might slip off every now and then, but I won't be far away. I do plan on remaining invisible to everyone but you, Peaches, and since no one else will be able to see or hear me, don't go embarrassing yourself by talking to me when you shouldn't or anything like that. And let me warn you, you're about to get one of the biggest shocks of your life, so be prepared."

She reached out and brushed off a spot of dirt he had missed on his shoulder. "There's something else I need to tell you, and this will come as a shock, too. The whole time you're here, in 1885, you're going to be in a fishbowl, so to speak. There'll be some folks watching you."

Howard didn't like the sound of this at all. "Watching me? Who? Why, for crying out loud?"

"They'll be watching you in a holograph, very similar to the ones I've shown you. As for who they are, and why they're watching— you'll just have to wait. I'll explain these parts when the time comes."

"Oh, wonderful." Howard grumbled. "You shove me back in time to meet some woman I couldn't care less about, and now you tell me I'll be performing in front of a live audience. I love you, too, Annette Placard."

Annette smiled at Howard and gave him the saddlebags. "It's show time," she said. "And a man in your profession should know what that means. Get over to that stagecoach, Peaches. And be prepared for the shock of your life as you come face to face with your destiny."

* * *

Lori stared in disbelief at the holograph playing out in front of her. "Things are getting a little deep here, Sam," she said. "First you bring Howard Placard into my family room and make me sit here and watch him. Then you hit me with this science-fiction time-travel thing. No sooner do I accept that, then I learn Howard Placard is going back to 1885 to meet my very own look-alike distant aunt, Loraine Parker. Now comes another shocker. Howard even knows I'm watching him."

"Not exactly," Samantha attempted to explain. "Howard knows *someone* is watching him, but he doesn't know who. And by the way, when Annette said she would be invisible to everyone but Howard, that doesn't apply to us. We'll be able to see her just fine on our end."

Lori frowned. "I still don't like the thought of Howard Placard being introduced to my aunt. Loraine certainly deserves better than having Howard to contend with."

Lori wasn't ready for Samantha's next revelation. "You're wrong, Lori. Not introducing Howard to Loraine would be the most unkind thing I could do to her. What I know that you don't know is that Howard and Loraine are slated to share a forever contract with each other, exactly like you share with Brad." Lori caught her breath and stared at Samantha.

"I'm sure you'll agree that finding Brad is the greatest thing ever to happen to you," Samantha continued. "Would you deprive Loraine her chance for the same kind of happiness?"

Lori's face reflected her horror. "I—I . . . But Sam—! That's impossible! Loraine and Howard couldn't be contracted for each other. It's just not possible!"

"Why? Because they lived at different times? Look at Jason and me, Lori. We lived at different times and we ended up together. What's so impossible about Loraine and Howard doing the same?"

"That's not what I mean, Sam. I know how you and Jason got together, and I assume Loraine and Howard could do the same, but . . ."

Lori paused, trying to organize her thoughts. "What I'm saying is—Loraine is my family. And Howard is—you know—a jerk. He's not good enough for Loraine. You know that as well as I do."

Samantha looked over at Brad. "Are those your feelings, too?" she asked.

Brad shrugged. "I'd say that's putting it mildly."

"All right," Samantha conceded. "I suppose it's a little too soon to expect either of you to feel differently about the man. Let's move on, shall we? I'm going to move the two of you in for a close-up look inside the stagecoach before returning to the story. I want you to pay particular attention, Lori. It's important that you see just how much you and Loraine do resemble each other."

Lori turned to the holograph and saw it had panned to the inside of the coach. Loraine was still holding Amos to the floor, her face pressed hard against the boy's back. As Lori watched, Loraine slowly raised her head until her face came into full view. Lori gasped in disbelief. "It's—like I'm looking in a mirror."

Brad was no less impressed. "She could be your twin, Lori! I doubt if even I could tell the difference between the two of you."

"Nor could Howard," Samantha quickly pointed out. "That, in a nutshell, is the problem here. Howard mistook you for your distant aunt, Lori. That's why he thinks he's in love with you."

Lori looked confused. "I—I just don't understand, Sam. Even if Howard and Loraine were destined for each other, it makes no sense why he would be attracted to me. I mean—Howard's never even seen Loraine Parker. How could he possibly know about her ahead of time?"

"It happens, Lori. Not every time, necessarily. But often when two people are destined for each other, they know that person even before meeting them in the mortal world. That was the case with Howard and Loraine. And so, when Howard saw you that day on his father's ranch, he unknowingly mistook you for the woman he really was destined for. That's why he's been so relentless in his effort to win your affection. To put it bluntly, you lit a fire inside Howard that's actually burning for Loraine Parker. He just doesn't know it yet."

"Oh!" Lori gasped. "This is all so unnerving. I just can't believe it! Howard Placard nearly destroyed my marriage because he mistook me for my distant aunt, Loraine Parker?"

"Let me ask you this, Brad," Samantha said, turning to him. "What if you had met Loraine Parker before you met Lori? Could you have been fooled into thinking Loraine was the one for you?"

Brad blew out a loud breath. "That's an unfair question, Sam."

"It's a perfectly fair question, Brad," Samantha insisted. "Take a good look at Loraine, and tell me you couldn't have fallen in love with her."

"If I'd never met Lori, you mean?" Brad said, stalling for time.

"That's what I mean."

Brad shook his head. "I honestly don't know, Sam. I've loved Lori all my life. Ever since she and I were children. Maybe if conditions were such that I'd have met Loraine when we were small . . ."

Lori didn't like hearing this at all. "You mean you might have fallen in love with her instead of me?!" she accused. "I never thought I'd hear you say something like that, Brad Douglas!"

Brad's face softened, seeing that he had hurt his wife. "I'm sorry. I'm just trying to answer Sam's question. You and Loraine do look an awful lot alike, so yes, I might have fallen for her, circumstances being right and all."

"Listen to what he's saying, Lori," Samantha said gently. "He doesn't mean he loves you less, and he doesn't mean he could fall in love with Loraine after knowing you first. But he is saying she might have fooled him if he hadn't known you first—exactly as you fooled Howard because he hadn't met Loraine first."

Lori's face was stubborn. "I'm sorry, Sam. How do you think it makes me feel, hearing Brad say he might have fallen in love with another woman, regardless of who she is? And I still think Howard's a jerk!"

Samantha sighed. "I knew this was going to be an uphill battle," she admitted. "But you're a hard one to convince, lady. Tell you what . . . let's just watch the story a while longer, then we'll tackle the subject again."

Lori folded her arms in frustration and looked back at the holograph, only to discover that the scene had moved from the stagecoach back to Jeremiah Samuels.

CHAPTER 13

Jeremiah loosened the bandana he had tied around his leg to slow the bleeding. To his relief, he found the bleeding had stopped. Examining the wound more closely, he saw that the bullet had passed cleanly through the calf muscle of his left leg. Fortunately, it had missed the bone; otherwise, the leg would have been completely useless. At least this way there was some hope he could make his way through the desert.

Jeremiah was no stranger to the desert. He'd spent his whole life here and had been in plenty of scrapes under the hot sun before. This time would be tougher than most, that much he had to admit. Mesa was the nearest town, and it was a good twenty miles away. He had no water and he could barely walk.

Thoughts of his passengers came painfully to mind. How could he have been so careless to get himself shot and allow the team to run away? He had only one hope for the young woman and her little brother, and that was for the team to outrun the holdup men all the way back to the station they had left this morning. He knew it was a long shot, but not impossible. He could only hope. One good thing, there was plenty of water on the stage. Even if they were stranded somewhere along the trail, they could survive until another stage happened by.

Jeremiah glanced upward at the sky. Noon, he figured. Maybe a little after. Pulling himself to his feet, he tried the bad leg. The pain was excruciating. If he was going to walk, he would need some sort of crutch. Expecting to find a crutch on the desert might seem a little farfetched to some, but not to Jeremiah. He knew exactly what to look for. Shielding his eyes from the sun, he searched until he found it—a fallen saguaro. To his relief, it was only a few feet away.

The saguaro cactus is one of the wonders of the Arizona desert and often lives a hundred and fifty years or longer. Sometimes, however, a saguaro falls victim to some unexpected act of nature, usually a bolt of lightning. Such was the fate of the saguaro Jeremiah spotted now. The misfortune of this cactus would be his good fortune. When a saguaro dies, it decays into an unusual, almost skeletal shape. These remains are especially popular for artistic decorations, but can be suitable for countless other uses—a makeshift crutch, for instance.

Limping to where the fallen giant lay, he searched until he found just the stick he wanted. Wrapping his bandana around the end that would fit under his arm, he tried out his makeshift crutch. It was far from perfect, but it did allow him to take some weight off his injured leg. He turned to the west and set out walking. Painful as it was, it was his only hope. He needed water to ease his already burning thirst, but unfortunately his canteen was still on the stagecoach. Jeremiah knew that making it off the desert without water wouldn't be easy, but he also knew a few tricks that would improve his chances. Using one such trick he had learned from an old Indian chief, Jeremiah picked up a small pebble and placed it beneath his tongue. This would at least keep the saliva flowing enough to prevent his mouth and throat from becoming unbearably dry. He also knew there were some types of cactus that offered up a little moisture when the pulp was chewed. He'd just have to keep a sharp eye for any of these along the way.

"Things could look a mite better, I suppose," he said to himself. "But this desert's never beat me yet, and it's not going to beat me this time."

And so—in spite of the pain—he placed the makeshift crutch under his shoulder and began his long, painful journey.

* * *

Watching Jeremiah was interesting, but Lori couldn't help wishing this part of the scene would hurry by so she could get back to Howard and Loraine's first meeting. Samantha must have sensed her feelings. "All right, Lori," she said. "I won't keep you in suspense any longer. I just needed to bring you up to date on Jeremiah since he's an important part of the story, too."

The scene shifted back to the stagecoach. By this time, Howard and Annette were walking toward the stagecoach, but Lori was glad to see they hadn't reached it yet. She didn't want to miss the big moment.

* * *

On reaching the stagecoach, Howard twisted the handle and pulled the door open. Annette had tried to prepare him for a surprise, but she certainly hadn't prepared him for anything like this. "Lori?" he gasped in astonishment. "What are you doing here? I—don't understand."

Seeing Howard, Loraine quickly pulled Amos to her. "Are you one of the robbers?" she snapped. "Because if you are—"

"Robbers?" Howard asked in total surprise. "I don't know anything about any robbers, Lori. I was brought here to stop the stage. I had no idea you were inside."

Howard glanced back at Annette, who stood smiling at him. What was his crazy sister up to? She told him he'd be meeting a lady who could be part of his destiny, but he certainly hadn't expected her to mean Lori Parker herself. If that was so, then why had Annette berated him for pursuing Lori?

"I asked you if you're one of the robbers," Loraine pressed again. "I demand an answer!"

Howard was dumbfounded. "You know perfectly well I'm not a robber, Lori. Why would you even have to ask?"

Doubt remained in Loraine's eyes. "I'm sorry if I've accused you falsely," she responded cautiously. "But you've obviously mistaken me for someone else. My name isn't Lori."

"Not Lori?" Howard gasped, his eyes fixed on her face. "But—that makes no sense at all."

Suddenly, a very strange thing occurred. As Howard looked on in complete astonishment, the lady he assumed to be Lori and the young lad became perfectly still, as if they had been frozen in time.

They reminded him of ice statues. "What's happening?" Howard muttered, looking back to his sister for an explanation.

"Another one of my angel antics," she grinned. "I've just put time on hold. I assume the process has been explained to you, since you've been dealing with angels for some time now."

Howard wiped his mouth. "The captain explained it to me," he observed. "But seeing it firsthand is—you know—weird." Howard looked again at Loraine and Amos. "They don't know a thing that's going on right now, do they, Annette?"

"No, and when I start time again they won't know so much as one tick has passed off the clock. Amazing what we second-level angels can do, eh, Peaches?"

Howard eyed her suspiciously. "Has anyone ever done this to me?" he asked. She smiled but didn't answer. "They have done this to me, haven't they?" he complained, his voice a pitch higher. "It was that pesky lady angel, Samantha, wasn't it?"

Annette shrugged. "I can't say Samantha never put time on hold while you were around. But even if she did, what did it hurt?"

"What did it hurt? For crying out loud, Annette. Can you imagine the humiliation of being frozen like this for anyone present to gape at? I'll never trust myself in Samantha's presence again. Come to think of it, how do I know I can trust you?!"

"Put it to bed, big brother. We have more important things to discuss than my putting time on hold. I warned you that you were in for a surprise. Was I right or what?"

Howard's cheeks puffed out as he blew out a breath. "You're darn right I was surprised. Why wouldn't I be when the very woman you tell me is part of my destiny turns out to be Lori?"

"Well, let me explain something to you, Peaches. The lady you're looking at isn't Lori at all." Annette paused, letting this sink in. "Appearances can be deceiving, you know," she added.

"You're lying, Annette," Howard said, staring at the frozen figure of Loraine. "I'd stake my life on it. I don't know what your game is this time, but this is the woman I'm in love with and nothing can convince me otherwise."

"Oh, she's the woman you're in love with, all right," Annette smiled. "But she's still not Lori. You know I'm telling the truth, Peaches. I've never lied to you in your life, and I'm not lying to you now."

Annette's words came with the force of a wild stampede. She had him and he knew it. Annette was a first-class kidder, but she never lied. If she said this woman wasn't Lori, then Howard knew she was telling the truth. But—if this woman wasn't Lori, then . . . ? To acknowledge surrender was humiliating, but he had to know. "If she's not Lori—who is she?"

"I'll let her answer for herself," Annette responded. "But let me fill you in on this much. The reason she thinks you may be a robber is because the stage was held up a few miles back. The driver was injured and the horses bolted. That's how the runaway occurred. The only other thing you need to know about her right now is—she represents your destiny. Admit it, Peaches. She's the most beautiful woman you've ever seen, and it's all you can do to take your eyes off her."

"Well, of course she's beautiful!" Howard spit back, glaring at his sister. "Why wouldn't I think she's beautiful when she looks exactly like Lori?" Howard felt a sudden surge of anger as the reality that this wasn't Lori framed in his mind. "This is a cheap trick, Annette. Finding someone who looks like Lori and trying to pawn her off on me. My destiny indeed. Ha! It's just your poor attempt at playing matchmaker. Well, it won't work, so you might as well hang it up right now."

But Annette didn't answer. Instead, Howard was stunned to see Loraine come to life and ask a question as if there had been no time lapse at all. "If you're not one of the robbers, then who are you and where did you come from?" Annette had put time back into motion as quickly as she had stopped it earlier.

"Where did I come from?" he stammered. "Well you see, I . . . That is, . . . I'm the one who stopped the stage."

Annette laughed at her brother. "Don't just stand there gaping at her, Peaches. Offer the lady a hand out of the coach."

Howard glanced nervously at his own hand, then extended it toward the young woman. Cautiously, she reached out to accept his hand and allowed him to help her from the stage. Amos hopped out on his own. "How did you do that?" he asked excitedly. "Stopping the stage like that? And how'd you get up there? I didn't even hear your horse come up."

"I wasn't on a horse, son. That is, I . . ." Howard paused, trying to figure a way to explain how he had gotten on the stagecoach. Explaining he was put there by his sister, an angel, wasn't going to cut it. Since he couldn't come up with another sensible solution, he sidestepped the issue. "My name's Howard. Howard Placard." Turning to Loraine, he added, "And you are Miss . . . ?"

"I'm Miss Parker," she said, still keeping a cautious eye on Howard. "And this is my little brother, Amos. We're certainly grateful for your stopping the stagecoach. I'm sure you saved our lives by doing it."

Miss Parker? The name rang in Howard's mind like bells from a cathedral. Annette said the woman wasn't Lori, but the woman had just introduced herself as "Miss Parker." Confused, he looked to Annette to clear up this strange matter.

"They share last names, Peaches," Annette said gently, "which is only natural since the lady here is Lori's distant aunt."

Howard's knees felt like rubber. He wished for a place to sit, but there was none. "Miss Parker, you say? I hope you'll forgive me if I seem a little perplexed. It's just that you remind me of someone I know quite well. The resemblance is extraordinary. And the irony is, her last name is Parker, the same as yours."

"That's not entirely true, Peaches," Annette quickly pointed out. "Lori is a Douglas now. She gave up the name Parker when she married Brad. I wish you'd stop ignoring that fact."

Howard glared at his sister, but didn't argue for two reasons. First, he didn't want to look like a fool in front of Miss Parker and the boy—and second—he knew Annette was right.

"And this is your little brother?" he asked.

Loraine smiled and placed a hand on the back of Amos' head. "He's my only brother, and he's a fine young man."

"I'm sure he is." Howard rubbed his chin. As he contemplated the strangeness of this situation in his own mind, he had no idea she was doing the same.

* * *

What was it about this man that seemed so familiar, Loraine

wondered. She was certain she had never seen him before, but the feeling of familiarity was overwhelming. It was also a little frightening. She had had the same question Amos had voiced earlier, but it had gone unanswered. How had this fellow gotten onto the stagecoach so completely unnoticed? She had wanted to ask, but couldn't bring herself to do so. Trying not to be obvious, she looked into the stranger's eyes and found that she was almost powerless to look away. Her mouth went dry and her heart raced.

"You said your name is Howard?" she asked shyly.

"Yes, my name is Howard—Howard Placard. I'm pretty well known in my parts as a motion picture producer," he went on to explain.

Loraine was stunned. Motion picture producer? What was he talking about? She had never heard of any such thing. "I'm afraid you have me at a loss," she meekly responded. "I'm not familiar with the term you used."

* * *

Annette broke out laughing. "You're handling this well, Peaches. "Why not tell her about the stretch limo you once owned or about your personal computer network? What the heck, she'd love to hear about your computers."

Howard could have kicked himself for the slip. This situation was proving harder than he had supposed at first. To his relief, Annette provided him an excuse for ignoring any explanation about motion picture producers. "Looks like you're about to have company, Peaches," she said, pointing off in the distance along the road. "It seems the bank robbers didn't get what they were after the first time around. They'll be here any minute, big brother. And they look a little dangerous to me."

Howard turned his attention to the road where he saw two horsemen rapidly approaching. "We may have a problem, Miss Parker," he said, pointing toward the approaching men. "They could be the robbers coming back for another try."

"Oh my!" Loraine gasped. "What shall we do?"

"I don't think they've seen us. Maybe we can hide over there in those rocks." Howard motioned to some large rocks off to one side of the road.

"Yes!" Loraine agreed. "We'll hide!" Grabbing Amos' hand, she hurried toward the rocks. Howard glanced back at Annette, who waved at him to go ahead with Loraine and Amos.

"Go on, Peaches," she said. "You can't depend on me to protect you from these culprits. I've already explained the rules."

Howard wasted no time in catching up with Loraine and her brother. As soon as he was sure Loraine and Amos were safely hidden, he peeked over the top of the rock at the men who were just riding up.

* * *

"Whoa!" Clay Derringer called as he and his partner, Grayson Hobbs, reined up alongside the disabled stagecoach. Clay and Grayson had been partners in crime, so to speak, ever since the two of them were teenagers from the same cattle town in the Texas panhandle. The larger and meaner of the two men, Clay was the self-designated leader of the pair. Both were sons of cattlemen who earned their living doing backbreaking work from sunup to sundown on other men's ranches. This sort of life had never appealed to Clay or Grayson, who learned early in life that it was much easier to let another fellow earn his wages by hard work, then simply steal them from him.

Of course, stealing didn't always turn out to be as easy as they expected. Such was the case when they set out to relieve the old miner Sylvester Black of his gold dust after a month's digging. They didn't reckon on the tenacity of Sylvester's stubborn mule, where the sack of gold dust hung seemingly in wait for an easy snatch. But when Clay and Grayson tried snatching it, they thought they had tackled a Texas tornado. Clay met a pair of hind hooves that sent him on an airborne trajectory terminating smack in the middle of a prickly cactus patch. It took weeks to remove all the pesky needles from his backside. Still, he was better off than Grayson, whose left ear was bitten off by the not-to-be-bested beast. That little episode came as close as anything ever had to reforming the two culprits. Close—but, unfortunately, no blue ribbon. The prospect of working for a living was just too much for either of these lazy scoundrels to face.

Grayson lost more than an ear that day with the mule. He lost his first name while he was about it. From that day on he was tagged with the nickname Scar, because of his stub of an ear left by the mule who'd been protecting his master's gold dust.

The two men quickly dismounted and checked around the outside of the stagecoach. "Where do you reckon them saddlebags are?" Clay asked at last.

"Don't rightly know, Clay," Grayson answered. "But they gotta be here someplace. One thing for sure, that driver didn't have no bags on him. You look inside the stage while I scout around out here. One of us is bound to find 'em."

* * *

Loraine scooted next to Howard, where she too could get a look at these men over the top of the rock. "The bandanas are gone," she whispered. "They were wearing bandanas before."

"That's good," Howard responded also in a whisper. "That means they probably don't know anyone was in the stage. All we have to do is stay hidden until they leave, and they'll never know about us."

As Howard and Loraine watched, the one called Scar approached a suitcase lying on the ground a few feet from the stagecoach. Ramming his boot into the suitcase with a hefty kick, he broke it open, spilling some of the contents onto the dusty ground.

"That's my suitcase!" Loraine hissed. "Of all the nerve! What right does that man have going through my personal belongings?!"

"Shhhh!" Howard warned. "These men are dangerous. They're after anything of value, and nothing is going to escape their scrutiny. Not even your luggage, Miss Parker."

"Hey, Clay, get a load of this." Grayson called out, holding up a revolver, still in its leather holster, that he had scavenged from the suitcase.

Clay, who was just about to check inside the coach, stopped to look. "It's a pistol," he responded with a shrug. "So what? We're after the payroll, you idiot. Pistols ain't worth nothin'."

Grayson pulled the revolver from the holster and looked it over. "This ain't no ordinary pistol," he declared. "Look how shiny it is.

And check out these purty-lookin' white handle grips."

"That's my target pistol," Loraine grimaced. "That man is planning on stealing it."

Howard did a double take. Miss Parker might look like Lori, but here was one place where she was a much different woman from Lori. Lori would never have anything to do with guns. Howard voiced his surprise. "You carry a pistol in your luggage, Miss Parker?"

"Yes, I carry a pistol," Loraine came right back. "Why shouldn't I? I happen to be a sharpshooter, Mr. Placard. A very good one, if I might be so bold as to add."

Howard looked impressed. "A sharpshooter? A lady like you? I—I would never have guessed."

Howard knew in an instant he had said the wrong thing, as both his sister and Loraine jumped on his remark in synchronized unison. "I'm a sharpshooter!" Annette snapped. "Are you saying you don't think of me as a lady?"

Loraine's response came as a loud whisper and was no less critical than Annette's. "You think I can't handle a gun just because I'm a woman?"

"I'm sorry, Miss Parker," Howard stammered. "I didn't mean . . ."

"My father gave me that pistol for my eighteenth birthday. He had it specially made at no small cost, I'll have you know."

Howard strained to get a better look at the pistol. No stranger to guns, he had little trouble recognizing that this one was indeed special. It was a chrome-plated revolver with ivory handles, and he could see why she would be upset at the thought of losing it to these men. Still, no gun was worth putting her life in jeopardy. Loraine stiffened as she watched the outlaw reholster the pistol and shove it under his belt.

"That's my pistol," she said softly, but with fire in her eyes. "That man can't have it!"

Howard took hold of her arm and pulled her down lower. "No, Miss Parker! It's only a gun. Let it go."

Loraine pulled her arm free and peered over the rock to see the outlaw digging even deeper into her suitcase. He reached down and picked something up. "Would you take a look at this, Clay?" he called to his partner. "It's a pink lace petticoat. Ya-hoo! I'd say there must have been a fancy-smelling lady passenger aboard this stage."

Clay walked over to where Grayson stood and took the garment from him. "I believe you're right, Scar," he said, his voice rumbling with newly aroused interest. "And you know what I'm bettin'? I'm bettin' that fancy-smelling lady just might be somewhere hereabouts. If she was on this stage, there ain't much place she could have disappeared to, now is there?"

"We're not looking for no fancy-smelling lady, Clay," Grayson objected. "We're looking for the payroll money."

Clay waved a hand in front of Grayson's face. "We'll get to the money; it ain't goin' no place. I'll bet a month's supply of tabacky that fancy-smellin' lady is hidin' out somewhere in them rocks. Let's go have ourselves a look-see, whaddya say?"

Howard swallowed hard as Clay took a step in their direction. He ducked and pulled Loraine down with him. Clay's footsteps drew nearer, eventually coming close enough for Howard to hear his heavy breathing and actually smell the vile aroma of tobacco on his breath. For a second or two, Howard closed his eyes, drawing up his courage. Then he suddenly stood and rounded the rock, where he found himself looking straight in the startled eyes of the outlaw.

"You're mistaken, gentlemen," he said, trying to remain calm. "I was the only passenger this trip. The suitcase is filled with clothes I'm taking to my sister."

Clay's gun was instantly out and aimed directly at Howard's head. For a long moment, he stood staring at the big man. "Well, looky here," he said at length. "I think we've found our missin' money, Scar."

At first, Howard didn't make the connection. Why would these men think he had anything to do with the money they had expected to be on the stagecoach? Then it hit him. He still held the saddlebags Annette had sent along with him. These men had mentioned looking for saddlebags, and Howard suspected that the saddlebags they were looking for actually did contain money. He pulled the saddlebags off his shoulder and held them out in front of him. "You think there's money in here?" he asked. "No, these bags contain some personal items, but no money."

Grayson didn't even bother with a reply to Howard. He merely grinned and asked his partner, "You want to shoot him, Clay, or shall

I do it?"

"Now hold on!" Howard exclaimed. "There's no need for gunplay, no need at all. Just take a deep breath and don't get excited. I'll do whatever you ask. Here, take the saddlebags if you like."

Clay looked at the saddlebags in Howard's outstretched hand, but didn't take them just yet. "It ain't like we got anything personal against you, friend," he sneered. "It's just that you seen our faces. You leave us no choice. We got to shoot you now."

Howard stared at the gun in Clay's hand. This was the first time he'd ever found himself looking down the business end of one of these things. "Put the gun down, fellow," he reasoned calmly. "I'm sure we can talk this out man-to-man. I have no interest in turning you in to the law—you have my word on it."

The shot came so fast, Howard didn't have time to react. He was suddenly gripped with an excruciating pain in his upper chest. His knees buckled, his head throbbed, his stomach tightened in hard knots. Placing a hand over his heart, he slumped to the dusty earth and soon slipped into unconsciousness.

* * *

Horrified, Loraine shoved Amos hard to the ground. *They've killed him in cold blood,* she told herself. *How could they have done that? Mr. Placard didn't do one thing to antagonize them. Something like this could never happen in Boston.* Wide-eyed, she raised her head just far enough to see around the rock. The one called Clay gave Howard a kick. "He's done for, Scar," Clay reported. "Ya got 'im dead center. Good shootin', I'd say."

"'Course I hit him dead center. That's what I was aiming for. Get them saddlebags and let's see what's inside. Ten'll get ya twenty, it's the payroll cash."

CHAPTER 14

"They shot him!" Lori cried, staring at the holograph still playing in her family room. "Why didn't Annette protect him, Sam?"

Samantha smiled. "You want Howard protected? Why? After all, what's one jerk more or less in this world?"

"Sam! Just because he's a jerk doesn't mean I wanted this to happen."

"Me either," Brad interjected. "Why would his sister take him back to 1885 just to get him killed, Sam? It doesn't make sense."

"No one took him back to 1885 to get him killed, you two. He's not dead; he only thinks he is."

Lori looked again. "Well, if he's not dead, he's doing a good job pretending."

"If you had been paying attention," Samantha said, laughing softly, "you'd know what saved his life."

"The medallion!" Brad cried out. "That's what saved his life, isn't it, Sam?"

"There you go," she responded. "Makes a nice-sounding plot for one of your movies, wouldn't you say?"

"The medallion?" Lori repeated. "Sam? Are you trying to say . . . ?"

"If you were watching, you would have seen Annette put the medallion in Howard's shirt pocket, right over his heart."

Lori felt her pulse quicken. "The stranger who saved my great-grandfather's life . . . ," she stuttered. "It was . . ."

"Pretty embarrassing, isn't it? Having your own great-grandfather's life saved by such a jerk. Not to mention that same jerk saved your distant aunt's life as well."

"I can't believe this," Lori mused. "All my life I've heard the story of how the medallion stopped a bullet and saved a stranger's life—the same stranger who saved Amos and Loraine Parker's life. But—Howard Placard? Please, Sam, tell me I'm dreaming. Tell me I'll wake to find this whole thing is a nightmare."

"Lori, I'm an angel, sworn to tell the truth. I can't tell you you're dreaming when you're not," Samantha scolded her.

Lori glanced across the room at a glass trophy case setting atop the bookshelf. The case contained a chrome-plated revolver, which had been given to her on her eighteenth birthday—the same day she had received the medallion. "That pistol in the trophy case," she asked. "Is it . . . ?"

"It's the same pistol you just saw in the holograph," Samantha responded. "Interesting, isn't it? Loraine got the pistol from her father on her eighteenth birthday, and you got it from your father on your eighteenth birthday."

Brad picked up the Polaroid photograph he and Lori had been talking about earlier. The one said to be a picture of Loraine Parker. "What about this, Sam?" he asked. "Is this authentic, too?"

"It's authentic," she assured him. "We haven't reached that part in the story yet, but we're almost there. You'll get a firsthand look at how the picture came to be, Brad. You have my word on it."

Samantha turned back to Lori. "Let me ask you another question about the stories you heard from your daddy's lap. Do you remember him telling you about the time Loraine bested the now famous Annie Oakley in a shooting demonstration?"

Lori's head was swimming. She hadn't yet settled in on the idea of Howard being the one whose life was saved by the medallion, and here Samantha was pushing another off-the-wall idea, something about Annie Oakley. She tried to clear her mind. "I remember Daddy telling me something about Annie Oakley," she said. "I think he did say Loraine once met Annie and somehow outdid her with a gun. I never put much stock in his story. I know how things like that can get exaggerated."

"Nothing exaggerated about the story, lady," Samantha said briskly. "I checked it out myself while I was doing my homework for this assignment. Went straight to the source."

Lori's eyes narrowed. "Are you saying you talked with the real Annie Oakley?"

Samantha nodded, smiling. "I did. And Annie makes no bones about being glad that Loraine never chose to go into show business as her competition. Annie likes being remembered as the top female gun in the Old West."

"Are you serious, Sam? You really talked with Annie Oakley?"

"Sure I did. She was more than willing to help with my research. Very nice lady."

"Oh, my. This dealing with angels gets stranger by the minute. Next you'll be telling me you've seen Elvis."

"Funny you should mention Elvis. I just happen to have tickets for one of his multi-universe concerts. It's coming up tomorrow night, as a matter of fact."

"What? Elvis performs on your side now? And you have tickets?"

"What's so hard to believe about that? Life on my side is a lot like life on your side. Things are just done on a higher level over there, that's all. And yes, I do have tickets to the concert—although there is a slight chance I might not get to use them." Samantha shrugged. "Jason wants to attend some stiff chefs' convention that's scheduled for the exact same time as Elvis."

"A chefs' convention? In place of an Elvis concert? Doesn't Jason have any heart at all?"

"Not when it comes to his cooking," Samantha huffed. "I've outsmarted him on this one, though. We have a little bet going to see which event we'll attend. He wins, we go to the Sominex Festival; I win—it's Elvis, here we come."

"Amazing," Lori said, shaking her head. "An Elvis concert on your side."

"Yep. We have Elvis on my side, and we have Annie Oakley in our story. In fact, Annie plays a big part in our story. She and a fellow by the name of William Frederick Cody."

"William Frederick Cody?" Lori repeated. "Buffalo Bill? He's part of the story, too?"

"There," Samantha said, pointing to the holograph. "See for yourself."

Lori looked to see the holograph had switched again. This time she was watching a wagon train moving toward her down a dirt road that appeared to be the same one the stagecoach had been on. She counted six wagons in all. The lead wagon was close enough for her to get a good look at the woman driving it. "That's her!" Lori shouted. "I recognize her from pictures in the history books."

Lori then noticed the rider on a horse next to Annie's wagon. Her attention was drawn to the clothes he was wearing. There was a buck-skin coat with leather tassels hanging from the sleeves, a large brimmed hat, a pair of leather gloves with more tassels, and the fanciest boots she'd ever seen. His hair was full and he wore a mustache and chin whiskers. "And that's Bill Cody!" she added, with no less enthusiasm.

"That's him," Samantha agreed. "One of the greatest showmen ever to live. Annie Oakley and her husband, Frank Butler, joined up with Bill's Wild West Show in 1885. Frank was a sharpshooter, too, but it was Annie who went on to become famous. Frank's not with them at the moment; he's in Phoenix making arrangements for a proper greeting when the train of celebrities arrives there sometime tomorrow."

Lori was spellbound at the thought that she was actually looking into the faces of Buffalo Bill and Annie Oakley. She had always been fascinated by stories of these two. "Sam?" she asked, almost afraid to voice the question hanging in her mind. "Are Buffalo Bill and Annie Oakley my ancestors, too?"

"No," Samantha laughingly assured her. "But they do play an important part in our story."

Lori's face showed her disappointment. Buffalo Bill and Annie Oakley were two of her favorite characters from history. She had written an essay on Bill Cody in high school, so she knew something about him. When Bill was nine, his father had died; two years later young Bill got a job riding with supply trains. From there, he went on to become a Pony Express rider. At eighteen, he enlisted in the Union Army and became a scout and guide for the Fifth Cavalry. At twenty-six he won the Congressional Medal of Honor for his scouting.

But his real fame came when a novelist by the name of Ned Buntline tagged him with the nickname "Buffalo Bill." Buntline used Buffalo Bill as a hero in several of his stories and actually talked Cody into playing his own part in a few stage presentations. That was Bill's first experience with the entertainment world. One taste and he never left it again. Every history student knows how he put together the most famous "wild west" show ever conceived. He and his troupe toured the country, entertaining people everywhere.

Lori sighed. "There is one sad part about his story, though. A year before he died, the U.S. Congress withdrew his medal of honor. Their excuse was that he hadn't held any service rank when the medal was awarded. It broke his heart. I only wish Bill Cody could have known the U.S Government would restore the validity of his medal in 1989," she said.

"He does know," Samantha smiled. "I talked to him not more than a month ago when he came by our galaxy with his new universally expanded show. Annie's still with him, too."

Lori caught her breath. "They have wild west shows on your side, too?"

"Oh yes. It's a nostalgic thing for some and a history lesson for others. Very popular entertainment."

Samantha nodded toward the holograph to draw Lori's attention back to it, since by this time, the front wagon was near enough for Bill and Annie's conversation to be clearly understood.

* * *

"Whoa!" Annie called, reining in her team and bringing the wagon to a stop. "Up there, Bill," she said, standing up from her seat and pointing off in the distance at an approaching dust cloud. "What do you make of it?"

Bill looked for himself. "Don't rightly know, Annie. It looks like a team of horses headed our way, but I don't see a wagon hitched to 'em."

Annie strained even harder. "I think you're right, Bill. It is a team. Runaways, I'd say. Better get some of the hands up here so's we can rein 'em in."

"Shorty!" Bill called back to the driver of the second wagon. "Pass the word back. We got a team of runaway horses comin' at us from up ahead. Everyone out of the wagons. Spread out. Let's rein them rascals in and see if we can figure out what they're doing."

Word spread through the wagon train like wildfire through a pine forest. Everyone sprang into action, forming a human blockade. It worked. The approaching horses slowed, finally coming to a stop only a short distance away.

"Easy there, big fellows," Bill called to the team as he dismounted and eased his way up to them. "Take it easy now." Very carefully, he reached for the bridle on the lead horse. "What's got you fellows spooked, anyway?" he asked, stroking the horse ever so gently along its neck. Once he was sure the team had no intention of bolting again, he walked to the rear and examined the broken tongue.

"These fellows were a stagecoach team," he exclaimed as some of the others joined up with him. "From the looks of things, I'd say there's been an accident. My guess is there's a busted-up stagecoach not far from here. Some of you fellows get these horses watered and cooled down. I'll ride on ahead and see what I can find out."

Annie was off the wagon in one bound. Moving straight to her own horse, kept leashed to the back of her wagon, she pulled him free and led him over to where Bill was just mounting up. "I'm riding with you, Bill," she said, slipping a foot in the stirrup and pulling up to the saddle. "One of the fellows can drive my wagon."

Bill looked at her only once, then with a nod of agreement, shouted for Shorty to get someone to drive Annie's wagon. "Reckon I'd like your company, Annie," he said. "No telling what we might find waitin' for us up there." Digging his heels into the animal's side, Bill nudged his stallion forward into a full gallop with Annie right behind.

* * *

Lori watched as the two of them rode off in the distance. "Aren't we going with them, Sam?" she asked.

"We'll get back to them later," Samantha explained. "Right now it's time to return to Howard and Loraine."

"I'd forgotten how realistic these holographs are," Brad mentioned. "It's amazing how we can actually feel what Annie and Buffalo Bill were feeling at the time."

"You have to understand, Brad," Samantha explained. "These holographs are the way we preserve history on my side. Preserving history is important, as is preserving it accurately. These holographs are the means the higher authorities have chosen for the job."

Brad laughed. "Who knows, when it comes my time to cross the line, I might just be involved with the making of holographs. It should be right up my alley after being a film director all these years."

Samantha thought about it. "Stranger things have happened," she acknowledged. "I was a schoolteacher during my time in the mortal world, and my first job over here was as a teacher. It wouldn't surprise me one bit if your first assignment does involve holographs."

"Maybe I should pay some close attention to how they're put together," Brad reasoned. "Roll 'em, Sam."

CHAPTER 15

Clay Derringer took one last look at the man he had shot, just to be certain he was dead. He looked dead enough, so Clay turned his attention to the saddlebags, and what he supposed was the payroll money. Opening one side of the bags, he dumped the contents on the ground at his feet.

"What is this junk?" Grayson grumbled. "Open the other side, Clay. See if the money's in there."

"That's what I figured on doin', Scar," Clay retorted as he dumped the contents of the second side.

"More junk!" Grayson spat out. "There ain't no dough in them bags!"

"Well, that money's got to be here somewhere," Clay growled. "We'll just have to keep looking till we find it."

Howard's head was beginning to clear, but his chest felt as if it had been hit by a charging rhinoceros. Carefully, he moved a hand to his chest, feeling for signs of blood. There was none. Somehow the bullet hadn't broken his skin, but right now wasn't the time to question why. Out of the corner of his eye, he spotted two pairs of leather boots. He quickly surmised it was the robbers. He noticed something else, too. The saddlebags. The outlaws must have dumped the contents on the ground. His eyes lit on the can of pepper spray and the handcuffs, and instantly a plan formulated in his mind. Very slowly, he reached for the pepper spray, retrieving it without either of the men seeing him. Then in a low voice, he called out to them. "You want to know where the money is?"

Clay and Grayson looked at each other. "Did you hear something?" Clay asked.

"Yeah, I think so," Grayson said.

Clay allowed his eyes to settle on Howard. "It sounded like it came from him."

Grayson also looked at the supposedly dead body. "Don't make no sense, Clay. Dead men don't talk."

"I'm not dead," Howard said, without moving so much as an eyelash. "And I know where the money is."

Clay lay a boot alongside Howard's ribs and gave a gentle shove. Howard still didn't move. "He said something, Scar. I'll swear he said something 'bout the money."

Both men looked at each other again, then in unison slowly knelt with their faces close to Howard's. "The money, you say?" Clay asked. "You know where it is?"

Sitting up, Howard opened fire with the pepper spray. Screaming in agony, both men frantically rubbed their eyes. "Get him, Scar!" Clay bellowed at the top of his voice. "The darn fool's blinded me!"

"Get him yerself!" Grayson screamed back. "He's blinded me, too! What in tarnation did he hit me with?"

Howard wasted no time. Shoving both men to the ground, he quickly disarmed them, remembering to take the fancy pistol that belonged to Loraine as well. Grabbing the handcuffs, he snapped one bracelet on Clay and the other on Grayson.

"What's he doin' Clay?" Grayson cried out. "Do something—do *anythin'*—just get me to some water so's I can wash my eyes out!"

Howard took a step backward, cocked the hammer on Clay's revolver, and aimed it at the hapless pair. "Button it up!" he shouted at them. "Don't move so much as a toenail, or I'll see if this gun works any better on the two of you than it did on me."

Clay managed to open one eye just enough to realize he was staring down the barrel of his own revolver. "You're a dead man, mister," he growled. "No one takes my gun from me and lives to tell about it."

"I beg to differ with you, fellow," Howard shot back. "But from where I'm standing, it looks like I just made a liar out of you. In case you hadn't noticed, it's you looking down the stinger end of your revolver at the moment—not a good time to be threatening the man whose finger's resting on the trigger."

Loraine was astonished at the way this stranger handled these two outlaws. She wasted no time coming out of hiding. Rounding the rock, she went straight for her own pistol, removing it from the holster.

"I'm glad to see you're all right, Mr. Placard," she said, stepping next to Howard and adding a second gun to his. "I thought they'd killed you."

"So did I," Howard half joked. "Personally, I don't think these two like me very well."

"I knowed it, Scar!" Clay shouted. "That sweet-smelling lady was here the whole time."

Loraine leaned down and picked up the can of pepper spray. "Now here's a weapon I've never seen before," she observed. "What's it called?"

Howard searched his mind for an explanation. What could he say?

"Tell her what it is, Peaches," he heard his sister say. "She has to learn the truth about you sometime. She might as well start now."

Tell her the truth? Now there was a thought, Howard mused ironically. *Wouldn't the average nineteenth-century woman understand how a man could come from more than a hundred years in the future to save her and her little brother from the runaway stage? Yeah, right.* But if Annette said Loraine had to learn the truth, Howard would accept that. Taking a deep breath, he decided to go for it. "You said you came from Boston, isn't that right, Miss Parker?"

Her face showed her bewilderment at his question. "Yes, I come from Boston."

"Boston's a very long way from here," Howard went on. "And you have things in Boston that are more advanced than some of the things they have here in the Arizona Territory, wouldn't you say?"

"This is true, Mr. Placard," she agreed. "But where is this conversation leading?"

"I come from a place far from here, too, Miss Parker. And we have things more advanced even than what you have in Boston. What you're holding is a can of pepper spray. By simply depressing the top of the can, it sprays out a stream of highly irritating liquid. As you can see by these two, once the liquid hits the eyes . . ."

Loraine examined the can more closely. "What makes the liquid come out?" she quizzed. "Is there a spring in the can?"

Howard laughed. "No spring," he said. "The can is sealed so tightly, it can be pressurized inside."

"Pressurized?" she repeated. "You're right, Mr. Placard. I've never seen anything like this in Boston. Where exactly is it you come from?"

Howard coughed. Explaining the pepper spray was one thing; explaining her next question was quite another. So he sidestepped the issue instead. "It's not really important where I come from, Miss Parker. Let's just say it's a long way from here, and let it go at that, may we?"

"Very well," she responded. "But there is one thing I want to know. How did you survive this culprit's bullet?"

Howard wanted to know the answer to that one himself. As he contemplated the mystery, his sister spoke up. "Check your shirt pocket, Peaches. You might be surprised at what you find there."

Howard shifted the revolver to his left hand, then reached inside his shirt pocket with his right hand and removed the medallion. "Well, I'll be," he murmured. "This is what stopped the bullet."

Loraine took the medallion and examined it. "You're a very lucky man, Mr. Placard. It's incredible that this little medallion was in the right place to save your life."

By this time, Amos had grown tired of crouching behind the rock so he climbed on top of it to see what was happening.

"Good Gabriel's ghost," Clay grumbled, seeing the boy. "Now a kid shows up. How many more of 'em are out there?"

Ignoring the bandit, Amos went straight to Loraine, who was still looking at the medallion. "Can I see it?" he asked excitedly. Loraine handed it to him. "Wow, look at this, sis. This medallion has our family crest on it."

"What?" Loraine asked, glancing down at the medallion in her brother's hand. "You're right, Amos!" she exclaimed. "This is the official Parker crest." Her eyes held a silent question as she looked at Howard.

"I didn't know that," he answered honestly.

Amos spoke up. "This is really nifty, Mr. Placard. Can I keep it?"

"Amos!" Loraine scolded. "That's not polite asking for something that belongs to Mr. Placard."

"No, it's all right," Howard insisted. "Let the lad keep it." He smiled to himself, thinking of the story of the medallion as he had heard it from Lori all those years ago. She said the stranger, whose life the medallion had saved, gave it to her great-grandfather. And here he was—fulfilling that very part of the folk tale at this very time. What a strange thing time travel was. What a strange thing, indeed.

"Are you sure it's all right for Amos to keep it?" Loraine asked.

"Let the lad have it," Howard smiled. "I'm sure he'll make better use of it somewhere down the road than I ever would."

"All right, Amos," she agreed. "You may keep it. But say thank you to Mr. Placard."

"Thank you, Mr. Placard," the lad said, beaming. "Where'd you get it, anyway?"

"Where did I get it, indeed?" he responded, glancing over at his sister. "It was given to me, Miss Parker. By an angel, if you will."

"An angel?" Loraine looked at him curiously. "Your mother, perhaps?"

Annette gave Howard a playful shove. "What do you want, Peaches? Here's the perfect opening. Go ahead, tell her your story."

Howard's eyes shifted from his sister to this lovely woman standing next to him. He studied her face meticulously. It was still hard for him not to think of her as Lori Parker. Every line, every curve, every tiny feature told him he was looking into the face of the woman he loved. But she wasn't Lori. She was Loraine Parker, from Boston. She was the sister of Lori's great-grandfather. And strangest of all, she belonged to a completely different century from Lori.

Howard wet his lips. "I wasn't referring to my mother when I said an angel, Miss Parker." Without explaining this further, he asked, "Doesn't it seem strange to you how I managed to get on top of the stagecoach in order to stop it?"

"I had considered that," she admitted. "And yes, I would call it strange. I have no idea how you managed it."

"Let me ask you another question," he said, moving ahead with what was probably the most difficult explanation of his life. "What is today's exact date?"

"Monday, October the fifth," she said with no hesitation.

Howard had every intention of using this date as a jumping-off point for explaining when and where he had come from. But just as he was about to make his point, he was distracted by Clay Derringer who was attempting to stand. "Hold it right there, mister!" Howard snapped. "Don't even think about it!"

Clay glared at Howard, his eyes still red from the pepper spray. "If I was you," he sneered, "I'd be considering how you reckon on keepin' the two of us in hand. You don't strike me as the sort who knows much about using a gun. Maybe we can cut a deal here. What do ya say, pal?"

Before Howard could answer, Loraine stepped between them. She leaned down, resting the barrel of her gun against the tip of Clay's nose. "Hold your tongue!" she ordered. "I can't speak for Mr. Placard, but I know how to use this. And just so you know—it's a twenty-two magnum, nine-shot, high-standard revolver with a hair trigger set for a one-ounce pull. There will be no deals with the likes of you two. We're turning you over to the authorities."

Clay laughed. "A slick-looking gal like you using a gun? I have a hard time believing that one, sister. Scar and me will go easy on you if you cooperate with us. Ya got my word on it."

Loraine glared at him. "The word of a snake like you?" she scoffed. "That's a laugh. And as for my knowing how to use this revolver, maybe a little demonstration is in order." Loraine reached down and removed Clay's hat.

"That's going to cost you, lady," he growled through clenched teeth. "No one messes with my hat."

"Humph, funny, I'd swear I just did. Here, little brother," she said, handing Amos the hat. "Give this a toss in the air, will you?"

"Sure, sis," Amos grinned. Then, with a flip of his wrist he sent the hat sailing high into the air.

Howard watched with keen interest as three shots spat from Loraine's revolver in rapid secession. With each shot, Clay's hat jerked violently. The hat hardly had time to hit the ground before Amos had retrieved it.

"Nice shootin', sis," he boasted. "Three shots dead center. I'd say this fellow better not expect this hat to keep out much rain. No sir!"

Loraine took the hat and tossed it on the ground next to Clay. "If you're not happy with the hat demonstration, I'll do it again—using a dime."

Clay stared at the hat, his eyes bugging out from their sockets. He swallowed once, then swallowed again. But he didn't say a word.

By this time, all thoughts of explaining when and where he came from were forgotten. Howard's interest now was in the demonstration Loraine had just given. "That was some fine shooting, Miss Parker," he said. "Where did you learn to use a gun like that, if I might ask?"

Amos broke in. "In Boston," he grinned. "My sister has been shootin' since she was twelve. Nobody can beat her. She's just too good for everybody."

"Amos is right," she smiled. "From the time I was twelve, I was a member of the local Ladies' Sharpshooters Academy. I love the sport. From my second year I was the top markswoman in our group. I wasn't kidding about being able to hit a dime." She smiled. "Bet you never knew a woman who could handle a gun."

Howard checked out his sister's smile. He might have let the subject drop, but Annette had other ideas. "The lady's good, Peaches. Almost as good as me. And might I point something out to you, brother dear? All the years you made a fool out of yourself chasing after Lori Douglas, did you ever find one thing you and she shared in common? No, you didn't. You and Lori have nothing whatsoever in common. But take Loraine Parker here. You've known her less than half an hour, and already you've found something you share in common with her."

Pointing a finger at Howard in a gun-like fashion, she smiled mischievously. "Bang, bang," she said, then pretended to blow the smoke away from her finger.

Howard cleared his throat. "I've done some shooting, myself, Miss Parker. Maybe we can set up a contest sometime."

Amos looked at up at Howard with keen interest beaming from his face. "You shoot, Mr. Placard? Are you good at it?"

Howard lay a hand on Amos' shoulder. "Not to be bragging, son. But, yes, I am good. And you know, I had a sister, too. We were raised on a ranch, right here in Arizona. The two of us took up the sport when we were kids. Your sister is good at shooting. Well, my sister was good, too—" Howard glanced over at Annette, and added, "almost as good as me." She glared at him but said nothing.

"You were raised on a ranch here in Arizona?" Loraine broke in. "I thought you said you were from somewhere a long ways off."

Howard was momentarily speechless, then he gathered his wits about him. "Ah, yes, well—I was raised in Arizona but I haven't lived here in years." Howard knew this wasn't the real answer to her question, and he knew he'd have to give her a better answer later on.

Evidently Loraine accepted it as she went on to another thought. "You have a sister who's a markswoman? How interesting. Is she good?"

"Oh, yes. My sister is—or was—almost as good as me," he said for a second time.

"There's that 'almost' again," Annette scolded. "If there's an 'almost' involved, it's that you're almost as good as me. And don't go using the past tense about my ability, either. I was good then and I still am."

Howard paid her no mind and continued speaking to Loraine and Amos. "My sister died when she was only twenty. But to answer something you said earlier, Miss Parker, yes I did know a lady who could use a gun."

Loraine's expression softened. "I'm sorry about your sister. It must have been a terrible loss."

Howard nodded. "Her name was Annette, and she was my twin. Her death was like losing half of myself."

"Oh, I'm really sorry," Loraine said sympathetically.

"I've kept up my shooting, through the years. Some of my filming crew went in with me to form our own club. They're good, but to be honest, not one of them can hold a candle to me."

"Filming crew?" Loraine asked, puzzled. "There's another of your terms I'm unfamiliar with."

Howard bit his lip, angry with himself for slipping again. "I know," he said. "I'm trying to explain, but it's quite difficult." He shoved the revolver he was holding under his belt. "Tell you what—let me hobble these fellows a little more, then we'll talk. Keep them covered, okay?"

"All right," Loraine said, holding her revolver on the men. "What's your plan?"

"The long-range plan is turning them over to the authorities, just as you suggested. But for now, I have something else in mind."

"Ha!" Clay hooted. "Turn us over to the authorities? That's what you think, pal. There ain't no authorities in these parts, and from the looks of you, I'd say you wouldn't make it two miles over this desert on your own. You got more to think about than just yourself, ya know. You got the woman and kid here. Just how do you plan on getting the three of you back to civilization alive?"

"I guess that's my problem, isn't it, mister?" Howard said calmly. "You want to pull off those boots and toss them over here?"

"My boots? Are you crazy?!"

"That's what I said, pardner. It's a little something I learned from a friend of mine named Dusty Lockhart. With your boots off, you'll be a lot less likely to cause us any unnecessary problems. Now get 'em off. And that goes for you, too, Mr. Scar, or whatever your name is."

"Listen, pal," Clay protested. "Just forget about the boots, okay? And forget about turning us over to the authorities while you're at it. Get these handcuffs off us, let us ride out of here, and I give you my word to stop by the nearest town and tell them where to find you."

Howard glared at the men. "The boots," he said slowly. "Let's have them—now!"

Clay never took his eyes off of Howard. "Just how do you expect us to get the boots off when we're cuffed together like a couple of Siamese twins?"

Catching even Howard off guard, Loraine fired a shot at the ground only inches from Clay's foot. "Figure it out," she said. "If I fire another warning shot, I guarantee it will be even closer than the first."

Clay let out a quick breath of disgust. Reaching down with his one free hand, he removed the first boot. "I'll see to it you pay for this, little lady," he grumbled, pausing before reaching for the second.

Loraine cocked the hammer on her revolver. "I think she means it," Howard laughed. "Look at her eyes. You can always tell when a woman's serious just by reading her eyes. Off hand, I'd say you'd better get that second boot off sort of sudden-like, pardner."

Clay removed the boot. Grayson quickly did the same with his. "That's more like it," Howard said, picking up the boots and handing them to Amos. "Here, young man, take these out in the desert and find a place to toss them where they'll be a little difficult to retrieve."

"Yes, sir," Amos laughed, grabbing the boots. "I spotted a cactus patch back there on the other side of the rocks where we were hiding. I suppose anyone would think twice before going in there after a pair of boots."

"Good thinking, Amos," Howard laughed. "Go give 'em a toss."

Howard rubbed his hand over his mouth and stared after Amos. What Clay had said was true; handing these two over to the authorities wasn't going to be easy. Just saving himself, Loraine, and Amos from the jaws of this barren desert would be tough enough. All things considered, he might not be able to turn these culprits over to the authorities at all. It might come down to leaving them to fend for themselves. It was just a matter of survival.

One thing was in his favor—he had grown up in the shadow of the Superstition Mountains. And with them in sight now, he knew the city of Mesa was due west roughly twenty miles.

"Okay, Peaches," Annette said, breaking into his thoughts. "Enough stalling. It's time for you to explain some things to Miss Parker. And don't go getting the idea you can weasel out of it. You can do it the easy way or the hard way. And I think you know I have what it takes to back up my word when I threaten to help you do it the hard way. I might even contract the evening news to tell the world your nickname, Peaches."

Howard glared at her. "You wouldn't!" he grumbled under his breath.

"Oh yes I would, brother dear. So why not do it the easy way and save face?"

Howard had no doubt his sister would make good her threat if he gave her the slightest bit of trouble. He decided on the easy way. "Miss Parker," he said. "Would you mind stepping over by the stage-coach with me? There's something I'd like to discuss without our audience listening in." He nodded toward the men on the ground.

Loraine understood. She lowered her pistol until it nearly touched Clay's face. "Don't go doing anything stupid," she warned. "Mr. Placard and I are going to walk over to the stagecoach. We may be out of earshot, but we won't be out of pistol range. Get my point?"

Clay grunted and Loraine pulled back the gun. She nodded at Howard, and the two of them moved over next to the stagecoach. "You wanted to talk?" she asked.

"Yeah." Howard exhaled and stared at the ground. "There are a few things about me that need clarifying," he began, "and what I have to say won't be easy." He lifted his eyes until they met hers. "They're not easy for me to say, and they certainly won't be easy for you to understand. When I showed up on the stagecoach," he said, "I didn't do it entirely on my own. I had some help." Howard hesitated briefly, then just said it, "Do you . . . believe in . . . angels, Miss Parker?"

Loraine caught her breath. "Do I—? Angels? You mean, like with wings and a halo?"

"No, no, not that at all. Real angels don't have wings or halos. Real angels look more like . . ." He stopped, just staring into her disbelieving eyes. "I told you this wasn't going to be easy, didn't I?"

"Are you saying—that—you're an angel, Mr. Placard?"

Howard coughed. "Me an angel? No, Miss Parker. Not hardly. I'm certainly no angel. What I'm trying to say is, I had the help of an angel. And before you decide I'm some sort of nut, consider this—if I'm not telling the truth about my angel—how else could I have gotten onto the stagecoach?"

"I—I'm not sure, Mr. Placard. But angels? I don't know, I've never met anyone who claimed to have seen angels."

"Tell her she's wrong, Peaches," Annette spoke up. "Tell her she's seen an angel herself. It was her grandfather. He came to her once when she was nine years old. He had only been gone a month or so at the time, and she was having a hard time dealing with his death. He came to her in a meadow behind the house where she lived in Boston. He told her he loved her and that he was happy where he was."

When Howard hesitated, Annette pressed the issue. "Tell her what I said, Peaches. Take my word for it, it will open doors."

"I—uh—happen to know about a time you saw an angel yourself," Howard said, after gathering his courage. "It was your grandfather."

Loraine froze and stood looking at Howard without speaking. "You were nine years old. He came to you in a meadow behind your house in Boston. He comforted you and told you he was happy where he was living then."

It was a long time before Loraine could speak. "I never told that story to a living soul," she said, once her voice would work. "Not even my mother. How could you possibly know about that?"

He smiled. "My angel told me. Just now."

"Just now?" Loraine asked. "You're telling me your angel is here now?"

"Standing right there," he said, pointing at Annette. "I'm not sure why she's chosen to remain invisible to everyone but me, but . . ."

Loraine stared into space where Howard was pointing. "My grandfather told me something else that day," she stated cautiously. "Can your angel tell me what that was?"

"Her grandfather's name was Lesley," Annette said. "He told her that after she had grown up, she would meet a very special man. And that man would come to her with an unbelievable story. The way she would know the man was telling the truth is that the man's middle name would be Lesley."

Howard felt a sudden urge to drop the subject. He had always hated his middle name and had made it a point for many years never to use it. So it was with great apprehension that he followed his sister's prompting now. "I know what else it was your grandfather told you, Miss Parker," he said, reluctantly. "Not many people know this about me, but my middle name is . . ." He stopped. He had a hard time getting the name out, he hated it so badly.

All the color drained from Loraine's face, hearing him say this. "Your middle name is what?" she prompted him.

His eyes lowered. "It's Lesley," he said. "The same as your grandfather. And by that, you should know I'm telling the truth about my angel."

"Oh, my!" Loraine breathed. "You are telling the truth. You do have an angel with you."

"Yes, and my story doesn't stop there, I'm afraid. It gets even more bizarre than just having an angel with me, Miss Parker. When I asked you the date, you told me today is Monday, October the fifth. But you didn't mention the year."

"I assumed you would know this is 1885, Mr. Placard," she replied.

"The only reason I know this is 1885 is because my angel told me," Howard said. "You see, Miss Parker, I don't belong in 1885. My angel has brought me here from another time."

Loraine's face grew pale. "Another time? But how can that be?"

Howard looked at Loraine frankly. "I don't know how it can be, Miss Parker. All I know is she brought me here. I'm from a very long time in your future, you see. That's what I meant when I told you I came from a faraway place. It would have been more correct to say I come from a faraway *time.*"

Loraine turned her back on Howard and walked a few steps away, then stopped. For nearly a minute, she said nothing. When she did speak, she remained looking the other way. "You're absolutely positive your middle name is Lesley?" she asked soberly.

"I'm positive," he said. "But I'd just as soon you didn't broadcast it."

It was another long moment before she finally turned and walked back to where he stood. "Pepper spray?" she asked. "And filming crews? These are things from the future?"

"Yes."

"Okay, Peaches," Annette said. "It's time to move things up a level. You brought a Polaroid camera along on this trip. Now's the time to use it."

"That's right!" Howard exclaimed excitedly. "Why didn't I think of that? I can show you something from the future, Miss Parker. Wait here a moment."

* * *

Loraine's head was spinning at the things that had transpired since Howard Placard had shown up so suddenly in her life. Never had she been faced with anything like this. Tales of angels, of time travel, of strange inventions, and terms like "pepper spray" and "filming crews." And the incredible part was, she believed it all. How could she help but believe when her grandfather's test of proof had been so completely laid out in front of her?

Loraine watched as Howard hurried back to the saddlebags belonging to him and began picking up the items dumped on the ground by the outlaws. She had no idea what he was up to, but she was certain whatever it was would bring even more surprises. As she watched him retrieving the things, her mind drifted back to that day in the meadow when her grandfather had come to her as an angel.

Loraine and her grandfather had always been close, and his death had left her devastated. There was a lot more to his visit than Mr. Placard had alluded to. Her grandfather had told her much more about the man with the middle name of Lesley than the simple fact that his amazing story would be true. Grandfather Lesley had actually described the man, and as Loraine looked at Mr. Placard now, the description fit him perfectly.

Through the years, Loraine had remembered that meeting with her grandfather. She had always wondered about the man he said would come someday. As a child, she had pictured the man as a valiant prince who would ride in on a powerful steed to sweep her away to a castle in the sky. As she grew older, this image diminished—as did her belief the man would ever actually come. But now, without a doubt, he had come. And if not on a steed, then on a runaway stagecoach. She could only wonder why fate had brought them together.

There was more about this man than just his rugged handsomeness that attracted Loraine to him. When she looked in his eyes, it was as if she had known him all her life. And yet, there were so many mysteries about him. So many things she couldn't understand.

She watched as he picked up the saddlebags and started back toward her. He was carrying something outside the bags, but she didn't recognize what it was.

"Here," Howard said, stepping up to her. "This is what I wanted to show you. It's something to help you see what the world is like where I come from."

CHAPTER 16

"What is it?" Loraine asked, examining the strange object

"It's a camera," Howard responded.

"A camera? You mean like Mathew Brady used to capture the images of the Civil War scenes?" she asked curiously.

"That's right. Have you seen Brady's works?"

"I've seen some of them on display in our hometown museum. It's unbelievable that a little box can capture an instant in time and preserve it for anyone to see." She looked again at Howard's camera. "This doesn't look like the camera he uses. His is much larger and stands on three legs."

"No," Howard agreed. "This camera isn't like the one Mathew Brady used. This camera is much more advanced. Here, let me demonstrate." He aimed the camera at her. "Give us your best smile, okay?"

Loraine managed a nervous smile. Howard clicked the button and the flash went off. She jerked back with a start. She was even more startled by the whirring noise the camera made as it ejected the exposed print. "Oh!" she said. "Did you capture my image on a negative that fast?"

"No, not actually. You see, Miss Parker, unlike Mathew Brady's camera, this one doesn't need a negative. Nor does it need a laboratory to process the image. Here," Howard said, ripping off the exposed picture and handing it to her. "Hold it by the edges. You don't want to touch the surface just yet. It might interfere with the developing process."

Loraine stared at the paper. "I don't see anything," she said. "It's just a piece of thick paper."

"Just keep watching," Howard reassured. "You're in for a very pleasant surprise, I assure you."

"This is incredible," Loraine observed as her image began to form. "It's like magic."

"Yes, it is, sort of, Howard agreed. "I've always been a little amazed at how a Polaroid works myself."

Within seconds the image became clearer, and Loraine could see it was completely different from the drab black and white photographs she had seen in the museum. This image was in brilliant color. "It really is me," she said, stunned. "This is the most amazing thing I've ever seen."

Loraine was so taken up in watching the photo materialize that she didn't notice Amos had rejoined them until he was right next to her. "What ya got, sis?" he asked, staring at the picture.

Howard stepped in with an answer to his question. "It's what we call a photograph, son, Would you like me to take one of you?"

"Are you sure it's all right, Mr. Placard?" Loraine asked.

"Of course it's all right," Howard said, smiling. "There's plenty of film left."

Loraine reached out and smoothed Amos' hair with her fingers. "Face the camera, little brother," she said. "And smile."

Amos did as his sister asked. Howard then clicked the picture and handed Amos the blank print as it emerged from the camera. "Just keep watching, and you'll see a picture of yourself develop right in front of your eyes, son."

"Wow," Amos exclaimed as his own image began to appear. "How does it work, Mr. Placard?"

Howard laughed. "Well now, son, I don't know precisely how it works. I've used a lot of different kinds of cameras in my work over the years, but I'm not engineer enough to know how they capture an image."

"Mr. Placard was just telling me some things about himself, Amos," Loraine told the lad as he watched the last stages of his photograph appear on the paper. "He comes from a place where things are more advanced even than they are in Boston. That's how he happens to have this amazing little camera."

Amos looked curious. "What other kind of things do you have where you come from, Mr. Placard?" he asked.

Loraine took on a look of concern at Amos' question. "I'm not sure Mr. Placard wants to tell us about the place he comes from," she said.

"I don't see a problem telling you about where I come from," Howard responded, looking at Annette to see if he might be treading on thin ice. She gave him a quick nod. "It's a place with technologies and advancements like you probably can't even imagine, Amos," he began. "For instance, we don't use stagecoaches. We have what we call 'automobiles.' Automobiles are like stagecoaches, but they don't need horses to pull them. They move down the road all by themselves."

"That's not possible," Amos countered.

"Yes it is, son. Not only that, once you're inside the automobile you stay perfectly comfortable regardless of how hot or cold it gets outside. In the winter, the car has a way of remaining warm inside. In the summer, it remains cool. Even on the hottest days."

"That sounds incredible, Mr. Placard," Loraine responded. "Almost unbelievable, in fact."

"Wait!" Howard said, yanking out his wallet. "I may have some pictures. Yes, here's one of my sister standing in front of Mom's BMW. BMW is a particular brand of automobile. They make hundreds of different kinds."

Howard pulled the picture from his wallet and handed it to Loraine. She seemed more interested in the woman in the picture than in the car. "Is this Annette?" she guessed.

"Yeah," Howard said. "This picture was the last one taken of her before the accident that took her life."

"She was a very beautiful young woman," Loraine observed.

"Can I see it, sis?" Amos asked and Loraine held out the picture.

"This is one of those automobiles that go without horses," he asked.

Howard nodded yes. "Could I have this picture to keep?" Amos asked hopefully.

"No, Amos!" Loraine quickly said. "That's a very special picture for Mr. Placard, and he's already given you the medallion."

"Really, it's all right," Howard affirmed. "I have several other copies of this picture. And I have the negative in case I ever want more. Amos can have the picture. And you know, automobiles are only the beginning." He smiled at Loraine. "Think about this, Miss

Parker. How would you like to have something so small you could hold it in one hand, and yet so powerful it would allow you to talk to someone at any other point in the entire world? Say for instance, you wanted to talk to someone back in Boston. You could do it from right where you're standing. Pretty incredible, wouldn't you say? We have those devices, Miss Parker. We call them 'telephones.'"

Howard turned to Amos. "And there's something you might be particularly interested in, son. We have something called 'television.' You can think of it as a little theater right in your own room. You can watch plays or see other people doing what they do in their lives from anyplace in the world. You can watch any number of things. Television has sound, too. So you can hear what's going on as well as watch." Howard wished he could describe Saturday morning cartoons, or the Super Bowl, but he couldn't think of any way to do it that a boy from 1885 might understand.

He thought of something else he might describe. "We also have airplanes," he said. "Some can carry hundreds of people. They fly through the air just like giant birds. They even fly across the oceans."

"People fly in the air like birds?" Loraine repeated. "Oh my! How frightening."

"Yes, and they travel fast that way, too. Do you have any idea how long it would take you and your brother to travel from Boston to Mesa in one of our airplanes, Miss Parker? Just about five hours. Not five weeks or five days. Five hours."

"Five hours from Boston to Arizona? I can't even conceive such a thing, Mr. Placard."

"I think I have another picture here," Howard said, looking through his wallet again. "Yes, here it is." He pulled this one out and showed it to both Loraine and Amos at once. "This is me standing in front of my corporate jet. That's another way to say airplane. I once used it in my business."

Amos' eyes nearly exploded from his head. "This thing flies like a bird? And people can ride inside it, like in a stagecoach?"

"Well, actually this one only holds eight people, but we have much bigger planes that hold hundreds. I never compared flying to riding in a stagecoach, but I suppose you could." Howard smiled. "They're both forms of public transportation."

"Ha!" Amos laughed. "I'll bet these guys would have a hard time holdin' up a stage like this one, wouldn't you say, Mr. Placard?"

Howard patted the lad on the head. "Actually, son, there are men who hold up airplanes. They're not called robbers; they're called skyjackers. Funny name, isn't it?"

"Yeah, it is a funny name." Amos' eyes glazed into a far-off look. "I wish I could fly in one of those things," he said.

"Yes, son, I wish you could, too. Flying is quite a kick. I love it."

Loraine caught her breath as she noticed another picture still inside Howard's wallet. "Oh, my!" she exclaimed. "Is that a picture of me you have in there?"

Howard grew solemn as he realized what picture Loraine had noticed. "No," he said softly. "This is a picture of someone who looks a great deal like you. In fact, her name is even similar to yours. Her name is Lori. This picture was taken more than ten years ago, when Lori and I were at Carmel by the Sea together."

Loraine reached out and took the wallet from Howard to get a better look. "She does look like me, doesn't she?" Loraine said. "Is this the lady you mistook me for when we first met?"

Howard removed his hat and ran his fingers through his hair. "I apologize for that mistake, Miss Parker. But as you can see, the resemblance is striking.

"And her name?" Loraine asked. "You said it was Parker?"

Howard wiped his brow, then replaced his hat. "Actually, her maiden name was Parker." Having said this, Howard retrieved his wallet and placed it back in his pocket. After a moment, he grinned. "You know what else we've done in my time, Amos? We put men on the moon. What do you think of that?"

"Please, Mr. Placard," Loraine said, holding up one hand. "I think we've heard enough about your technology. But there is something else I'd like to ask if I might. This angel you say you talk to? Can you tell me about her?"

"Angel?" Amos asked. "You talk with an angel, Mr. Placard?"

Howard knelt down to Amos' level. "Yes, son, I do. I've already explained this to your sister. It was an angel who brought me here to stop the runaway stage."

"Go ahead, Peaches. You can tell them all about me, I don't mind.

Just be sure you keep what you say accurate. No more of this stuff about you being a better shot than me."

"Your sister once saw an angel, son. Did you know that?" Howard asked Amos, who shook his head and looked at his sister.

"It was a long time ago, Amos," Loraine confirmed. "Our Grandfather Lesley came to me."

"It's sort of interesting that your angel was your grandfather, Miss Parker," Howard said. "My angel, you see, is my sister."

"Your sister?" Loraine asked. "The one you said died when she was twenty?"

"That's her," Howard smiled. "And I have to be careful what I tell you about her, since she's standing right here next to me with a clenched fist."

"Liar!" Annette shouted. "I do not have my fist clenched. But I can, if you don't watch yourself, big brother."

Amos looked around. "Where's an angel?" he asked. "I don't see one."

"That's because Mr. Placard is the only one who can see or hear her, Amos," Loraine explained.

"Oh," Amos responded, looking confused but not pushing the subject any further.

Looking at Howard, Loraine asked, "What's your sister's name?"

"Annette."

"That's a lovely name. I wish there were a way I could see her." Loraine's voice was wistful.

Annette spoke up again. "You don't need to mention this, Peaches. But it wouldn't surprise me if the time doesn't come when I'll show myself to Loraine—if you live up to everything you're supposed to, that is, and if the plan goes according to the way destiny wants it to." Howard found this interesting, but he merely nodded and said nothing.

"How come your sister brought you here, Mr. Placard?" Amos asked "Just to stop our stagecoach?"

Howard looked back and forth between Loraine and Annette. "I'm not sure if she had other reasons than stopping the stage or not. My sister's never made it clear to me why I'm here."

Annette threw up her hands. "Give me a break, Peaches! How much more explicit can I be?"

Loraine looked puzzled. "Why wouldn't she explain her reason for bringing you here, Mr. Placard? That doesn't make sense to me."

"Okay, one more time, big brother," Annette said slowly and clearly. "I brought you here because you and Loraine Parker share a forever contract with each other. You're destined for her, and she's destined for you. What's not to understand about that?"

Howard grew quiet. Why would his sister say such a thing? Howard was in love with one woman, and that woman was Lori. It was true, Loraine Parker did look like Lori, but she wasn't Lori. To think that destiny could pair him up with Lori's look-alike was absurd.

"I'm sorry, Miss Parker," he said. "I haven't the slightest idea why my sister has brought me here." Looking back at Annette, he finished the thought. "I'm not even sure she knows the answer to that one."

Annette folded her arms and glared at Howard. "I swear, big brother, I'm going to tell the world about your nickname if you keep it up. And you know I mean it."

Howard glared back at her, but he didn't budge. "All right, Peaches," Annette sighed. "Let's try a different approach. I want you to look at Loraine's eyes." Still Howard didn't move. "I said look at her eyes, big brother. Now do it!"

This time he relented. He turned to Loraine and looked straight into her eyes. "All right, Peaches," Annette went on to say. "I want you to think about what you feel when you look in her eyes."

Think about what he felt? Humph! That was preposterous. Still . . . Loraine was a lovely woman. And Howard had to admit, she was lovely because she was Loraine Parker, not just because she resembled Lori. In fact, looking deeply into her eyes like this somehow revealed a completely different woman from Lori behind that lovely face. Something about her was captivating, and after the first few seconds, Howard discovered he didn't want to look away. Suddenly, he heard himself say, "I've been calling you Miss Parker," he said. "I've just assumed you're not married. Are you married?"

Hearing himself say that, he cringed. What on earth had prompted him to ask such a thing? He wanted to turn and run someplace where he could hide. Instead, all he could do was stand there feeling like a bigger fool than the circus clowns in some of his films.

Loraine's face turned a brilliant red at the question. "Uh, no. I'm not married, Mr. Placard. Not yet, anyway."

Howard shifted his weight nervously. Why should he care whether or not this lady was married? But the truth was, he did care. And now that he had himself backed into a corner, there was no way out other than pressing forward. He asked another very stupid question. "Is there someone special then?"

It was Loraine who broke eye contact first. At this second question, her eyes quickly lowered. "Well, yes, sort of," she answered nervously. "There's a fellow back in Boston—Mark Brown. Mark hasn't actually asked me to marry him. But I've always supposed he would ask me . . . someday."

"Oh, I see," Howard responded, more than a little annoyed at himself for letting the mention of Mark bother him. "I hope your Mark doesn't wait too long before proposing to a lovely woman like you. He could just find himself on the outside looking in, if you get my drift."

Loraine's blush deepened, leaving Howard even more embarrassed for starting this conversation. But what he had said was true. He was reminded of his own mistake in not approaching Lori when he should have. What he would give for a second chance to rectify that mistake. "I'm serious, Miss Parker," he continued. "If I were Mark Brown, I'd be on the first stage headed west. You can bet on it."

Out of the corner of his eye, Howard caught sight of his sister who stood smiling—but perfectly silent.

* * *

Loraine knew she had never really been in love with Mark, but he was the only man she had ever considered marrying. Now, in light of having met this stranger from another time and place, Mark was drifting ever further to the back of her mind. Another thing that concerned Loraine was the twinge of jealousy she had felt on seeing the picture from Howard's wallet—the picture of this Lori. Loraine realized that regardless of how she herself felt about Mr. Placard, he was already in love with another woman. Ironically, he was in love with a woman who bore a remarkable resemblance to Loraine.

It was obvious what Loraine had to do, and that was to put all thoughts of this man out of her mind. And to do that, she needed to get the subject back on more serious matters. "I'd say we're facing a pretty serious problem here, Mr. Placard. What do you propose we do about getting out of this desert? Don't you think it would be best to spend the night here near the stagecoach and hope we're found? Surely someone must be looking for us."

* * *

Howard drew a sigh of relief that Loraine had taken the initiative to bring the subject back to their current problem. "I'm not sure about waiting for someone to find us, Miss Parker. This is the Arizona Territory, not Boston. Who knows how long it might take for us to be found?" Howard pointed to the mountains off to the north. "I was raised in the shadow of those mountains over there," he said. "They're the Superstitions. In my time, there's a city of Mesa about twenty miles west of here. I'm almost positive Mesa was there in the year 1885."

"I know Mesa is there," Loraine said excitedly. "That's where Amos and I were headed. My folks live there now. We expected to be there by nightfall—that was before the holdup, of course."

"The Superstition Mountains?" Amos cut in. "Is that where the famous lost gold mine is?"

"The Lost Dutchman," Howard responded. "It's supposed to be in those hills somewhere, though no one's ever had the good fortune of finding it."

"I'd sure like to find it," Amos said energetically. "Yessir!"

Howard smiled, then looked off to the west where he knew Mesa would be. "Twenty miles is nothing back in my time and place. But here, in 1885 . . . You can forget getting there by nightfall, that's for sure. Still, I think we should get started in that direction. I think that's our best bet."

"Am I being presumptuous, Mr. Placard. Shouldn't your sister— the angel—be of some help to us in our situation?"

Howard looked at Annette, who only shrugged. "No," he answered, disgusted. "My sister can be pretty stubborn at times. She's indicated to me that I have to handle things on my own. She got me to the stagecoach so I could stop it, and that's the extent of her involvement, it seems."

"I see," Loraine replied. "Well, I suppose we can't argue with an angel, can we?" She looked back at the two outlaws still on the ground where they had left them. "What about them?" she asked. "It's going to be hard enough worrying about the three of us, without having them to think of. What do we do about them?"

"I haven't made up my mind what to do about them, Miss Parker. But one thing for sure, I do plan to borrow their horses. Twenty miles will be a lot closer with two horses than it will on foot. You can ride, I assume?"

"The horses? You're right, we do have two horses. I hadn't considered that. And yes, I do ride. I'm as at home in the saddle as I am with a revolver."

Howard stared at her. This Loraine Parker was becoming a more interesting lady as they went along. He had to laugh inside. A combination between Lori and his sister, Annette, Loraine looked like Lori but could ride and shoot like Annette. Something Annette had said earlier came to mind now. *You and Lori have nothing whatsoever in common. But take Loraine Parker, here. You've known her less than half an hour, and already you've found something you share in common with her.* It galled Howard to admit it, but Annette was right on this point.

"And I can ride as good as my sister," Amos announced proudly.

The three of them started walking back toward the robbers. As they walked, Loraine asked, "How about you, Mr. Placard? You can ride, I assume."

Loraine's question triggered something from the depths of Howard's memory that took him back through time to his teenage years. Back to a time when riding was his life. He used to love riding alone through the hills behind the ranch. There was one place in particular, a rise overlooking a desert valley that stretched out as far as the eye could see. The view from the rise was breathtaking. It was there Howard would ride to watch the sunrise in the morning or the sunset at dusk. The air was sweet and crisp, like no other place in Howard's world. At night, the stars were like millions of tiny diamonds pressed majestically against a fold of black velvet.

"Yes," he replied. "I can ride." He cleared his throat and then added, "Amos and I can share one horse, and that will leave the second for you, Miss Parker."

By this time they were standing next to Derringer and Grayson. "Now hold on here, mister!" Clay loudly objected, having heard what Howard said. "Them horses belong to Scar and me. Do you have any idea what we do to horse thieves in these parts?"

Loraine shot a glance at the men. "What do they do to stagecoach robbers in these parts?" she asked sharply.

Ignoring her remark, Clay pointed to the water barrel beside the crippled stagecoach. "How do you expect to make even two miles, let alone twenty, across this desert with no water?" he asked

Howard glanced at the water barrel. He hadn't noticed before, but it had been shaken loose in the accident from where it had been tightly tied down and had fallen off the stagecoach, spilling its contents onto the thirsty sand.

"Now you listen to me, both of you," Clay continued. "The best you can do is let Scar and me be on our way. I give you my word, we'll send help back for you."

Howard continued to stare at the empty barrel. "I hadn't realized we were without water," he admitted.

"I left a half full canteen inside the stagecoach," Loraine was quick to point out. "But the outlaw's right, I fear. We do need more water than that."

Howard stepped to the water barrel and righted it. Not a drop left. "You suppose the driver had a canteen?" he asked.

"I'll see," Amos said, rushing to the stage and climbing to the driver's seat. "Yeah!" he shouted. "There is one and it's half full."

Loraine spoke up. "I noticed there were two canteens among the things in your saddlebags, Mr. Placard. I don't suppose they happen to be full?"

Howard quickly checked inside the saddlebags. There were two canteens, but both were empty. "Thanks a lot, sis," Howard said, no longer caring if the others heard. "A couple of empty canteens should come in real handy about now."

"Is he talking with his angel?" Amos asked, wide-eyed.

"I think so, little brother," Loraine answered.

Annette grinned. "I didn't need to send water with you, Peaches. I figured I'd just give it to you after we got here." Suddenly, the air was split with the sound of rolling thunder. "I figure you should know what that sound means, Peaches. You and I have both seen enough monsoons to know exactly what that thunder means."

Howard shaded his eyes and looked up at the sky. "There, off to the south!" he exclaimed. "Clouds! Do you see them, Miss Parker?"

Loraine looked. "I see them," she responded as a flash of lightning suddenly streaked across the sky, followed by another clap of rolling thunder. "What do you think? Is there a chance of rain?"

Howard continued looking at the darkening sky for another moment before answering. "Have you ever heard of a monsoon?" he asked.

Loraine shook her head. "No, I can't say that I have."

"Monsoons are usually over with before October," he explained. "It seems my little sister has struck up a deal with Mother Nature. I'd say we're going to get a monsoon a little late this year, Miss Parker."

Loraine watched as another flash of lightning burst across the sky, followed instantly by a booming clap of thunder. Howard went on with his explanation. "A monsoon, Miss Parker, is a storm associated with only two places in the world—Southern Asia, and this particular desert. And from the looks of that sky, I'd say you're about to learn firsthand exactly what a monsoon is."

"Are you saying we're about to get rain?" she asked again, repeating her earlier question.

Howard laughed. "You're in for more rain than you've ever seen in one place in your life, Miss Parker. Come on, Amos. We have work to do. Miss Parker, you can keep an eye on our friends here."

Howard quickly searched the wreckage for something suitable for funneling water into the barrel. He spotted it instantly. It was a canvas tarp at the rear of the stage, used to protect the luggage carried there. Howard had already noticed a coil of rope near the driver's seat. "Grab that rope, Amos," he said pointing to it. "We're going to make ourselves a little rain trap."

"Yes, sir, Mr. Placard," Amos said, scooting off after the rope.

Howard grabbed the tarp and tossed it to the top of the stage. By the time he had climbed up there himself, Amos had the rope. Howard removed a small pocketknife from his pocket and tossed it to the lad. "Cut me off a couple of short lengths," he called down. "Something I can use to secure the canvas to the top of the stage."

Amos cut off two pieces of rope and tossed them up to Howard, who quickly secured the canvas at the corners, one to the front of the stage and one to the back. Then Howard jumped down and grabbed the empty water barrel, which he positioned a few feet from the stage. Taking the end of the tarp, he formed it into a funnel shape and placed it in the empty barrel.

* * *

Loraine looked on with keen interest as Howard worked. She found herself drawn to him as a kitten might be drawn to a warm spot in the sunlight. Why was this happening to her? It made no sense. She couldn't keep her eyes or her mind off Howard. And she couldn't shake the feeling she had known him from somewhere in her past—somewhere long before he appeared atop a runaway stagecoach to save her life. But—that was impossible. She couldn't have known him before. And there was absolutely no reason why she should be attracted to him now. It angered her that she couldn't shake these feelings.

* * *

"Here, hold this tarp in place," Howard said to Amos, "while I get some rocks to weigh down the barrel."

Amos obliged and Howard set off in search of some large rocks. One by one, he cleaned the rocks off, then hefted them into the barrel. It took five rocks before he was satisfied that the barrel was heavy enough to remain in place. "Okay," he said. "All that's left is to tie the lower end of the tarp to the barrel so it won't slip out."

Amos cut a couple more lengths of rope, and between the two of them they had the canvas secured within a matter of minutes. Howard stepped back and surveyed their work. "Yes," he said confidently. "This will do."

Amos closed Howard's knife and handed it back to him. "Lucky you had this, Mr. Placard. We would've had a hard time building this rain catcher without it."

"Yes," Howard agreed, looking at the knife. "I've carried this little gem for more than ten years. It has special meaning for me. I found it one evening on a stretch of beach in southern California."

* * *

Loraine watched as Amos returned Howard's knife and heard his remark. A stretch of beach in southern California? Could this be the same beach he had mentioned earlier? The beach where he had spent time with the woman called Lori? Something inside refused to let the question go unasked.

"The beach in southern California? Is that the same beach where you photographed the picture of Lori you carry in your wallet?" she asked.

Howard looked up and their eyes met. "Yes," he said with a certain gentleness in his voice. "It's called Carmel by the Sea. I was overseeing the filming of a picture there at the time."

Loraine thought about this. "I know you told me some marvelous things about the world where you come from, Mr. Placard. But I still don't understand what you mean by filming a picture."

Howard smiled. "No, I'm sure you don't. Let me explain. Where I come from, we take stories—you know, like from books—and film them as motion pictures. I was the one who made all the decisions about which story to use, who the actors would be to play the parts, everything like that. And I put up the money for the filming. For one motion picture, running about an hour and a half, the cost sometimes reached millions of dollars."

A million dollars? The thought of that much money astounded Loraine. "How could you afford a million dollars, Mr. Placard?"

Howard removed his hat and ran the edge of his hand through the crease, smoothing it. "At first it was a matter of loans," he explained. "But, in time, I built my assets up so I was able to finance everything myself." He replaced the hat. "You see, Miss Parker, there are huge profits to be made in producing motion pictures. Once the picture is finished, it's leased to theaters all over the world. Hundreds of thousands of people pay to see it. Sometimes the audiences can reach into the millions."

"I think I understand," she responded, but at that moment she had something else on her mind besides scientific achievements. Something that embarrassed her for not being able to let it go, but she just couldn't. "Was Lori with you when you found the little knife?" she asked. "Is that why it has special meaning for you?"

Howard hesitated. "Yes," he said at length. "I invited Lori to go with me. She was a set designer, and . . ." Howard suddenly looked up and caught Loraine's eyes. "A set designer," he explained, "is a person who decides how a certain scene in the motion picture should appear. You know, a chair here, a table there, that sort of thing."

"I see. Lori works with you in producing these motion pictures, then."

Howard rubbed the back of his neck nervously. "Not exactly, Miss Parker. Lori helped me for a brief time, but that was it. I wanted her to stay on working with me, but it just didn't work out. But, yes, the reason the little knife is special is because I found it while Lori was with me. The time we spent together in Carmel is one of the fondest memories of my adult life."

Still Loraine couldn't drop the subject. "And that was ten years ago?" she asked.

"More like eleven now. But I remember it like it was only yesterday."

Loraine bit her tongue and tried to force her thoughts from the subject. It was no use. She felt compelled to pursue it further. "I, uh, don't mean to pry, Mr. Placard. But if that happened that long ago, whatever became of you and Lori? You obviously never married."

Howard's eyes grew hollow and he blew out a sharp breath. "No, we never married. Not that I didn't try my best. But . . ."

"But the lady said no?" Loraine pressed.

Howard kicked at the dirt with the toe of his boot. "There's more to it than her simply saying no, Miss Parker," he painfully confessed. "You see, I fell in love with Lori when she was a teenager. But I was a fool. I let her slip through my fingers into the arms of another man."

Another man? Had Loraine heard him right? "Are you saying Lori married someone else?"

Howard forced a smile. "Sum and total of the problem," he said bluntly. "You see, Miss Parker, Lori made a mistake. The man she married is nothing but a loser. I could have offered her the world, if she'd only let me."

Loraine searched Howard's eyes for his meaning. "Does her husband mistreat her? Is that your meaning, Mr. Placard?"

Howard shuffled his feet nervously. "Brad's not an abusive man, I didn't mean that. I'm sure he loves Lori in his own way. He's just a loser. What else can I say? "

"A loser?" Loraine repeated, mulling Howard's possible meaning around in her mind.

"The life Brad offers Lori is about as exciting as roller skating across this desert. I, on the other hand, could have given her the life of a celebrity. I was a motion picture magnate. At my side, Lori would have been a queen. The world would have been at her feet." Howard's jaw tightened, and fire blazed in his eyes. "I'll never understand why she would throw her life away for a man like Brad Douglas, when she knows how I feel about her."

Loraine couldn't believe what she was hearing. Could this man be so obsessed with money and power as to think he could use it to buy Lori's love? Common sense told her to let the subject drop, but something inside refused to let her do that. "I'm sorry to have to say this, Mr. Placard, but I think you're overlooking the obvious. Lori is undoubtedly in love with Brad."

"She thinks she loves him," Howard snapped. "She could love me if she'd give it a chance." Howard kicked at a rock with his foot. "It's all academic now anyway," he conceded dejectedly. "I'm no longer in a position to give Lori—or anyone else—the luxuries I had at my disposal a year and a half ago. I lost everything to an arrogant female named Samantha." Howard pulled out his bandana and wiped his hands. "And for your information, Miss Parker, Samantha is another angel I've been forced to deal with for the past eighteen months."

Another angel besides his sister? How many more surprises was this man going to come up with? Putting two and two together, she reasoned some things out. Lori was married to another man, and Howard had made a play for her on the assumption that his power and wealth could win her over. Apparently Howard had somehow lost his fortune, and this had put an end to his pursuit of Lori. All this must have happened a year and a half ago. The part about an angel named Samantha, she didn't understand. Nor could she figure out why his sister, who was also an angel, had brought him back here to 1885, when he belonged far, far in the future.

One thing was obvious. Mr. Placard certainly didn't understand the power of love, or he wouldn't have assumed he could take Lori away from her husband with the promise of the world at her feet. Loraine thought about it and decided to speak her mind on the matter. "You're wrong, you know, Mr. Placard," she said outright. "Thinking you need to offer a woman material things to make her happy. A woman wants to be loved, not showered with expensive gifts."

Howard stared at Loraine and opened his mouth to speak, no doubt to disagree, but no words came out. Watching him, Loraine wanted to kick herself. Why couldn't she just keep her mouth shut? And why did it bother her to hear Howard say he was still in love with Lori? It was none of her business, for heaven's sake. And as for Howard himself . . . Who knew the answer to that one? He was brought here by an angel, from another dimension. Who could say when he might be swept away again by his angel, never to be seen again? This whole thing was like a dream. A dream that could last for one brief instant and then be gone forever.

"I—I'm sorry," she stammered. "I had no right to say what I did."

* * *

Howard was astounded at the impact of Loraine's words. So astounded, in fact, that he didn't even hear her apology. Never had anyone, or anything, so completely shattered his self-imposed logic about his ability to make Lori happy, not even his pushy sister. He suddenly felt like a naked man, standing in full view of the whole world. Without question, he had come to a point in life where he had assumed an open checkbook could buy anything he might desire, even the love of a woman like Lori. With Loraine's simple statement, he suddenly realized the fallacy in his thinking. And for the first time, he understood: Lori was genuinely in love with Brad Douglas. Howard saw himself for exactly what he was in his attempts to destroy that love—and he wanted a place to hide from the world.

Another flash of lightning streaked against the darkening sky, mercifully draining his thoughts away from Lori and his misdeeds against her. This time the thunder came sooner, followed immediately by several large drops of rain slamming noisily into the dry desert sand. Howard glanced upward, shielding his eyes with his hand. "I suggest the three of us get inside the stagecoach. It's about to get very wet out here. We'll have some shelter there, at least."

"Hey! What about us?!" Clay screamed. "Are you just gonna leave us here to get soaked?"

"Looks that way," Howard called back as he escorted Loraine to the door of the coach. "Not to worry. Since you're not made of sugar, there's no chance you'll melt."

Suddenly, Amos darted toward his and Loraine's suitcases, their contents strewn across the ground. "We can't just leave these things to be soaked," he called back. "I'll gather them up before the storm gets here. We can put everything in the coach with us."

"Good idea, little brother," Loraine said, as she stepped up into the stagecoach.

Once she was inside, Howard went back to help Amos with the suitcases; he also brought his own saddlebags inside. They barely made it before the scattered drops gave way to a deluge. Soon the heavens opened in a raging fury of wind and water gushing down with stinging force.

"I've never seen anything like this," Loraine gasped as she huddled close to Amos. "It's like we were under a waterfall."

Howard only laughed. "If you plan on making Mesa your home, Miss Parker, you'd better get used to this. It happens every monsoon season."

CHAPTER 17

Mumbling obscenities under his breath, Clay grabbed his bullet-riddled hat and shoved it hard onto his head. Angrily he yanked his arm against the handcuff that held him bound to his partner who had taken a seat on a nearby rock. "OW!" Grayson cried out in protest. "What are you trying to do—pull my arm off?"

"Shut up!" Clay shot back. "And get on your feet. We're getting out of here while the getting's good."

"What? You want to get me shot?!"

"You ain't gonna get shot! They're too busy trying to stay dry to notice what we're up to. Come on, Scar, let's get to those horses."

"Horses? How we gonna mount up when we're shackled together?"

"We'll have to ride double. We'll take my mount; he's the fastest. Now come on!"

Bare feet splashing through already deep pools of trapped rainwater, the two desperados made a dash for Clay's horse. Just as Clay had suggested, in the cover of the driving, wind-blown rain, they were able to escape unnoticed. After an almost clown-like struggle to mount the horse with their hands handcuffed together, the two of them made their getaway through the raging storm.

"What about the money?" Grayson yelled as they rode. "We ain't just gonna leave it, are we? And my horse? That's a darn good mount, Clay. I want my horse back."

"You'll get your horse back, Scar. We'll get the money, too. After that, I got a score to settle with that fancy-dressed city slicker. And the lady, too. No one messes with Clay Derringer and gets away with it. We'll hightail it for the hideout, where we can bust these cuffs off. Then we'll grab some boots, guns, and another horse, and catch up with 'em before they get ten miles down the road."

* * *

Grimacing in pain, Jeremiah picked out a large rock at the edge of the road and sat down to rest. So far he had managed to hobble no more than a mile or so. At this pace, there was little hope he could ever make it off the desert alive.

One thing to be thankful for, at least, was the rain. The constant lightning and rolling thunder he could have done without, but the stinging force of wind-driven rain against his flesh was a small price to pay for the benefit that came with it. Pulling the bandana from around his neck, he held it up until it was saturated. Then, squeezing the cool liquid into his mouth, he let it trickle soothingly past his parched throat. Again and again he soaked the bandana and drank from heaven's gift until his thirst was quenched. Eagerly, he searched for a container; anything that would work as a makeshift canteen. With a deep sigh, he glanced down at his boots only to see just how worn they really were. Large cracks in the leather would prevent either of them from holding water for more than a few minutes, at best. His hat was out of the question, too, since it was anything but watertight. At least his thirst was quenched for now. That was something.

He rose to his feet and set out again. By keeping the weight off his bad leg with the help of the makeshift crutch, he was at least able to walk, in spite of the powerful gusts of wind and driving rain. He could see the rocks up ahead where he had tossed the saddlebags full of the payroll money. A slight grin crossed his lips. He had deprived the robbers of the money, but what good did it do in the end? If he were found dead here on the trail, who would know what happened to it?

Still, he decided his best bet was to retrieve the saddlebags. Carrying them would make walking more difficult, but if worse came to worse whoever found him would also find the money. That way the money would stand some chance of finding its way back to its rightful owner. Lifting his face into the stinging rain, he let out a burst of laughter. "Now ain't you the noble one, Jeremiah Samuels? Worrying about the money getting back into the rightful hands when you're probably gonna die here on this forsaken stretch of desert." But crazy as it sounded, that's exactly what he was worried about—simply because he was Jeremiah Samuels. Jeremiah Samuels was just made that way.

* * *

Howard glanced up at the troubled sky as the last few straggling raindrops fell listlessly to the already-soaked desert sand. Bright streamers of sunshine broke through, scattering billows of spent thunder clouds. It was a marvelous sight and one not unfamiliar to Howard, who had witnessed these desert monsoons many times before. He was always amazed at the amount of water one storm could bring in such a short time—in this case, not more than twenty minutes. All that remained now was a cool breeze brushing against his face in intermittent gusts.

Slipping out of the coach, he turned and helped Loraine down. Amos jumped down on his own. The first thing they did was check the water barrel, which was filled to overflowing. "You did it, Mr. Placard!" Loraine shouted. "We have all the water we need and much more."

"Hey!" Amos called out. "The robbers must have gotten away. And they've taken one of the horses!"

Howard slapped a hand to his forehead. "I should have known better," he scolded himself. "Of all the rotten luck. Now we have water, but half our transportation is gone."

"It's all right," Loraine quickly cut in. "We have all the water we need, and we still have one horse. We're in a lot better shape than we were before the rainstorm."

"Yeah," Howard agreed after some thought. "I guess you're right. At least you and Amos can ride. I'll just have to keep up the best I can."

Loraine shook her head. "I have other ideas for the horse," she stated emphatically. "He can carry my luggage out of here. Everything I own is in those suitcases, and I refuse to leave them."

Howard couldn't believe it. "Miss Parker! Our lives are at stake here. I'm sure your things will be fine until the stage line can send a salvage crew out. Don't you think—"

But Loraine had already pulled one of the suitcases from the coach, and gathering her skirt off the wet ground with her free hand, she set off in the direction of the one remaining horse. "I'll not argue the point further," she stated firmly. "Are you going to help me tie these to the horse, or do I have to figure it out myself?"

Howard opened his mouth, but the words froze in his throat as a staggering thought crossed his mind. Loraine had more in common with Lori than simply her looks. It was suddenly evident that Loraine Parker had that same streak of unyielding determination Howard had so often faced with Lori.

"She won't change her mind, you know," Amos said. "That's just the way my sister is."

Howard placed a hand on the boy's shoulder. "No, I don't suppose she will. Why don't you fetch the rope while I take care of the rest of these suitcases?"

"Good plan," the boy grinned. "I'll get the rope."

Howard paused, just watching this lovely woman, marveling again how much like Lori she really was. He pondered again how cruel fate had been in depriving him of the chance to share his life with Lori. How he envied Brad Douglas.

Grabbing the three remaining suitcases, he stepped over to where Loraine was standing next to the horse. "All right," he said. "I don't like it, but we'll do it your way."

While Howard tied the luggage to the horse, Loraine and Amos filled the four canteens with water from the barrel and hung them over the saddle horn. "My handbag and parasol," Loraine said as an afterthought. "I left them inside the stagecoach."

"I'll fetch them for you, sis," Amos said, bounding for the open door of the stage and returning immediately. He gave them to Loraine, then handed Howard's saddlebags to him.

Howard hung them next to the canteens. "Thanks, son. I'd have forgotten the bags if it weren't for you."

Loraine looked surprised. "What about your sister? Wouldn't she have reminded you, Mr. Placard?"

"My sister's gone," Howard said. "Haven't seen her since the rain started."

"You know, I've been wondering," Loraine said. "If you and Annette were twins, why do you refer to her as your little sister?"

"She is my little sister," Howard laughed. "I was born three minutes before her, and that's all it takes."

"Did you know you have dimples in both cheeks when you laugh?" Loraine asked, sending a wave of embarrassment through Howard.

"Uh, no," he answered, red-faced. "No one's ever mentioned that before." He quickly changed the subject. "Do you want to hang your handbag on the horse while we're about it?"

Loraine handed Howard her bag, which he fastened to the saddle. "They're quite becoming, you know," Loraine went on to say. "Your dimples, I mean."

Howard cleared his throat loudly and glanced down at Loraine's feet. She was wearing a pair of button-up high-top shoes with two-inch heels. "You're sure you won't reconsider about riding the horse? Walking in those shoes won't be easy, you know."

"I'll make do," she said. "I love these boots."

"You may love them," Howard argued. "But they're not made for walking in sand. Hold on a minute," he said suddenly. "There's something I had forgotten about!"

Howard unsnapped his saddlebags and removed the three pairs of walking shoes his sister had sent along. "Unless I miss my guess, these shoes are going to be perfect sizes for each of us."

"Here," he said, handing the lady's pair to Loraine. "Slip these on. They'll be a darn sight better to walk in than what you're wearing."

Loraine stared at the shoes Howard had handed her. "What do you mean 'walking shoes'?" she asked. "I've never seen anything like these. The shoes I'm wearing happen to be the latest fashion, straight from Boston."

"Just try these on," Howard said. "I think you'll see right away what I mean about how comfortable they are."

"I don't want to try them on," she said. "They look hideous. I'd be a laughingstock if anyone from Boston ever caught sight of me wearing something like these."

Howard's smile warmed. "I assure you, Miss Parker. A woman as lovely as you could never be thought of as a laughingstock because of her shoes."

Now it was Loraine who blushed. "You think I'm lovely?" she asked.

"Actually, lovely is not the word to describe your beauty, Miss Parker. There are no words that would do you justice. Describing your beauty would be like trying to describe a morning sunrise over a green meadow, or a rainbow over a field of wild flowers after a summer shower."

Loraine lowered her eyes. "But it's not really me you're describing, is it, Mr. Placard? You're describing Lori, aren't you?"

"Yes," Howard admitted. "I am describing Lori's beauty. But I'm describing your beauty, too. Describing one is describing the other since you're both mirror images of each other. Now please, put on the shoes. You won't be sorry, I promise."

Loraine eyes raised again. "You really don't think I'd look hideous?" she asked one last time.

"No, Miss Parker. I could never think that." Howard handed a second pair of shoes to Amos. "How about you, son?" he asked. "Are you going to give me trouble over these, too?"

A giant grin filled Amos' face. "No, sir, I won't argue about a pair of nifty shoes like these. Where did you get them?"

Howard chuckled. "Let's just say a fellow named Michael Jordan recommended them. You called these shoes 'nifty,'" he said to the lad. "You know what someone your age would call them where I come from, Amos?"

"What?" Amos asked.

Howard thought a moment. "Some young men your age would call them 'cool.' Others might call them 'awesome.' Either way, it would mean the same thing as you calling them 'nifty.'"

"Hmmm," Amos said thoughtfully. "Cool or awesome? I like that."

Howard grinned at Amos as the boy admired his feet. "These are nifty shoes!" he loudly exclaimed. "No, they're better than nifty. They're *awesome!*" Howard couldn't help but laugh. "I'll bet I could run a hundred miles an hour with these on!"

"I'm not sure about the hundred miles an hour, young man. But I guarantee walking will be a lot more pleasant in those shoes."

Springing to his feet, Amos tested the shoes with a brisk walk to the stagecoach and back. "Wow! These really are awesome!"

"I think it's time to be heading down the road," Howard said. "We have a long way to go, and standing here talking won't get us there."

* * *

"Oh, no," Samantha groaned, burying her face in her hand. "How could she have done this to me? No woman in her right mind would wear those shoes with a red dress."

"Excuse me, Sam," Lori said, seeing that Samantha was upset about something. "What's bothering you?"

Samantha stood up and blew out a long dejected breath. "Do you know what you just witnessed, Lori? Your distant aunt actually put those hideous shoes on her feet. Can you believe it?"

"I admit, the shoes do lack style, Sam. But Loraine has a problem. She has to walk through the desert. The Nike shoes are going to make it a darn sight easier than it would be in her stylish boots. Why send the shoes with Howard, if you thought Loraine wouldn't use them?"

"Remember the bet I told you about that I made with Jason—over the Elvis concert? Well, these shoes were the bet. I asked Annette to send the hideous things along with Howard on purpose. Jason was the only one who thought Loraine would actually wear them. I was dead sure she wouldn't. Do you know what she just cost me by putting on those shoes, Lori? She cost me a night at the Elvis concert, that's what. She just let Jason win the bet."

Lori glanced over at Brad and realized he was having the same problem she was at the moment—that of not breaking out laughing. Lori had never seen Samantha so upset. "You bet Jason that Loraine wouldn't wear the Nike shoes?" she asked.

Samantha threw up her hands. "I can't believe Loraine did this to me. I'm going to be spending tomorrow evening at a chefs' convention when I could have been listening to Elvis." When she realized that both Lori and Brad were staring at her, she gave an embarrassed grin. "Sorry," she said. "I guess this is my problem, not yours. What do you say we get back to Jeremiah?"

* * *

Finding the saddlebags was easier than Jeremiah had supposed. The bags had ended up behind a rock just a few feet off to the side of the road. He picked up the bags and examined them, glad to find that the money had remained dry in spite of the storm. Tossing the bags over his shoulder, he glanced up at the sky.

"About four o'clock, I'd guess," he said to himself. "That means it'll be dark in four hours or so. Not good. Here I am fixing to spend a night in the desert with a bum leg, no food, no water, and no horse. Not exactly what I'd call a cozy evening."

He touched his wounded leg and quickly jerked back his hand as the pain shot all the way up his thigh. "Jeremiah Samuels, you really did yourself a good one this time. You knew the payroll money was on board, and you knew old Benson was too sick to ride along. All you had to do was swallow your pride and ask for a substitute shotgun. They'd have got you someone. But no, you were too darn fool stubborn for that. Well, Mr. Samuels, you're paying for your stubborn streak big time now."

Jeremiah's thoughts turned to his family. Thirteen-year-old Brittany Ann would be home from school by now, probably helping her mama with supper. Visions of his wife, Stephanie, flashed before his eyes. She'd be baking an apple pie right about now. Stephanie always fixed apple pie on days Jeremiah was due home from a long haul. The custom had begun the first year they were married. Jeremiah loved Stephanie's apple pies almost as much as he loved her. At least, that's what she always said.

What else would she be fixing for tonight's supper? Jeremiah wondered. Fried chicken? Chicken and dumplings? Or maybe rabbit stew. No matter. Right now Jeremiah would give a week's pay for anything she might be cooking up for his arrival home.

A heartsick pain filled his soul as he pondered how long it would be before Stephanie began to worry about him. He closed his eyes and pictured her working in the kitchen. What he would give for the welcome home kiss he knew was waiting for him. Would he ever kiss her again? Would he ever see her again? Would he ever see Brittany Ann again? These questions raced through his mind with tormenting force. Death held no fear for Jeremiah Samuels. But what of Stephanie and Brittany Ann? They needed him.

He took a breath and turned his face heavenward. "No!" he shouted. "Don't be sending no angel of death for me this trip. I got a wife and daughter waiting for me, and by blazes, I'm going home to them! One way or another, I'm going home."

He balanced the saddlebags on his shoulder and moved back to the trail. Grimacing in pain, he picked up the pace. "I may be eating your pie cold, Stephanie Samuels. But by blazes, I'll be eating it!"

* * *

Cresting a dusty hill, Annie and Bill reined their mounts to a stop. "Looks like your hunch was right, Bill," Annie said. "That's definitely a disabled stagecoach."

"Yeah," Bill agreed, staring at the coach a half mile or so ahead. "So it is. What do ya say we get down there, gal, and have ourselves a closer look?"

"I'd say that's a right good idea, Bill. Come on, I'll race you to it." Annie urged her steed into a run with Bill not two seconds behind. They reached the stagecoach in a matter of minutes and quickly dismounted. Annie went straight to the stage for a look inside, while Bill checked out the makeshift funnel and the barrel still mostly filled with rainwater.

"No sigh of anyone in here," Annie allowed.

"Maybe not," Bill responded. "But someone's been here, you can bet on it. They even found themselves a way to make up a water supply from the monsoon that passed by earlier. Look at all these footprints. Off hand, I figure there were at least five, maybe six of 'em. One was a lady, and there was a kid. A boy, I'd guess."

Annie agreed. "There's been a couple of horses here, too. And it looks like they headed out of here in two different directions." She looked closer at the set of tracks leading off down the trail to the west. "Take a look at this, Bill. I don't quite know what to make of it."

Bill walked over where Annie was kneeling and examined the tracks she was referring to. "Humph," he mumbled. "Reckon you're right, gal. Don't rightly know what sort of tracks those are myself. Definitely human. But the strangest sort of shoe soles I ever seen."

"They're strange, all right," Annie said. "But I agree—they are human. I'd say they're pretty fresh. Not more than an hour or two old."

"Yep. Looks like three of 'em went this way on foot. No tellin' how many may have been on the horse. No matter, I suppose. One thing for sure, these people could use our help, Annie."

"What about those who left on the other horse? Reckon they need our help, too?"

Bill considered it. "At least none of them were walking, Annie. And they headed off through the desert. They'd be pretty hard to find before nightfall. I'd say we stick to looking for those ahead of us on the road."

"I agree," Annie said. "Maybe one of us should ride on ahead to try and catch up with them. The other should stay here and wait for the wagons."

Bill squinted at the afternoon sun already hanging low on the horizon. "You stay here," he suggested. "I'll go after 'em and try to turn 'em around to meet up with our wagons, so we'll have a place to spend the night in reasonable comfort."

Annie nodded. "I'll keep the wagons rollin' till dark. If we don't see you by then, I guess you'll just have to use a rock for your pillow tonight. One way or another, we'll catch up to you. If not tonight, then tomorrow."

CHAPTER 18

Loraine and Howard walked side by side down the wet, sandy road. Howard led the horse, and Loraine couldn't help being thankful she had given into his persistence about wearing the shoes. Granted, they were ugly, but she had never had anything so comfortable on her feet. She couldn't help but be amused at Amos. He was having the time of his life experimenting with his shoes. She wondered where he got all his energy. He was up and down hills, over rocks, through gullies, you name it. At first, she had considered having him sit behind the baggage on the horse, but after watching his antics she gave up on the idea. Right now Amos was several yards ahead of them up the road. Loraine didn't mind, just as long as he kept in sight.

She glanced up to see that the sun was just entering the lower part of the western sky. "How much more daylight do you think we have, Mr. Placard?" she asked.

"Two hours—two and a half at the most," Howard responded.

"That would be my guess, too," she said, moving her parasol around to shade her eyes from what sun was left. "What do you think? Should we plan on walking all night, or should we get some rest and start out first thing in the morning?"

"A lot depends on how much light we have, I'd say. I have no idea what kind of moon to expect since I wasn't in the year 1885 last night, so I don't know what stage your moon is in right now."

"We're in luck in that department," she stated. "The moon should be full tonight."

"Full moon, eh? Well—that just might make walking all night a little more attractive. But we can make that decision when we get to it."

The two of them walked without speaking for a short time. All the while, Howard was still smiling. At last he spoke. "If you don't mind my saying so, Miss Parker, I certainly admire the way you've handled this situation. You have no idea how much like Lori you really are."

Loraine arched her eyebrows. "May I take the comparison as a compliment, Mr. Placard?"

"You may, Miss Parker. That's precisely how it was intended." Howard reached down and picked up a small rock. "I'm sure that my being here under these strange circumstances is hard for you to understand," he said, staring at the rock. "I'd like to apologize for that. Popping in on you the way I did was my sister's idea, not mine."

"No matter whose idea it was, I'm glad you're here," Loraine said earnestly. "Amos and I would have been in a bad way if you hadn't. But I do agree, this is a difficult situation to understand—you and your angel and your coming here from another time."

"I know my coming here from another time is the hardest part for you to understand, Miss Parker. But there is something I'd like to tell you about if I may. Actually what I want to tell you is about Lori."

The sound of Lori's name again left Loraine with mixed feelings. Part of her wanted to block out anything further about Lori, while another part wanted to hear what Howard had to say. "All right, Mr. Placard," she agreed. "What is it you'd like to tell me about this lady who looks so much like me?"

"There's a reason why she looks like you, Miss Parker. You see— and I find this very hard to explain—but your brother is part of the reason you and Lori are so much alike. A big part of the reason, I might add. I'd prefer that he not hear this part of our conversation."

Loraine's curiosity was on fire. She glanced up the road to see that Amos was still quite a ways ahead of them. "Where I come from," Howard went on to explain. "All that's happening right now—well— it's history, you see. And your little brother, well . . . Let me approach the subject like this. Lori's maiden name is the same as yours. Your name is Loraine Parker. Her maiden name was Lori Parker."

"That's right," Loraine said with a slight nod. "You mentioned that before."

Howard cleared his throat. "There's more," he said, his voice lowering until it was barely more than a whisper. "I'm told that Lori was—you know—named after you."

"She was named after . . . ? You mean to say . . . ?"

"I mean to say—your brother, Amos, is Lori's—great-grandfather."

"Oh, my!" Loraine gasped, the color draining from her face. "This is most difficult to conceive. Are you making this up, Mr. Placard?"

"No, Miss Parker, I'm not making it up. You are Lori's distant aunt."

"Oh, my!" Loraine said again. "Are you sure you were supposed to tell me this? Did you clear it with your sister? It would almost seem this is more information than anyone ever should know about themselves."

Howard shrugged. "Annette has given me the green light to tell you everything."

"Green light?" Loraine asked. "I don't understand."

"Oh, yeah, I guess that wouldn't mean much in the days of stagecoach travel. Green light means Annette gave me permission to tell you everything."

"Oh my," Loraine said still again. "This has been quite a day. Quite a day, indeed."

* * *

Jeremiah stopped dead in his tracks. His throat ached for a drink of water, and his leg throbbed with pain. It was no use; he could go no farther. A voice inside his head kept telling him he had to rest. He leaned heavily on his makeshift crutch and drew in several deep breaths. There was little doubt in his mind that if he stopped now—there would be no starting again. He glanced at the trail ahead of him. Nothing but miles of dirt road. How could he keep going? But how could he stop when he knew it meant never seeing his beloved Stephanie's face again?

Suddenly, Jeremiah felt an urge to turn around and look down the road behind him. He had no idea what prompted him to do this, but whatever the prompting was it was much too strong to throw off. Jeremiah turned and shaded his eyes for a better look. To his total disbelief, he spotted something. No, not something! It was someone!

"What the . . . ?" he stopped, staring. "It's a boy. Nah! It can't be a boy. Where would a boy come from out here in this desert?" Jeremiah squinted and looked all the harder. "It is a boy," he reasoned aloud. "It's the boy who was on the stage." Jeremiah removed his hat and wiped his brow with the back of his hand. "Well, at least one of my passengers made it out alive, and he's headed my way."

Jeremiah waved his hat. "Hey, boy!" he hollered. "This way! Just keep on coming!" Jeremiah could only hope the woman was behind the boy and that he just hadn't seen her yet. "That's right, son!" he called again. "Keep on coming this way."

* * *

"Hold still, Scar," Clay grumbled. "I gotta cut the chain on these cuffs, and you ain't making it easy with all your jerking around."

"You ain't left-handed, Clay," Grayson said nervously. "You're gonna cut me, tryin' to swing that hand ax with your left hand. It's my right hand that's free. Give me the ax, and I'll cut the chain."

"Shut up, Scar, and hold still. I'm perfectly capable of cuttin' this chain with my left hand."

Grayson lowered his hand to the rock between him and his partner, laying the short length of chain between the cuff on his hand and the cuff on Clay's hand across the rock. As Clay raised the hand ax, Grayson's eyes closed and his jaw tightened. The hand ax struck the chain with a loud report, and Grayson felt his hand pull free. Opening his eyes, he was relieved to see his hand was still attached to his wrist.

Making their way back to the hideout, handcuffed and on one horse, hadn't been easy, but fortunately they had a good horse. They had a good hideout, too. It was an old miner's shack that supposedly once belonged to the late Mr. Jacob Waltz. Waltz had been dead more than twenty years, and the stories of his Lost Dutchman gold mine were widespread by this time. Wherever that gold mine lay, it was hidden good. And so was this old shack. Deep in the wasteland of the rugged Superstitions, it proved to be a great refuge from more than one posse who came looking for these two.

With the handcuff chain severed, the men were at least separated from each other. Later, when there was time, they'd have to pay a visit to their old locksmith buddy, Ralph Slate. Slate could have the bracelets off in no time at all. But that could wait. There were more pressing matters on the fire right now. There was still the payroll money to be found, and those two meddling fools to be dealt with.

They wasted no time saddling up another horse from the corral behind their hideout. Fortunately for them, they each had an extra pair of boots, and guns were no problem since they always kept plenty of firepower at the hideout. Clay mounted up and glanced back at Grayson who was still busy loading his revolver. An evil grin crossed Clay's face, revealing a large gap between his tobacco-stained upper front teeth. "The woman's mine, Scar. I'll leave the killing of the man and boy to you. But the woman is mine, you got that?"

"You can have the woman," Grayson huffed. "I don't want nothin' to do with a spitfire like that one. And killing that city slicker will give me great pleasure. But the kid's another matter. I ain't never killed a kid before."

"Get on your horse, Scar. If you ain't got the stomach for killing the brat, I'll do it for you. Them folks are varmints. Makes no difference to me how old a varmint might be. If he gets in my sights, I'll gun him down." Clay talked big, but knew that when push came to shove, he'd overlook shooting the kid. Even he wasn't that heartless.

* * *

Young Amos was still ahead of the others. Rounding a turn in the road, he slowed his pace to allow the others to catch up. To his astonishment, he spotted a man in the road ahead. The fellow was waving his hat and calling out to Amos. Amos rubbed his eyes and looked again. "It's the stagecoach driver," he said to himself. "Awesome." He turned to look back at his sister and Howard, who were still a hundred feet or so behind. They hadn't reached a point in the road where they could see the man yet.

"Sis!" Amos yelled. "Hurry up! It's the stagecoach driver—just up ahead!"

"What did he say?" Howard asked. "Something about a stage-coach driver?"

"Yes," Loraine responded anxiously. "The man was shot during the holdup. Come on, let's hurry. He may need our help."

* * *

Jeremiah couldn't believe his eyes as two more people joined the boy. To his relief, one of them was the woman passenger from the stagecoach. He didn't know who the man was that was with her. But would you look at that? They had a horse! Jeremiah's piercing cry of a hearty "Yaaa-hoooo!!" rent the air as he waved his hat more violently than ever.

CHAPTER 19

Jeremiah lowered the canteen and wiped his mouth with his sleeve. "I'm mighty grateful," he said. "I can't remember when a drink tasted so good." He screwed the lid back on the canteen and hung it over the saddle horn with the other three. Leaning on his crutch, he extended a hand to Howard. "Name's Jeremiah Samuels," he said. "I was the stage driver."

Howard gripped his hand and responded. "Howard Placard." Howard eyed the blood stain on Jeremiah's pant leg. "Looks like you took a shot. That happen during the holdup?"

"Humph!" Jeremiah grunted. "You mean *attempted* holdup, pardner." He slid the saddlebags off his shoulder and dropped them to the ground near his feet. "They were after the payroll money in these bags. As you can see—they didn't get them. As for the leg—no broken bones at least. The bullet passed clean through. Makes walking a little difficult, though." Jeremiah's eyes shifted to Loraine, then to Amos. "Would someone mind telling me how you managed to get that stage stopped?" he asked. "And those two polecats who held me up—what happened to them?"

Loraine stepped forward. "Mr. Placard came along just in time to stop the stagecoach. He also apprehended the two outlaws, although they later escaped during the storm."

"The monsoon," Jeremiah observed. "Yeah, I got my share of that one, too."

"They left one of their horses behind," Loraine added.

Jeremiah's attention shifted to Howard. "Oh," he said. "I just assumed this was your horse, Howard. You did have a horse . . . ? How else could you have caught up with the stage?"

Howard lifted his hat and nervously brushed back his hair while considering the best way to address Jeremiah's question. He certainly didn't want to go through the whole complicated, and unbelievable, explanation of his sister the angel again. It was hard enough the first time, for Miss Parker's sake. "My horse?" he stammered. "Well, you see . . ."

To Howard's delight, Loraine came to his rescue. "That's a long story, Mr. Samuels," she said. "Perhaps I can explain it to you another time. Right now we're faced with the more pressing problem of how to get out of this desert."

"You're right," Jeremiah agreed. "I'm not sure how much help I can be in my present condition."

Howard glanced down at the saddlebags near Jeremiah's feet. "You say these bags contain payroll money? That's what the outlaws were after?"

"Yep, but I outsmarted 'em. In round one, at least."

"I'd say you did at that, Jeremiah," Howard complimented him. "I'm sure the owner of this money will be very grateful."

But Jeremiah waved away his praise. "Well, let's don't go counting our winnings before the last hand is dealt. We're not home free just yet. Unless I miss my guess, those two will be back looking for the money once they discover it's not on the stage."

Howard dismissed the idea. "They won't be back. They have no guns, only one horse, and I deprived them of their boots. I'd say we've seen the last of them, Jeremiah."

Jeremiah laughed. "You stole their boots? There's a dandy idea. I'll have to remember that." The smile left his face. "But I know these two," he warned. "Recognized 'em in spite of their masks. Clay Derringer and Grayson Hobbs. Two bad ones. Bad to the core."

"You're right," Howard quickly concluded. "One of them was called Clay. The other one was called Scar."

"Grayson Hobbs," Jeremiah explained. "Scar is a nickname Grayson goes by. You might have noticed, he had a big chunk missing from one ear."

Howard nodded. "Yeah, I did notice."

"Those two have a hideout somewhere up in the Superstitions. It won't be any trouble at all for them to get weapons, boots, horses, whatever they need. They'll be back. I'd wager a month's pay on it." Jeremiah glanced at the luggage and paraphernalia on the horse. "You say you disarmed these men?" he continued. "Did you by chance hang onto their weapons?"

"Two revolvers," Howard affirmed. "I have them tucked away in my own saddlebags, there on the horse."

"Two revolvers, eh?" Jeremiah reasoned aloud. "Not much fire power, but maybe enough to hold 'em off."

"Make that three revolvers," Loraine broke in. "I have my own."

"Three revolvers," Jeremiah corrected himself. "And I see you have four canteens of water. The way I see it, our best bet is to find a place where we can hole up and defend ourselves. We can keep a lookout tonight, and at daybreak Miss Parker and the boy can take the horse and ride into Mesa for help. The two of us should be able to hold them off until help arrives—if our ammunition don't run out, that is."

"I have plenty of extra ammunition for my revolver," Loraine stated. "And I think Amos should ride for help by himself. One rider will be faster than two."

Jeremiah started to object when Amos cut him off. "It won't do any good arguing with my sister, Mr. Samuels. Once she makes up her mind, there's no changing it. No sir-ree. No changing it at all. And besides, she can outshoot any ten outlaws who ever lived. You'll be better off with her here. I can ride for help. And the way I see it, I'd be better starting off right now. No use in waiting for morning. No sir, no use at all."

"No, Amos!" Loraine responded sternly. "I won't have you riding across this unfamiliar desert at night. You can wait until sunup tomorrow morning, then go."

Jeremiah shrugged. I suppose one rider would be faster," he conceded. "But I agree with your sister, son. You should wait until morning. When you get to town, I want you to look up the sheriff. His name is Scott Engels."

"Scott Engels?" Howard asked. "That name sounds mighty familiar. I wonder where I've heard it before."

"Scott's been our sheriff for the past couple of months. Young fellow, but plenty capable for the job."

Howard couldn't figure out where he had heard the name Scott Engels, but he was sure he had heard the name somewhere. He quickly put it out of his mind and had a good laugh at himself. He'd always wanted to play Dusty Lockhart, and here he was on the brink of a possible chance for doing just that. With one big exception. If the bullets started flying, they would be real lead and not just puffs of imagination like in his movies. Nevertheless, as he thought about it, he was surprised at how little this bothered him. Maybe because he knew he had an angel looking after him. Or maybe just because he felt more at home in 1885 than he had ever felt back in his own century. But that was absurd, wasn't it?

He shook off the thought and took a good look at their surroundings. He didn't like what he saw. "Where would you suggest we hole up, Jeremiah?" he asked. "I don't see any rocks, and I've never considered a cactus all that good at stopping bullets."

Jeremiah frowned as he looked across the desert. "You're right. We do need some cover. I know every inch of this road. The only rocks big enough to offer the protection we need are a half mile back. That's where the saddlebags were hidden."

"I remember seeing those rocks," Howard acknowledged. "Do you really think that's our best shot? Doubling back?"

"I wouldn't have thought so when I was by myself. But with the four of us, and with a horse, I'd say backtracking to the rocks is our only real hope. That is, if you're up to helping me walk a little faster than I've been managing on my own."

Howard looked at Jeremiah's bad leg again. Just as he did, he was surprised to hear Annette's voice. "This man's leg needs attention, Peaches. That's why I sent along the medical supplies."

"Guess who's back," Howard said, speaking in a low voice that only Loraine caught the meaning of. "And she's reminded me of something. Could you bring me my saddlebags off the horse while I have a look at Jeremiah's leg?"

Howard remembered what Annette had told him about the hypodermic needle she'd sent along. She said it contained a combination of an antibiotic and a tetanus shot. Howard was no doctor, but he did have enough savvy to give a shot in the arm and administer a few first-aid tactics common to the twenty-first century

"Why not let me have a look at that leg, Jeremiah?" he suggested. "I've, uh, had some medical experience, and I may be able to make you a little more comfortable." It really wasn't all that much of a lie. Howard had produced a couple of movies about medical centers. And he'd kept a medical staff on hand while filming to be sure every medical detail was correct. That should count for something.

Jeremiah appeared surprised by Howard's suggestion. "You can look at the leg, if you like," he agreed with a shrug. "But I'm not sure how you can help."

"Let me be the judge of that," Howard said, taking Jeremiah's arm and helping him sit down. Howard removed his pocketknife and opened the blade. "I need to split your pant leg far enough to uncover the wound," he said.

Jeremiah grunted. "Split away," he assented. "The trousers are done for anyway, thanks to the bullet hole and blood."

Howard split the pant leg up to Jeremiah's knee and examined the wound. There was only a small puncture where the bullet had entered the calf, but where it had exited there was a large tear in the flesh. Howard's concern increased when he found the wound covered with dirt from Jeremiah's pants. "This leg definitely needs attention," he said. "Infection is bound to set in, and that could spell real trouble."

"Sure, it's going to get infected," Jeremiah responded. "Gunshot wounds always do. Ain't much I can do about that, just pray gangrene don't set in."

Howard had to remind himself he was dealing with a man probably not even trained in the medicine of his own day—such as medicine was in the late nineteenth-century. He opened the saddlebags Loraine had brought to him and removed the first-aid kit, which not only contained the hypodermic needle, but also two small bottles, one marked hydrogen peroxide, the other marked alcohol. There was also some spray antiseptic and an abundant supply of clean bandaging.

"Have you ever heard of Dr. Joseph Lister?" he asked Jeremiah.

Jeremiah thought a moment. "Nope, can't say as I have."

"I've heard of Joseph Lister," Loraine spoke up. "He's the doctor who uses carbolic acid to treat open wounds. He's well known back in Boston. Dr. Lister has saved hundreds of lives, and he's been able to save people's limbs from amputation with his remarkable new medical techniques."

"Very good, Miss Parker," Howard responded.

"Do you have some carbolic acid with you?" she asked.

Howard grinned. "I have something better," he said. "Something from my dimension, if you get my drift."

Loraine gave him a wink of understanding. "I think you should let Mr. Placard treat your wound, Mr. Samuels," she said. "I can vouch for him. He knows what he's doing."

"She's right," Howard added. "I do know what I'm doing. And I have some things here that will help you heal much faster."

Jeremiah stared at the paraphernalia Howard had taken out of the saddlebags. "What have I got to lose?" he shrugged. "It would seem the two of you know some things about modern medicine that I don't."

Howard opened the bottle of alcohol and used it to disinfect his hands and the area around the wound. Next, he removed the cap from the solution of hydrogen peroxide and poured the contents directly onto the wound. It instantly began to boil. "What's it doing?" Jeremiah asked.

"It's doing exactly what it's supposed to do," Howard reassured him. "It's boiling out the wound." Howard gave the solution a couple of minutes to work, then using a clean bandage, wiped the wound dry. He then sprayed it with antiseptic and applied a bandage, holding it in place with several layers of medical tape.

"There," he said, wiping his hands on an extra bandage. "That's the easy part. The next step is even more important. I'm going to give you a shot that will help the wound heal much quicker and virtually eliminate the possibility of complications."

Howard picked up the hypodermic needle and removed its protective cover. Jeremiah's eyes grew even wider at the sight. "Uh, what is that thing?" he asked nervously.

"It's called an injection," Howard explained. "I need to stick this needle in your arm and inject this liquid."

"You want to stick that thing in my arm? Why?"

"For one thing, it's to protect you from lockjaw, Jeremiah."

"Lockjaw? Sticking me with that cactus spike is going to protect me from lockjaw? Doesn't make sense to me, pardner." Jeremiah looked dubious.

"Trust me," Howard said, taking hold of the other man's arm. "It's only going to sting a little." At the thought of how many times he had heard these same words before, Howard smiled to himself as he shoved the needle in and depressed the plunger.

"Ow!" Jeremiah grimaced. "That hurt almost as bad as getting shot in the first place."

"It'll help later, I guarantee it," Howard assured him.

"I sure hope you know what you're doing," Jeremiah objected again, rubbing the sting out of his arm.

Howard pulled out a Band-Aid and laughed when he realized what Annette had done. She'd sent along children's Band-Aids. Each one contained a full-color depiction of Bugs Bunny and friends.

"What in blazes is that thing?" Jeremiah asked loudly as Howard applied one over the puncture mark where he had injected the needle.

"Sorry, Jeremiah. All I have is the children's version. You can live with it."

Amos moved in for a closer look at the Band-Aids. "Nifty," he said. "May I have one, Mr. Placard?"

Here," Howard said, smiling, as he handed the rest of the box to Amos. "You can have them all."

"Awesome!" came Amos' reply as he took the box from Howard.

Howard laughed and replaced the protective cover on the needle as he considered how he could safely dispose of the thing. Then he remembered—this was 1885. There was no need to worry about a used needle getting into the wrong hands here. He grinned to himself and tossed it into a nearby cactus patch where no one could happen onto it by accident.

Jeremiah rubbed his arm again. "I want you to know I'm much obliged to you for stopping that stage and setting those outlaws to running. I don't much like having my passengers roughed up. What can you tell me about the horses?" he asked, genuinely concerned. "They all right?"

"The horses broke free," Howard responded. "The last I saw of them, they were headed east at full gallop."

"Good," Jeremiah said. "They should find their way home, okay."

"Look!" Loraine shouted, pointing back down the road. "There's a rider coming our way! Could it be one of those men?"

Howard shielded his eyes and stared at the approaching rider. This definitely wasn't one of the outlaws. This man rode tall in the saddle, and the animal he was riding was no ordinary horse. Howard was a good enough judge of horseflesh to realize, even from a distance, that this was a magnificent animal. Howard continued to stare as the rider drew nearer. Something about the way he was dressed looked very familiar. It took only a moment or so for Howard to realize what it was. The man was dressed very much like some of the pictures Howard had seen of the famous Buffalo Bill Cody. But, of course, it couldn't be Buffalo Bill. It was just a coincidence the way this man was dressed. Still, he certainly wasn't one of the robbers, Howard was sure of this.

"No," Howard assured Loraine. "Whoever this is, he's not one of the outlaws."

As the rider reined up, one gloved hand rose in a friendly gesture. "Hello, there!" he said. "Name's Cody." After a picture-perfect dismount, he extended a hand toward Howard. "Bill Cody, that is."

"Bill Cody?" Howard's eyes opened wide in astonishment. "Buffalo Bill Cody?"

"Well now, I see my reputation has preceded me, and I can't say as that bothers me, friend," the man said genially. "Good for business, you know. Me and some of my men brought in a runaway team a ways back. I rode ahead and found a disabled stagecoach. Found tracks leading this way and set out to catch up with whoever belonged to those tracks. Have I happened onto the right group of folks?"

Howard could only stare. Buffalo Bill Cody? If it were possible for Howard Placard to have a counterpart here in 1885, that counterpart could easily be Bill Cody. True, motion pictures were a few years down the road, but there was no question Cody was a producer in his own right. Probably the greatest producer of his day, with his very own world-traveling wild west show. That show was in its infancy in 1885, but Howard was well aware of the heights the show was destined to reach in time. Very respectfully, he reached out and accepted Cody's hand. "It is indeed a privilege to meet you, sir," he said in almost reverent awe. "I'm familiar with your show—you, Annie Oakley, and Sitting Bull. What a show business blockbuster the three of you make."

Cody eyed Howard carefully. "'Blockbuster,' eh? Hmmm. That's an interesting word. Never heard it before, but it does seem to match the occasion. By the way, how'd you know about Sitting Bull fixin' to join my show? It's true I've been negotiating with the army for approval to have the chief join up with me, but not many folks know about that yet."

Again, Loraine came to Howard's aid. "Mr. Placard knows a lot of things almost before they happen," she said, then quickly changed the subject. "And yes, we are the ones from the stagecoach. It was robbed, you see."

Cody tipped his hat toward Loraine. "Robbed, you say? I guess that would explain how the runaway happened. How much did the varmints make off with?"

"They got nothing," Jeremiah spoke up. "I'm Jeremiah Samuels, Mr. Cody. I'm the stage driver. I outsmarted those men the first time around, but I expect them back any time now. They won't rest until they've finished what they started out to do."

Cody and Samuels shook hands. "What were they after?" Cody quizzed. "If it's not too bold of me to ask?"

"Not at all, Mr. Cody," Jeremiah said, setting a toe of his boot against the saddlebags. "These bags are filled with payroll money bound for a bank in Mesa."

Cody looked down at the saddlebags. "Payroll money, you say. Pretty tempting bait for a couple of hornswoggling thieves, I'd say." Cody stroked his beard. "I suggest you folks join up with my wagon train for your own safety. The wagons are behind me, probably not more than an hour. We could head back down the road and meet them halfway. We'll spend the night in the safety of the circled wagons, then head on into Mesa tomorrow morning."

* * *

Loraine wasn't too happy about leaving her luggage by the side of the road, but Bill Cody convinced her they could pick it up the next morning when the wagon train passed by on the way to Mesa. She was somewhat consoled by his invitation to ride his horse, a truly magnificent animal. Jeremiah Samuels rode the second horse, while

Howard, Cody, and Amos walked. After everything that had happened to her today, Loraine had to admit she felt pretty safe in the protection of these men. Especially Howard Placard. It entered her mind again that she had never met a man quite like Howard. He just had a way of filling her with warmth and security. And the intriguing part was—she still didn't have the slightest idea why.

CHAPTER 20

It was shortly after dark when the little troupe came up on the six wagons already in place and readied for the night. Supper was fantastic that evening—stew so thick they could almost cut it with a knife. How long had it been since Howard had savored beef cooked to such perfection? And the flavor in the vegetables was like nothing he had tasted since leaving his father's ranch. After dinner, Cody and Annie joined their guests around a campfire, something else that reminded Howard of evenings on the ranch. Everyone sat in a circle around the fire, Loraine just to Howard's left, with Amos next, followed by Annie, Cody, and Jeremiah. Though seen by no one other than Howard, Annette was there, too, just to Howard's right, which made the camp-fire even more reminiscent of the days on the ranch.

Howard examined the faces of each one in the group and thought how wonderful it was to be a part of it. It was certainly a welcome change from the lonely nights he'd spent over the last year and a half on that dismal island.

Howard glanced up at the full moon gracing a star-studded evening sky. Its brilliance brought to mind other moonlit skies he had slept under as a young man. Filled with these nostalgic memories, he thought of the day he'd first laid eyes on Lori Parker. He closed his eyes and savored the moment.

It was the sound of Loraine's laughter that drew him back to the present. Opening his eyes, he thought for an instant that he was looking at Lori, but the illusion quickly passed, and he realized Loraine was laughing at something Annie had said. Howard missed exactly what it was, being deep in his own thought.

As reality told him he was looking at Loraine, and not Lori, he felt a surge of disappointment. But even so, it was impossible to keep his eyes off her. He listened now as Loraine ventured a question of Annie. "Is it really true you can shoot a dime out of the air?" she asked.

Annie smiled and nodded yes. "Would you like a demonstration?"

"Yes, I would," came Loraine's excited response. "I saw you on the stage once, but you didn't do the dime trick that day."

Annie stood. As usual, she was wearing her revolver. "It would be hard to see a dime in the dark," she said. "That's pretty much a daytime stunt." Annie reached into her pocket and removed two small white pebbles. "These aren't much bigger than a dime," she explained. "Would you settle for seeing me shoot one of these out of the air, Loraine?"

"Yes! I would. May I toss it up?"

"Sure, why not?" Annie said, handing one of the stones to Loraine. She removed her gun and cocked back the hammer. "Toss away," she said. "Just keep it in above the fire where I can see it."

The sound of Annie's gun was deafening. The white pebble instantly shattered, sending fragments sailing in every direction. "That's great shooting," Loraine said. "Can you hit it every time?"

"Pretty much," Annie confirmed. "I've been shooting since I was a girl. Won my first contest at age fifteen."

Amos sprang to his feet and moved quickly to where Annie stood. "My sister could have hit that pebble," he said, his face square-jawed with determination as he looked at the famous Little Sure Shot. "She's awesome. And she never misses the mark, either."

Annie looked a little taken aback. "Your sister?" she asked. "Miss Loraine Parker, you mean?"

Amos' chest expanded a size. "Loraine's my only sister. And she could hit that pebble, just like you did."

"Amos!" Loraine fussed. "Sit down and stop bothering Annie."

Annie turned to Loraine. "Is it true?" she asked. "Do you shoot?"

"A little," Loraine blushed. "But nothing like you."

"You're as good as her," Amos snorted, "and you're going to prove it." With that, he ran over to where Loraine's holstered revolver lay on the ground next to her handbag. He picked it up and was back in a flash, handing her the gun. "Go ahead, sis. Show these folks you can shoot, too."

"That's some six-shooter you have there," Annie observed. "A twenty-two magnum caliber, I'd guess."

"Yes, that's right. My father had it specially made for my eighteenth birthday."

"Chrome-plated. It must have cost your father a fortune."

"I—I suppose."

"Well, let's see what you can do with it. Here, let me toss up this other pebble."

Howard watched with keen interest as Loraine stood up and strapped on the holster. He had seen her hit Clay's hat, but this tiny pebble? Knowing Annie Oakley's history, he wasn't surprised she could do it. But Loraine? Well—maybe.

"All right," Loraine said. "Toss it up, I'm ready."

Annie gave her a look of surprise. "Your gun is still holstered," she observed.

Loraine blushed. "It's just the way I usually do my shooting," she explained.

"All right," Annie said, cautiously. "Let's see what you can do." She tossed the pebble up over the fire, just as Loraine had done earlier. Like a flash of lightning, the revolver was unholstered. The report rang out so fast, it was impossible to detect when she had cocked the hammer or squeezed off the shot. The bullet struck the pebble dead center. Then, just as quickly as the gun had left the holster, she replaced it.

"Awesome, sis!" Amos screeched. "I knew you could do it."

Howard's jaw dropped. Never had he seen anything like it, unless it involved some of his old Hollywood special effects crew. But with Loraine, there were no special effects. He had to admit, he would have been hard pressed to hit that small target in the dead of night himself. "Yes, Miss Parker," he quietly added. "That was an amazing display of speed and accuracy. Well done."

"Unquestionably well done," Annie meekly admitted. "I'm impressed you did it without having the gun unholstered. I see I'd better work on the presentation of my own act."

"You wouldn't by chance be looking for a job, would you, young lady?" Cody ventured. "I could use someone with your talent in my show. I'd be willing to bill you right alongside Annie, here."

Loraine quickly shook off his offer. "No, no. I'm not a show person. Marksmanship is strictly a hobby for me."

Annie laughed. "I can't say that hurts my feelings much," she confessed. "I like being known as the best woman alive with a gun. You just might put that honor in jeopardy, if you ever went into show business."

Loraine emptied the spent shells from her revolver and began reloading it from spare ammunition on her holster belt. "Oh no," she said modestly. "That honor belongs to you and you alone, Annie. You're the greatest."

"Miss Parker is right, you know," Howard said. "History will record you as the greatest female sharpshooter ever." *I wish I could tell you more,* he added to himself. *But how could you understand my telling you that Irving Berlin will someday write a hit musical about you? Or that the musical,* Annie Get Your Gun, *will even be made into a hit movie?*

Annie smiled. "Thanks to both of you. Marksmanship is my life. I'll take all the compliments I can get." Annie glanced at Loraine's feet. "May I ask where you got those unusual moccasins? I've never seen anything like them, and I was just wondering."

Loraine's face turned bright red. "These shoes were a gift from Mr. Placard," she explained. "I have to admit, they are most comfortable to walk in, but don't they look hideous?"

Annie's left brow raised. "Hideous isn't exactly the word I'd use to describe them, Miss Parker. Different, perhaps. But not hideous."

"Amos," Loraine said, still blushing. "Would you fetch my shoes from Mr. Placard's saddlebags, please?"

Amos hurried to where Howard's saddlebags lay near Loraine's handbag, but instead of rummaging through the saddlebags himself, he brought them back to Howard.

Howard had to smile at Loraine's discomfort with the shoes. That's something Lori would have shared with her. Just one more thing to show their similarity went much deeper than just their looks. True, there were some striking differences between the two women, but there were some striking similarities, as well. Howard opened the bags and removed Loraine's shoes, which he handed to her.

"Thank you, Mr. Placard," she said, quickly removing the walking shoes and slipping into her own. "I'll just give these back to you now."

Howard took the shoes and returned them to the saddlebags. As he did, he happened to notice the revolvers he had taken from the outlaws. Removing the guns, he offered them to Bill Cody. "I took them off the outlaws, and I certainly don't need them," he said.

"I'm much obliged," Cody said, taking the weapons. "I can always put these to use in my show."

Annette spoke up, catching Howard's attention. "Before you close up those saddlebags, Peaches, take out the tracking devices I sent along with you. I said you'd be needing them, and it's almost time."

Howard didn't argue. He removed both the sender and the tracker, then looked to Annette to see if she'd tell him more. She smiled. "Put them in your pocket, Peaches. That's all you need to know for now."

Howard shrugged and slipped the objects in his pocket. He lay the saddlebags on the ground behind him just as the sound of a fiddle reached his ears. It took only a second or two for him to recognize the tune as Camptown Races, an old Stephen Foster song. Glancing up, he spotted the fiddler. It was a young man standing just opposite the fire, stamping out the beat with one foot as he played. Jeremiah was the first to start clapping time, and within a few bars the whole camp had joined in. One couple and then another found their way to the make-do dirt floor where they danced. Off to his left, Howard saw Annie approaching young Amos.

"May I have this dance, master Amos?" she asked, extending a hand to the lad.

Amos turned bright red. "Go on!" Loraine said, pushing Amos to his feet. "Show this lady how they do the two-step in Boston." Amos moved reluctantly forward. At first he appeared awkward and nervous, but within seconds he had come to himself and soon proved this wasn't his first dance lesson. The folks looking on cheered and clapped all the harder.

"Would you look at that?" Howard laughed. "The boy knows what he's doing. Where'd he learn to dance like that, Miss Parker?"

"His older sister taught him," she beamed. "Dancing comes close behind shooting and riding in my book." Loraine unstrapped her gun belt and set the revolver down. "Come on," she said, taking Howard by the hand. "I'll prove it to you."

Howard's face went suddenly hot as he felt her hand in his. As a young man, Howard had loved dancing, but it was something he hadn't done in years.

"Come on," she said again, sensing his hesitation. "Dance with me, Mr. Placard. I won't bite."

"All right," Howard said, sliding an arm around her waist. "But I warn you, it's been a very long time. No telling what my feet may want to do."

Howard was surprised at how easily it all came back to him. More than this, he was surprised at how much he enjoyed dancing with this lovely lady, even if she wasn't Lori. He couldn't believe his disappointment when the first song ended. Nor could he believe his elation when the music picked up with another song, this one a perky rendition of "Turkey in the Straw." Not one of his favorites, but what could he expect from an 1885 fiddler—a Beatles number? "Would you like to dance again?" he asked.

"I thought you'd never ask," she smiled. "You're a good dancer, Mr. Placard. A very good dancer."

"As are you, Miss Parker. I can't remember dancing with anyone better."

"Thank you," she responded shyly. Howard took her hand and whirled her into a spin, her dress blossoming around her like a flower, and her face broke into a giant smile. For one brief instant, they faced each other, then stepped into the dance with all the vigor of two teenagers at a harvest festival. Dance after dance they spun, dipped, and skimmed over the dusty ground. Howard lost all track of time, and the rest of the world disappeared. There was only himself, and this beautiful woman on his arm. At first, he was sad she wasn't Lori. But after a while—it no longer mattered.

* * *

Loraine couldn't believe it when the fiddler announced this would be the last dance. How could it be time already for a last number? Where had the evening gone?

"You know our tradition," the fiddler announced. "Everyone sings along on the last number." With this, he broke into a slow rendition of a song Loraine remembered her father singing to her as a young girl. Howard took her in his arms, and together they sang as they danced.

> *From this valley they say you are leaving.*
> *I will miss your bright eyes and sweet smile.*
> *And they say you are taking the sunshine,*
> *That brightened our way for a while.*

In this man's arms, Loraine felt something she had never felt before. They were no longer dancing on a desert floor; they were somewhere in a fine hall in the city of Boston. Howard wore a splendid suit, and she wore a gorgeous flowing white gown embellished with French lace on the neck, sleeves, and hem. As they danced, her lips drew nearer to his until they almost touched. Again the words of the song rang to her ears.

> *Come and sit by my side if you love me.*
> *Do not hasten to bid me adieu.*
> *But remember the Red River Valley,*
> *And the girl who has loved you so true.*

The music ended. For another magic moment the two remained looking at each other, and the world was a wonderful place.

* * *

The sound of applause brought Howard to himself. He glanced around to see that they were the only two dancers remaining. All eyes were on them. Most were clapping, and a few of the men gave shrill whistles. Bill Cody approached and slapped Howard on the back. "Well done, young fellow," he said robustly. "You two put on some show, I must say."

Howard felt suddenly embarrassed. From the look on Loraine's face, he guessed she felt the same. "I—I'm sorry," he said to her. "I guess I got a little caught up in the music."

"Me too," she responded, blushing. "Thank you. It was great fun."

"Yes, it was, wasn't it?" Howard grinned. "More fun than I've had in one heck of a long time."

"If you'll pardon me," Cody said, "I've got some business that needs looking after before I can cash in for the night. You folks just make yourselves at home. The evening's still young. Don't let it go to waste." Having said that, Cody headed off in the direction of his wagon.

Looking around for Amos, Loraine spotted him by the campfire. "I should look in on my brother," she said, and Howard nodded.

As the two of them set out in Amos' direction, an amusing idea struck Howard. "Hey, you want to have some fun?" he asked. "I have a little trick up my sleeve we can play on Amos. It'll blow his mind."

"Blow his mind?" Loraine asked, a little disturbed by Howard's words.

Howard instantly perceived her concern. "Oops, did it again, didn't I? 'Blow his mind' is nothing bad; it's just an expression we use where I come from. It means—sort of—to add an element of surprise that Amos won't be expecting. Put a little excitement in his evening."

"Nothing that will get him hurt, right?" Loraine asked.

"No, nothing to get the lad hurt. Just a way to have a little fun with him." Howard reached into his pocket and pulled out the tracking devices. "Here," he said, handing her the half that emitted the signal. "Put this in your pocket. Then we'll have you and Amos go hide. As long as you have this in your pocket, I'll be able to find you, no matter where you hide. Poor Amos won't know what to think."

Loraine looked at the object. "But how can this help you find me? I don't understand."

"It's what we call a tracking device, Loraine. It sends out a signal that can only be picked up by this receiver that I'll keep. It's sort of like you were yelling at me, telling me where to look. I can't miss finding you."

Loraine's eyes softened, and it was several seconds before she responded. "You just called me Loraine," she observed softly.

Howard felt a jolt of embarrassment shoot through him. "I—I'm sorry, Miss Parker. It just slipped out. In my time it's common for a man to call a lady by her first name. I know it's not the proper thing to do in 1885. I'll try to be more careful in the future."

She paused again, looking into his eyes. "It's all right, I didn't mind. I've never been one to put much stock in silly rules, and I think not calling a lady by her first name is a silly rule."

As Howard stared at her, he thought that was exactly what he might expect from Lori, given this same situation. Loraine looked down at her hand, studying the transmitter more closely, then held it up to her ear. "I can't hear anything," she said.

Howard grinned. "That's the fun part of it, Miss Parker. No one can hear the signal. It can only be detected by this little receiver."

Loraine turned her attention to the receiver Howard was holding. "What if I hide too far away for your receiver to hear?" she asked. "What then?"

"Don't worry about that, Miss Parker. I'm familiar with these little goodies from some of my espionage movies. The range of this thing is between twenty and thirty miles, depending on how much obstruction may be in the way of the signal."

"Espionage movies?" she questioned.

"Yes," he responded, suddenly hearing himself speak as Loraine no doubt heard him. "It's just more stuff from the dimension I come from. I really do wish I could take you there to show you some of it, but . . ."

"But your angel won't allow that."

Howard noticed Annette shaking her head no. "I'm afraid not," he told Loraine.

Loraine smiled warmly. "It's nice you want to take me there to see those things. I like that."

"I assure you," Howard said, returning to the subject of the tracking devices, "these things will pinpoint you wherever you hide. Shall we give it a go?"

"Let's," Loraine grinned, shoving the signaling device into her dress pocket. As she did, her hand brushed against something else. She pulled it out and saw that it was the medallion Howard had given to Amos. Amos had asked Loraine to keep it for him, so he wouldn't lose it. Howard couldn't help noticing it in her hand now.

He stared at the medallion, as its meaning came clear. Howard had carried that medallion for more than ten years because it

reminded him of Lori. All those years he had known that the medallion carried a story with it of a stranger who had reportedly saved the
lives of Lori's great-grandfather and a distant aunt. He also knew the
medallion had stopped a bullet, saving that same stranger's own life.
The reality of it all hit him now with sudden impact. He was that
stranger. Amos and Loraine were the ones whose lives he had saved.
And it was his own life that had been spared when the medallion
stopped Clay Derringer's bullet.

The whole thing was mind-boggling. He'd first seen the medallion that day at the airport when it came off Lori's key ring inside his
pocket. But that day wouldn't happen for more than a century from
the day he was living now. He shook his head to push it all away.
Understanding the world of angels, and the rules accompanying their
world, was more than he was capable of.

Loraine returned the medallion to her pocket, bringing Howard
out of his thoughts. "Amos!" she called. "Do you want to play some
hide and seek?"

Amos quickly joined them. "Sure, sis. That sounds awesome."

She put her hands on her hips. "You've really taken to that word,
haven't you, little brother?"

Amos grinned. "Yes, I like the word. What's the matter with it?"

Howard stepped in. "I assure you, Miss Parker, all the young folks
where I come from use the word. I see nothing wrong with it."

"All right," she gave in. "I suppose there's nothing wrong with the
word. But if we're going to play hide and seek, you and I will have to
hide together, Amos. I'll need you to protect me from any critters that
might be out there. Mr. Placard will give us time to hide, then come
looking for us."

"All right," Amos exclaimed. "That sounds like fun. Come on,
let's go. Cover your eyes, Mr. Placard."

Howard was glad the others had all gone about their business by
this time. He had to admit, thoughts of this little game did sound like
fun. It almost made him feel like a kid again. But he certainly
wouldn't want an audience.

As Loraine and Amos moved away, Howard looked at Annette,
who was still standing nearby. Since no one else was near, he felt safe
speaking to her. "That medallion thing," he said. "It really blows my

mind, little sister. How is it possible that it saved my life in 1885, and yet it won't be until the late 1900s that I see it for the first time?"

Annette smiled. "I admit, Peaches, the properties of time are hard to understand. And don't think me being a second-level angel makes it any easier, because it doesn't. The higher authorities understand time, and they have complete control over it. The rest, I take on faith—the same as you'll have to do for now, big brother. But the higher authorities refuse to override the right that people have to make mistakes. There's always a way provided to correct our mistakes, but the higher authorities won't always prevent the mistake in the first place. Case in point: when you and I were born a century too late. Here you are back in 1885 trying to set destiny right because of that mistake. Take it at that, and let's drop it, big brother. Otherwise, it'll drive you nuts."

Howard considered this. "This does bring up another question, you know," he observed. "You mentioned once that you found the man destiny had picked out for you. And you said he lived back here in this time slot. So . . . ? How did the two of you get together, sis?"

"Very good question, Peaches. I'm glad to see you're thinking things out like this. I'm not going to tell you who my guy is, just yet because you might let a slip of the tongue mess something up. I'll tell you who he is when the time is right. But as to how he and I met, it's a long story. In a nutshell, it happened when I was a first-level angel. You've heard the stories about how Jason courted Samantha as an angel? Well, I courted my guy as an angel, too. Came back in time to meet him, I did. And if you're not confused enough already, let me take it a step further. Today is Monday, October the fifth, 1885. It'll be another year yet before I come back as a first-level angel to meet my guy. That won't happen until 1886."

Howard's head was spinning. "I'm really confused," he admitted. "You're a second-level angel now, but you won't be back to meet your destined fellow for another year? And then you'll do it as a first-level angel? I've produced some strange movies in my time, but nothing with a plot like this. Personally, I'd have trashed this plot. Too crazy. No one would buy it."

"Which only goes to prove, truth is stranger than fiction, Peaches." Annette glanced into the desert where Loraine and Amos had gone to hide. "You'd better start counting, big brother. I think they're about ready for you."

* * *

Clay and Grayson crouched low on the mesa overlooking the six camped wagons. "We gotta handle this just right," Clay spat out gruffly. "In and out without them ever knowin' what hit 'em. That's what we gotta do, Scar. Now see if you can spot that stage driver. Find him and we find the money. I'm betting on it."

"Yeah, reckon you're right about that. Hey! Ain't that him layin' out a bedroll over there?"

"Where?!"

"Right there, next to the second wagon. It's him, Clay. I'd swear to it."

"By snuff, I do believe you got him pegged, Scar. And look at what's layin' on the ground next to him. Saddlebags." Clay let out a low rumbling laugh. "Now what do you suppose is in them saddlebags, Scar?"

"Money, that's what. Let's get down there and get it."

Clay raised a hand. "Hold up, pardner. We gotta be sure we got all the angles covered. And I want that lady while we're at it."

"What about that city feller?" Grayson asked rancorously. "I still get to do him in, don't I?"

"Yeah, Scar, we ain't lettin' him off the hook. He's yours. We grab the money, I grab the woman, and you put a slug in the city slicker."

"And my horse? You told me I could get my horse back. I liked that horse, Clay."

"Forget the horse, Scar. We got plenty of horses. We can steal ourselves another one anytime. Right now, let's concentrate on the loot and gettin' even with those two meddlers."

"I don't like it," Grayson objected. "But I'll forget the horse just so long as I get to plug that troublemaker. And you know what? That looks like that's him standin' down there next to the campfire."

"I do believe you're right, Scar."

"And I got the girl pegged, too. Over there, behind that saguaro. That's her with that snot-nosed kid."

"Yeaaah," Clay agreed, the word dragging heavily off his tongue. "What do you suppose she's doin' out there?" He shrugged. "I guess it don't matter none. Let's get to it, Scar. Now don't forget, we hit hard and we hit fast. First the money, then you get that city slicker and I'll get the gal."

"Gotcha, Clay. Let's do it."

* * *

Howard pulled the tracking device from his pocket and moved it around until the signal peaked. It was pointing straight at a saguaro cactus about three hundred feet from where he stood. *I don't want to make this appear too easy,* he told himself. *I'll just wander around a bit, acting confused. Then I'll nail 'em.* He grinned and started walking in a circle like he wasn't sure which way to start looking. Just about the time he was ready to turn toward the saguaro, he was distracted by the sound of horses' hooves and an earsplitting cry of "Yeee-haaa!" His jaw dropped as he saw the riders. In one swift motion they rode by one of the closest wagons where Jeremiah was preparing to bed down for the night. Howard watched in disbelief as one of the riders leaned down and scooped up the saddlebags containing the payroll money on a dead run. To his utter dismay, one of the riders next headed straight for him. In an instant, he recognized Grayson Hobbs. Then, out of the corner of his eye, Howard noticed someone else. It was Annette.

"Hit the dirt, Peaches!" she cried. "This jerk aims to take you out."

Howard didn't argue. He dove for the ground just as Grayson's shot rang out. The bullet passed not six inches from his right ear. Howard quickly rolled over to face his assailant just as Grayson spun his animal around for a second shot. This time Howard didn't even have a chance to ask himself what Dusty Lockhart would do. There wasn't time. In one split second, he formulated a plan. Grabbing the cool end of a log lying in the campfire, he thrust the burning end directly in the face of the oncoming horse. The horse reared, causing Grayson's next shot to go completely astray. With a loud and startled whinny, the horse turned and bounded away, leaving Grayson helpless to do anything more than just hang on for dear life.

"They got the payroll money!" Jeremiah cried at the top of his voice, hopping up and down on his one good leg. "Someone's got to stop 'em!"

Bill Cody was the first to reach the scene, with Annie close behind. "What's happening here?" he demanded loudly.

"It's the robbers," Jeremiah shot back. "They're making off with the payroll."

Annie drew her gun, but by this time both riders had vanished into the shadows of a nearby mesa.

"They got my sister!" All eyes turned to see Amos, who was running at breakneck speed toward them. "They got my sister!" he cried again. "Someone's got to help her!"

A surge of fear gripped Howard as he quickly turned to look at Annette. "How could you let this happen?" he cried out, not caring who might hear or what they might think.

Annette smiled. "I thought you didn't care about her, Peaches. Of course, I was beginning to wonder, with the way you were holding her at the dance. Don't get your dander up, big brother. Just remember the lady has the sending device in her pocket. And you have the tracker in yours."

Annette's words hit Howard with the impact of a eighteen-wheeler. Of course! The tracking device! Annette had set it up just as sure as the sun rose in the morning.

"Saddle my horse!" Cody called out. "And be quick about it! Those varmints already have the jump on me."

Two men sprang into action, bringing Cody's animal out from where it had been tied up for the night. In less than a minute, the saddle was on and fastened, and two filled canteens were hung from the saddle horn. Cody stepped up to the animal. "Ain't no better tracker in the world than me," he said, throwing all modesty aside.

"That's true," Annie was quick to agree. "But even with a full moon, tracking those men at night will be pretty near impossible. Even for you, Bill."

Cody paid her no mind and grabbed the saddle horn in preparation to mount the horse. Then, without warning, he doubled over in tremendous pain. "Oh," he groaned, reaching a hand around to his back. "What in tarnation brought this on?" His knees buckled and he slumped to the ground where he crouched in near helplessness.

"What is it, Bill?" Annie asked in great concern.

"Don't rightly know, Annie. It's my back. Nothing like this has ever happened to me before. I—I don't think I can ride right now."

"Okay, Peaches," Annette said. "That's your opening. I have Cody out of the way now."

Howard grabbed up the saddlebags Annette had sent along. As he did, he noticed Loraine's revolver lying there. He picked up the revolver and crammed it into the saddlebags. Moving to Cody's horse, he placed a foot in the stirrup and mounted up.

"What are you doing?" Cody asked, his face grimacing in pain.

"Not to be arguing with you, Bill," came an answer that surprised no one more than Howard himself. "But you, sir, are the second-best tracker in these parts. Right now, I'm the best. I'm going after those men, if you'll permit me the use of your horse."

"Like Annie said, it's dark," Cody protested. "Tracking won't be easy, pardner."

"I've got a full moon, and I noticed a six-cell flashlight in the saddlebags." Howard reached down and felt the tracking device receiver in his pocket. "Plus, I have . . . uh . . . a certain intuition that will add remarkably to my tracking skills."

"A six-cell what?" Annie asked confusedly.

Howard ignored her question. "May I borrow the horse?" he asked again.

"Take him, man. And Godspeed to you."

"Please, Mr. Placard," Amos pleaded, moving to the horse and grabbing Howard's leg. "Save my sister!"

"I'll save your sister, son. You have my word on it."

"And the word of your angel?" the boy added.

Howard looked at Annette, who winked him a yes. "And the word of my angel, son," he said. Then, urging the stallion forward, he rode hard into the night.

CHAPTER 21

Moving through the treacherous Superstitions at night, even with a full moon, was no feat for the faint of heart. Even with the years of experience that Clay and Grayson had under their belt, they weren't fools enough to get in a hurry under these circumstances. Besides, there was no reason to hurry now. They had the loot, and no tracker alive could find them on this trail at night. An added reason for moving slowly was the fact that Clay had an extra passenger on his horse. Not a very cooperative one either, as the bite and scratch marks on Clay's face and upper body attested to. The first three or so miles proved to be the worst for the outlaws. Once they had put some distance between them and the wagons, they stopped long enough to tie and gag her, which made riding double a little more bearable for Clay. Only after she was bound and gagged did the subject of Howard come up.

"You put a slug in him?" Clay asked.

"Yeah," Grayson lied. "Clean through the heart." What the heck? He figured they'd never see the troublemaker again anyway. Why not let Clay believe he had gotten the job done?

Forced to move slowly, it was nearly dawn by the time they reached their hideout. It took both men to carry Loraine inside and tie her to a chair, and they felt like they had tackled a tornado by the time it was over. After lighting a candle and placing it in the center of the table, Clay removed the gag from Loraine and gave her a drink of water from a canteen. She spit it back in his face.

"Ain't you the feisty one," Clay snapped. "Taming you is gonna be great fun, missy. But first things first. Let's count the money, Scar. Then we'll split it up, sixty-forty, just like always."

"How come I always get less than you?" Grayson protested. "It ain't fair. I do half the work. I should get half the take."

"You'll get forty percent and like it, pardner. I'm the one with all the brains; I deserve a little extra for my effort. Now let's get this stuff counted."

"You'll never get away with this. You know that, don't you?" Loraine spat out.

"That's what they all say, sister," Clay retorted. "But as you can see, we've done a pretty good job getting away with it up until now."

* * *

Howard had never been more concerned in his entire life. True, he had an angel on his side—and he had the electronic tracking device. On top of this, he was a skilled horseman on one of the finest mounts he had ever ridden. What's more, the rugged terrain in these Superstition Mountains was not unfamiliar to him; Howard had ridden in these mountains many times as a youth. True, the darkness of night did make it more difficult, but at least he had the flashlight Annette had sent along. This permitted him to keep a close check on the tracking device and saved a great deal of time by providing him with better vision as he traveled.

Still, he couldn't help feeling apprehensive. So much depended on him catching up with these men. And after catching them, what then? He'd need a plan to free Loraine.

The morning sun was just peeking over the eastern horizon when he crested a hill overlooking a rustic old miner's shack. He had little trouble figuring out that this was where the hoodlums were holed up since their still-saddled horses were tethered in front of the shack. Howard dismounted and took stock of the situation. Besides the two horses he had first seen, he now noticed two more in a broken-down corral behind the house. He reasoned that this must be the hideout Jeremiah Samuels had mentioned.

Seeing one window in the side of the shack facing him, Howard raised his binoculars, which Annette had kindly provided in his saddlebags. He could just make out the flicker of a candle and the movement of a shadow or two. This at least assured him they were inside.

Howard sat back on his heels trying to decide his next course of action. What would Dusty Lockhart do? he pondered. But that was no good. Dusty Lockhart would simply rush the shack with guns a-blazing. That was fine for a movie, but this wasn't a movie. Howard had to think of something else. He looked thoughtfully at the saddle-bags draped over the horse. His sister had planned out everything he needed so far on this little journey; could she possibly have sent something along especially for this occasion?

He grabbed the bags and opened them up. There were his boots, along with Amos' shoes where he'd put them when they'd changed into the Nikes. Shoving these aside, he searched further and his hand touched a package of some kind. He withdrew it and was astonished to see that it was a huge package of firecrackers. Oh, brother, fire-crackers, he snorted. What he needed was firepower, not a package of noise makers. But wait. How would the outlaws know it wasn't gunshots—lots of gunshots, as if a posse had come after them?

Now some matches, Howard thought. He'd need matches. Had Annette remembered those, too? He turned the saddlebags upside down, dumping the contents onto the ground. Sure enough, the matches were there.

Looking at the shack, Howard smiled. "Dusty Lockhart," he said aloud. "Eat your heart out, pardner. I'm about to make your best adventure look like something off Sesame Street."

* * *

Loraine glared at the men still drooling over the stolen money that had been laid out on the table halfway across the room from where she sat tied to a wooden chair. She had heard Grayson say he shot Howard through the heart, but something inside told her it was a lie. She had to believe it was a lie; she couldn't bear thinking anything else. These men had tried to kill Howard before, only to be foiled by his sister, an angel who would most certainly protect him again. She forced herself to believe Annette would protect him.

Her mind raced trying to figure out some way of escape. What wouldn't she give to have an angel on her side about now? It looked pretty hopeless, but Loraine wasn't one to give up without a fight.

She'd just have to wait for her chance and see what came of it.

"Three hundred bucks!" she heard Clay shout. "We're rich, Scar. I always knew we'd hit the big one someday. That's two hundred for me and one hundred for you. Sixty-forty, just like I promised."

Grayson's eyes nearly burst from their sockets. "A hundred bucks," he gasped. "That's more cash than I've ever seen in one place. Yaaa-hooo!! I'm goin' to town and have me a party like I ain't never had before."

"Not yet you ain't," Clay commanded. "Not till this money has a chance to cool a bit. If you was as smart as me, you'd know that. This money will spend just fine in a week or so, after it cools some." Clay crammed his share of the money back in the saddlebags. Grayson left his lying on the table, where he could just look at it.

Loraine strained at the ropes, but it was no use; she was bound too tightly. She glanced up to see Clay looking at her, his eyes burning with ill intent. Clay wet his lips and stood up, shoving his chair aside as he did. The floor creaked as he moved heavy-footed to where she sat bound and helpless.

"I'd say it's time you and I got a little better acquainted, missy," he sneered, his jagged brown teeth showing through an evil grin. "Why don't you run out and put the horses away, Scar? The lady and me would like to be alone for a bit."

Grayson grumbled something under his breath and shoved his share of the money back in the saddlebags along with Clay's share. Standing up, he looked at Clay and there he hesitated.

Clay reached out and touched Loraine's cheek. His rough hand felt like sandpaper against her delicate skin. "You better be payin' me some mind, Scar," he warned his partner in a threatening tone. "The lady here is just dyin' for her first tamin' lesson."

Catching Clay completely unaware, Loraine yanked her head to the side and sank her teeth painfully into the flesh of his wrist.

"Yeee-ooowww!!!" Clay screeched, quickly pulling his hand away. "You little witch!" The words came out slow and spiteful. "I'll show you a thing or two about respecting your betters!" His arm cocked back, ready to deliver a vengeful backhand to her face. But right at that moment, he was cut short by a volley of explosions that sounded like gunshots coming from outside the shack. Instinctively, he abandoned his thoughts of Loraine and hit the floor, sending a blanket of dust flying. Grayson wasted no time following Clay's example.

"How in the bitter snuff did they find us?!" Clay growled, burying his head under his hands.

"I don't know!" Grayson whined back. "But from the sound of those shots, I'd say there's at least a dozen of 'em out there."

Hearing continuous volley of apparent gunshots, Loraine twisted her body around, toppling the chair over. Then she lay as low to the floor as possible and held her breath, fearing that a stray bullet might find her. As she lay there, she noticed something strange. In spite of all the gunshots, no bullets penetrated the shack. It didn't make sense. She was cautiously amused when neither Clay nor Grayson figured this out.

"We're sitting ducks in this shack," Clay noted loudly. "We gotta beat it out of here, fast! Take a peek out the back door, Scar. See if it's safe for us to leave that way."

"Check the door yourself!" Grayson bellowed. "I ain't getting my head blown off."

"Scar! You yellow-bellied coward! Check the door!"

"I ain't budging, Clay. You're the one who claims ta have all the brains. And you're the one who gets sixty percent of all our takings. You check the door."

"Imbecile!" Clay growled, as he crawled toward the back door. "I'm stuck with a yellow-bellied imbecile for a pardner! Next time we split seventy-twenty."

* * *

Reaching the door, Clay rose to his feet and opened it a crack. He peeked out. "Looks like it's clear back here," he said. "All the shots seem to be comin' from the front." He opened the door farther and poked his head outside. Then, drawing in a quick breath and crouching as low as possible, he broke into a run, heading straight for the corral and a horse that could take him out of there. Seeing Clay's course of action, Grayson was on his feet and after him.

Clay was grateful that the corral was far enough behind the house to keep him hidden from whoever was doing all the shooting out front. But his gratitude turned to frustration when he realized the corral was empty. A quick check revealed the gate had been left open and the two spare horses were nowhere to be seen. How could that have happened? He was always so careful about his horses. After all, they were a major tool in his trade, so to speak. Hearing footsteps behind him, Clay spun on his heels—gun drawn. "Scar!" he cried out. "You darn fool, you purt-near got your head took off sneaking up on me like that. I should shoot you anyway for leaving the corral gate open."

"How come you think it was me left the gate open?" Grayson retorted.

"You're the one who needed a horse to replace the one you lost back at the stagecoach."

"I closed the gate, Clay! It must have been one of them guys from the posse who opened it to let our horses out."

Clay gave it some brief thought. "Yeah, I reckon you could be right, at that. We best be hightailing it out of here on foot, afore they figure out we've left the cabin."

The two men quickly scurried to a ravine several yards behind the shack and made haste at putting some distance between them and the shooters, whoever they were.

* * *

Alone in the cabin, Loraine searched the room for anything sharp enough to cut the ropes binding her. It was no use, there was nothing. Her only hope lay with whoever was firing the shots. With any luck, they would find her. Suddenly, she heard footsteps at the door. Her heart raced as the door flung open and a man rushed inside. "Mr. Placard?!!" she cried out in disbelief. "You are alive! How did you find me?"

Howard rushed to her side and made quick work of the ropes with his pocketknife. "I told you, you couldn't hide from me with that little device in your pocket, didn't I? I had no idea you'd go to such great lengths trying to prove me wrong."

Loraine scrambled to her feet, then reached inside her pocket to feel the device still there. "This little thing led you to me?" she gasped. "I—can't believe it!"

Howard laughed. "You believe everything else about me, and you find this little tracking device hard to believe? That's one for the book. Come on! Let's get out of here before those guys figure out they're running from a posse of one."

"You're alone?" she choked. "But I heard . . ."

"Firecrackers, Miss Parker. That's what you heard."

"Firecrackers? You charged this hideout backed up by nothing but firecrackers? You're crazy, you know that?"

"So I've been told. Come on, let's go!"

Loraine spotted the saddlebags of money on the table. "Wait!" she said, making a fast detour to grab the bags. "We wouldn't want to leave these behind, now would we?"

Loraine bolted through the open door with Howard on her heels. Once outside, she spotted two horses saddled and ready to go. She recognized one as the horse she and Clay had ridden to the shack, and the second horse as Bill Cody's. "You take this one," Howard said, taking the reins of Cody's horse and handing them to her. "I'll ride Clay's horse." Loraine tossed the saddlebags across the horse, then mounted up. Howard mounted up, too.

"I've taken the precaution of spooking the other horses," Howard explained. "Hopefully it'll take those jerks a good long time to round them up."

"Good thinking," Loraine said, then added with a smile, "I love riding, but I'm getting so darn tired of doing it in this dress. I don't suppose you'd have a pair of ladies' riding pants in those famous saddlebags of yours, would you?"

Howard raised his shoulders in a shrug. "Sorry, Miss Parker. I don't believe that's something my sister included for this trip."

"Next time you see her, pass along my complaint, will you? Now, which way out of here, Mr. Placard?"

"Southwest," Howard responded without the slightest hesitation. "Mesa's about fifteen miles from here, and that's where we're headed." Howard set his heels and urged his horse into a gallop. Loraine did the same. Leaving a trail of dust behind them, both riders were out of sight of the cabin in a matter of minutes.

* * *

It had been a sleepless night for Jeremiah Samuels. There were just too many things bearing down on his worried mind. Thoughts of his wife, Stephanie, his daughter, Brittany Ann, and his newly discovered friends refused to give him any peace. What must Stephanie be thinking, with no word from a husband who should have been home before dark last night? And what of Miss Parker and Howard? Blast the luck that Jeremiah had been so foolish as to make the run with the payroll money and no one riding shotgun for him. How could he have been so foolish?

Jeremiah rubbed his wounded leg. Surprisingly, most of the pain was gone. The leg was still sore, but nothing like he figured it would be. Howard's medicine must have been more powerful than he had supposed. He tried the leg and was pleased to find he could walk with a fair amount of ease. He glanced toward the east. The sun was just breaking. He couldn't help wondering what this day would bring. Surely it couldn't be as bad as yesterday. Off to his right, he caught a movement and looked up to see Bill Cody emerging from his wagon. Jeremiah limped over to greet him just as Cody's feet hit the ground. "Mornin', Cody."

"Mornin', Samuels."

"How'd the boy do? Did he sleep at all?" Jeremiah knew that Cody had taken Amos into his own wagon for the night.

"He's a brave one, that lad," Cody replied. "Didn't get to sleep until the wee hours, but he's doing a good job of catch-up about now. Out like a lump of wet coal."

"That's good," Jeremiah said. "He'll need the rest. No telling what he's in for." Jeremiah paused for a breath. "His sister, you know."

"I got a good feeling about that fellow that went looking for her, Samuels. Don't know why, just a gut feeling. I'd lay odds he'll bring her home safe."

Jeremiah brushed his chin. "There is something about the fellow; I can't put my finger on what it is. But I agree. If anyone can bring her back, it's Mr. Placard." Jeremiah rubbed his leg. "The man sure come up with some powerful medicine for a gunshot wound," he said. "This leg's been better, but darned if I can't walk on it this morning."

"I see you're getting around a little better than last night. You say this Placard fellow did some doctoring on the leg?"

"Yep. You looked like you could have used some doctoring on your back last night yourself, Cody. Looks like you're doing some better this morning, same as me."

"Funny about that back," Cody said, his eyes squinted nearly closed. "I went to bed in absolute misery last night. By midnight, my back was purely normal. Not one hint of pain since. Strangest thing that ever happened to me. It's almost like it happened just to keep me from going after Miss Parker. Like fate wanted Placard to be the one on my horse."

Jeremiah nodded thoughtfully. "Yeah, it would seem that way, wouldn't it? So what do you figure? We gonna head on in today or wait?"

Cody considered it. "Don't see how waiting could do much good. If Placard manages to get the lady away from those men, he'll probably head straight for Mesa. If he don't, then the faster we get a posse rounded up and after them varmints, the better. I'd say we pack up and head for Mesa ourselves."

Jeremiah nodded in agreement. "I got a wife and daughter waiting in Mesa. Probably worried sick about me. I gotta admit, heading in suits me just fine."

* * *

Stephanie Samuels was a strong woman. It required a strong woman to be the wife of a stagecoach driver in this day and age. The long, lonely nights with Jeremiah on the road were trying enough, but at times like this when the stagecoach was late, it was almost unbearable. There were many reasons for a stage to be late, of course. There were breakdowns, weather conditions, road washouts, and the most dreaded reason of all—robbers. Even though Stephanie made every effort to remain optimistic, she couldn't help but fear the worst this time. She knew Jeremiah was transporting a substantial amount of cash in payroll money, and the stage was considerably later than should be expected, even under the worst conditions. The stage had been due in before sunset yesterday. The night had now passed, and morning was well into its waking hours. The one thing she didn't know—and perhaps it was best she didn't—was that Jeremiah was making this run minus his sidekick, Benson, riding shotgun.

Not wanting to worry Brittany Ann, Stephanie did her best to remain cheerful while explaining she would take the buckboard into town to see if there was any word yet. Brittany assured her mother that she was perfectly capable of getting her own breakfast and making her way to school. She would ride the mare as usual.

Stephanie pulled the buckboard up in front of the hotel, which doubled as the headquarters for the stagecoach line. Climbing down from the rig, she crossed the wooden walkway and entered the hotel. The clerk stood behind the counter, and James and Anelladee Parker were there seated on one of the two brown, overstuffed sofas in the lobby. Since Anelladee was still wearing the same hoop skirt and cute little perky hat she had worn the night before, Stephanie was certain they had spent the night in town. Not that Stephanie blamed them; she would have done the same if she hadn't needed to hurry home for Brittany Ann's sake.

The Parkers spotted Stephanie at the same time as she saw them and rose to greet her as she moved over to the sofa. "Any word at all?" Stephanie asked as Anelladee took both of Stephanie's hands in her own.

"No, nothing," Anelladee responded wearily. "The sheriff is over at the telegraph office now. He figures the office on the other end is open by this time, and he can find out if the stage got a late start." Anelladee's expression turned more serious. "Your husband is the stagecoach driver," she said. "You must be experienced at waiting for an overdue stage. Tell me, is it common for the stage to be this late?"

Stephanie forced a smile. "It happens, Anelladee. And there's something I want you to understand. My husband's been doing this for more than ten years now, and not once has he failed to show up with all his passengers aboard, safe and sound. Loraine and Amos will be all right, you can depend on it."

James Parker spoke up. "It is unusual for the stage to be this late though, isn't it, Mrs. Samuels?"

At that moment Sheriff Scott Engels entered the hotel lobby, which allowed Stephanie to avoid James' question. All eyes turned to the sheriff. "Did you learn anything?" Anelladee asked, voicing the same concern shared by all.

Scott wiped his brow. "The folks at the telegraph office have informed me the stage got away on time yesterday morning, but it ain't been heard from since. It seems Benson was sick, and Jeremiah made this run with no one riding shotgun."

Stephanie's heart raced at this knowledge. But not wanting to worry the Parkers, she tried not to show her concern.

"I wish I had better news," Scott went on to say. "My deputy's out now, rounding up some men for a search party. I'm sure we'll find 'em. Probably nothin' more than a thrown wheel."

Stephanie was glad that young Mr. Scott Engels was the town sheriff now instead of old Dan Rogers, who had retired only last month after fifteen years. Dan was a good sheriff in his day, but it was definitely time he stepped down and let a younger man have a crack at the job. Without question, Scott Engels was the right man for the job. He could ride, shoot, and track with the best of them. It left Stephanie with a feeling of security, having him on the job.

Suddenly from the lobby door came a cry of excitement, "MOM! DAD!" Stephanie turned to see a young man whom she didn't recognize.

It was apparent the Parkers recognized him. "AMOS!" Anelladee shouted, rushing to smother the boy in her arms.

By the time James had reached the pair, Anelladee had pushed Amos back and held him at arm's length so she could look him over, every inch. "Are you all right, son?" she cried.

"I'm fine, Mom," he said, obviously embarrassed by her outburst of affection.

Realizing who Amos was, and that he had been a passenger on Jeremiah's stagecoach, Stephanie looked behind him to see who else had entered the room. A man stood just inside the door, holding his hat in one hand. He was covered with dust, indicating he had probably just ridden in on horseback. Stephanie ran to him in three quick steps. "Did you . . . ?"

"Yes, ma'am," the fellow responded. "Name's Steven Lee. I work for a traveling entertainment group headed up by a man named Bill Cody. Maybe you've heard of him by his stage name. Buffalo Bill."

"Yes, I'm familiar with Bill Cody," Stephanie said breathlessly. "The boy came on the stagecoach. My husband, Jeremiah Samuels, was the driver of the stage."

"Your husband's fine, ma'am. Other than a bit of a bum leg, that is. He's back at the wagons with the main body of our company. They should be arriving in town in two to three hours. I rode on ahead to bring you word. The boy here asked to come along with me. He's a real horseman, that one."

Stephanie's eyes closed as she released a sigh of relief. Jeremiah was okay. "Thank you, Lord," she whispered.

James Parker, who had been taking all this in, lay a hand on Amos' shoulder. "Your sister?" he asked. "Is she . . ."

When Amos hesitated, Steven stepped forward to face James. "I have some bad news, I'm afraid. We rescued your daughter with the others, after the stagecoach broke down. But there were some complications. Some robbers, two of them to be exact."

"Robbers?" Sheriff Engels echoed. "Would you care to elaborate on this part, friend?"

"You the sheriff in these parts?" Steven asked, seeing Scott's badge.

"I am. And I don't cater much to stage robbers in my territory. Is that what we have here—a stage robbery?"

"Please," James interrupted. "What were you saying about my daughter?"

Steven wiped nervously at his mouth. "There was an attempted robbery," he explained. "Your husband, ma'am," he said, looking at Stephanie, "managed to foil it. The first time the robbers struck, that is. But they struck a second time after Jeremiah, Amos, and his sister joined up with our wagon group. They hit us just as we were buttoning down for the night. They made off with the money, and they—"

"They got my sister," Amos broke in. "But they won't get away with it, not with Mr. Placard looking out for her, they won't. He's awesome."

"Loraine's been kidnapped?" Anelladee gasped, clutching her heart.

"I'm afraid so," Steven responded dejectedly. "But as the lad said, Mr. Placard rode out in hot pursuit of the robbers. Mr. Placard appears to be a capable man. We can only hope for the best."

The sheriff shoved his hat back on. "Looks like the men in the rescue party are going to need deputizing. What we need is a posse. Would you be willing to ride with us, Mr. Lee? It would be helpful if you could show us where you last saw the outlaws."

"I'll be glad to ride with your posse, sheriff."

"Good. You stay here with the others while me and my deputy round up some more men."

Amos stepped up to the sheriff. "I want to ride with your posse, too," he said. "That's my sister out there."

"No!" Anelladee shouted, grabbing Amos by the arm and pulling him back. "You're only a boy, Amos. This is men's work."

"Mom! I'm fourteen. Loraine needs me."

"Please, Sheriff," Anelladee begged. "Tell Amos your posse is men's work."

"Your mother's right, young man," Scott replied. "Not that you're not man enough to be part of a posse, but with it being your sister out there—I figure it's best you leave her rescue to the rest of us men. Sometimes a fellow don't think too clear when the victim is someone he's close to. Besides, your mom and dad need a strong man here with them right now." As the sheriff spoke, he noticed something fall from Amos' pocket. He reached down and picked it up. It was a picture of some sort, the likes of which Scott had never seen. "What is this, young man?" he asked, spellbound by the image of the young lady in the picture.

"That's a picture of what's called an automobile," Amos replied. "Mr. Placard gave it to me."

Scott stared at the picture. "Do you know who the young woman standing by the—whatever you called it—is, Amos?"

"She's Mr. Placard's sister. I think her name is Annette. Do you know her?"

"I'm not sure," he said slowly. "It's just that she looks so familiar . . . like I should know her." He studied the picture of Annette a few seconds longer, then gave the picture back to Amos. "No doubt I'm just mistaking her for someone else," he decided. "Probably because that's the best photograph I've ever seen. I wonder how they managed to do it in color." Scott gave Amos a gentle push toward his mother. "You look after things here, son. I'll go see to the posse." With this, the sheriff exited the room.

"My husband's leg?" Stephanie asked. "You said he was hurt, Mr. Lee. Was he shot during the holdup attempt?"

"Yep," Steven said with a nod. "He was shot, but it's not serious. It seems our man, Mr. Placard, had some medical training. Placard gave your husband some sort of medicine that did wonders at getting him past the worst of it."

"This Mr. Placard," Anelladee observed. "He sounds like quite a man."

Steven cleared his throat. "He is that, Mrs. Parker. I'd say your daughter is in good hands with him out there looking for her."

CHAPTER 22

Loraine and Howard reined in their horses. "Is that a river up ahead?" she asked.

"Yeah. A branch off the Salt River, I suspect," Howard said. "The way I figure, once we cross it, we'll be within five miles or so of Mesa."

Loraine leaned forward in the saddle and studied Howard intently. After a moment, she spoke her mind. "Could I ask you a question? Being from Boston, it's not all that easy for me to come to a place like the Arizona Territory. You're from the future—can you tell me if this place will ever be as civilized as Boston?"

Howard fumbled with the reins and searched for the best way to answer Loraine's question. "I suppose that depends on your definition of 'civilized.' The Arizona Territory became part of the United States in 1912." He smiled. "Or maybe I should say it *will* become part of the United States in 1912, since 1912 is still in your future. In my day, I'd say most of Arizona is pretty much civilized. If you have to spend much time on their freeways, it's another matter. But that's something you needn't worry yourself about, Miss Parker. That's something you're better off not even knowing."

"Oh, my!" Loraine gasped. "In 1912? It's hard for me to think of anything so far away as the twentieth century. It all seems so distant."

"It's not really so distant at all," he assured her. "You could easily live well into the twentieth century, Miss Parker. In fact, I predict you'll live to see many of the things I've told you about—automobiles, motion pictures, airplanes, the works. You're in for a wonderful, exciting life."

Loraine shuddered. "You're frightening me, Mr. Placard. I'm not sure I'm ready to hear these things. I'm not sure I'm ready to think about living through the change of a century, either."

This brought a hearty laugh from Howard. "I lived through the change of a millennium, Miss Parker," he declared. "I went from the twentieth century to the twenty-first. And let me tell you this, if you have a fraction of the chaos moving into the twentieth century I had moving into the twenty-first, I don't blame you for being apprehensive. You can't believe the uproar generated over a simple matter of the calendar moving from 1999 to 2000. But everyone's fears proved unfounded. The sun came up January first in the year 2000 just like any other day." Howard paused in thought before continuing. "Would you rather I drop the subject?" he asked. "It gets a lot more complicated than anything I've told you so far."

"More complicated than what I've already heard?" she jokingly asked. "I may be sorry for this, but yes—do go on."

"By the time we were approaching the year 2000," Howard continued, trying to keep his explanation as simple as possible, "the whole world was run by technology we called computers. Computers are machines that do some amazing things to make life easier. But computers are built by people, and people make mistakes. One mistake was building the first computers without taking the calendar into consideration. As a result, on December 31, 1999, the eve of the new century—the new millennium even—millions of computers were programmed to go back to January 1, 1900. That's because the 99 starts over again with 00. Instead of moving forward one day, digital calendars would all move backward a hundred years. This might seem like a little thing to you, Miss Parker. But in the year 2000, this sort of computer failure could wreak havoc. Many experts of the day predicted things like airplanes falling from the sky, banks losing all their records, governments starting wars by inadvertently calling for attacks on other governments. None of it happened, of course. Like so many times in history, the experts proved themselves wrong in the end."

Loraine raised a hand. "Okay, you can stop," she said. "I was right. I am sorry I asked."

"Okay," Howard said with a grin. "But I haven't even scratched the surface yet. The bottom line is that January 1, 2000, wasn't much different from any other Saturday, other than cleaning up after all the parties the night before."

Loraine looked tenderly at Howard, her eyes filled with wonder. "You are the most amazing man I've ever met—you and your angel and your stories of a future that simply mystify my mind. Someday—maybe—I'll write a book about all this." She paused, thinking for a moment. "Yes, I will most definitely write a book. And I think I'll title it after the sister who brought you here. I'll call it *An Angel in Time*. What do you think, Mr. Placard? Will anyone from my day believe a word of it?"

* * *

Back in Brad and Lori's family room, the little group was still watching with keen interest as the story continued to unfold. Lori was astounded at the things she had learned from Loraine's manuscript and from Samantha's holographs. Not only had she learned about her own progenitors, she had learned things about Howard Placard as well. To her surprise, she was beginning to see Howard in a whole new light. For the first time, she understood why he had been so infatuated with her. He wasn't in love with her at all; he only thought he was. The woman Howard was really destined to spend forever with was Loraine Parker, not Lori. And to Lori's great relief, and even joy, she was watching Howard learn this truth for himself.

Lori had to marvel at how much alike she and Loraine really were. Much more alike than in mere physical resemblance, though the physical resemblance was remarkable. It occurred to Lori that except for the century's difference in the times they lived, they were actually identical twins.

Lori sighed, thinking of the many interesting things she had learned this day. She had learned the real story of the medallion passed down through her father. She had always known the medallion saved the life of some stranger, but she'd had no idea that stranger was Howard Placard. She'd also learned the significance of Loraine's fancy revolver kept all these years in the trophy case over Lori's fireplace. She had seen firsthand how the previously unexplainable Polaroid picture of Loraine came to be. And perhaps, the most interesting of all, she had learned about Loraine's own manuscript that told all these things in Loraine's own words. A manuscript she had just now heard Loraine declare her intention to write.

"*An Angel in Time?*" Lori said, repeating the title she had heard Loraine use for her intended story. "Then it's really true. Loraine did write the book?"

"Oh, yes," Samantha affirmed. "She wrote it, all right. But it had to be kept from the world until a day when the higher authorities would approve its release. Today is that day, Lori."

Lori picked up the old manuscript and examined it again. "I assume you plan to show us how this story ends, don't you, Sam? For the life of me, I can't figure how it can end."

"Lori's right," Brad agreed. "Even if Howard does realize Loraine's the one for him, how could he possibly remain with her in 1885? To my way of thinking, that would throw a major kink in the course of history. Like it or not, Howard Placard is a part of our time, Sam. He's made a major impact on my life, and on Lori's, that's for sure. How could any of that be if Howard remains in 1885?"

"You're right insofar as you've gone," Samantha explained. "There's no way Howard can give up the part of his life he's already lived. It would leave too big a hole in history, just as you said. But—" Samantha said, raising one finger for emphasis "—never forget this story is unfolding under the direction of the higher authorities, and the higher authorities can do whatever they choose to do. They're in control of time, just like they're in control of everything else."

"What if the life Howard's already lived in our time remains just the way it is, but he lives the rest of his life in 1885 with Loraine?" Lori reasoned, then snapped her fingers. "Better yet, why not bring Loraine here to our time?" she proposed excitedly. "That way, she and I could be real sisters—sort of."

"It's all speculation," Brad suggested. "But everything we've suggested could hamper the course of history. I hope you're right about the higher authorities knowing what they're doing, Sam."

Samantha laughed. "The higher authorities always know what they're doing, my friend. Never think otherwise. And I think you'll be happy with the ending they've approved for this story. But don't forget, the two of you are still slated to play a big part in it."

Lori and Brad looked at each other. She was beginning to understand what would be required of them, and she knew Brad was on the same wavelength with her. "Can we do it, Brad?" she asked.

"We have to do it, babe," he responded. "It's as much for our good as it is for Howard's."

Lori knew Brad was right. But just knowing what was coming didn't make it any easier to face. Settling into her seat, she turned her attention back to the holograph.

* * *

"You want to write a book?" Howard asked, obviously surprised at the thought. "About me?"

Loraine felt a little foolish for having mentioned a book. It was only a thought that had spontaneously popped into her mind. Still, it was a good thought. Why shouldn't she write a book?

"Why not?" she asked. "It wouldn't just be a book about you; it would be about us. All of us, I mean." She blushed. "I could write about everything that's happened. Amos and I coming from Boston, the stagecoach holdup, you being brought here by an angel to save us. All of it. I think it would make a great story."

"You might be right," Howard agreed after some thought. "I'm not sure how the story would be received in your time, but in my time it might possibly be a hit. Especially if the right producer got a hold of it and turned it into a movie."

"Producer?" Loraine responded, still smiling. "Like you, perhaps?"

Howard lifted his eyes toward the stillness of the azure sky. It was several seconds before he spoke. "You can't possibly imagine how I'd love to slip back into my old producer's chair, Miss Parker. And I would love filming the story of our brief acquaintance." He let his eyes meet hers again. "But that's most likely impossible now. In all probability, my career as a producer is finished."

Loraine was aware from the things Howard had already told her that he had somehow lost his wealth and power, but she couldn't figure why he couldn't earn it back again if given the chance. "How can you be so sure your career is finished?" she asked. "You're still a young man, Mr. Placard."

"It's a very long story, Miss Parker. I'd really rather not go into it right now, if you don't mind." Something in his voice and in his eyes told her not to pursue the subject, and she thought it would be wise to refrain from any further questions for the time being.

Many things about Howard were unclear to Loraine, but she strongly suspected the reason he was so uncomfortable on this subject had to do with his obvious fascination for this woman, Lori Parker. Not that it should matter; it was none of her business anyway. But if it didn't matter, then why couldn't she simply push aside her thoughts of his fascination with Lori? It made no sense, and it left her irritated with herself.

Loraine leaned over and stroked the mane on her horse as an amusing idea came to mind. A mischievous gleam shone in her eyes as she looked over at Howard. "Bet I can beat you to the river," she suddenly challenged. Without giving him a chance to respond, she urged her horse into a full run.

* * *

In his youth, Howard would never have let the challenge of a race go unanswered. As the years went by, however, Howard had grown more reserved. He had become a man of sensibility, position, and dignity. He had reached the point where subjecting himself to the indignity of a horse race was questionable. Or so he reasoned until Loraine Parker offered the challenge. With not so much as a second thought, he sprang into action. "You're on, lady!" he shouted, urging his horse forward as a boyish grin filled his face.

From the start, Howard knew Loraine was on the better animal—but he didn't care. Forcing his feet hard against the stirrups, he raised himself from the saddle and leaned forward with his face to the wind. "Heee-aaah!" he cried, seeing the gap between them gradually close.

It was like a slow motion scene from one of his movies as his horse inched forward; soon the two riders were neck and neck. There they remained—neither giving, neither taking—as the distance remaining to the riverbank continued to shrink. Then, at the last possible instant, Howard urged his animal ahead by no more than half a nose, and the race was over.

"Yaaaa-hoooo!!" Howard shouted as the two riders reined in their horses only inches from the water's edge. "I did it! I beat you, lady!"

"Only because I let you," Loraine shot back as she dismounted, stepping onto the soft riverbank.

"You let me?!" Howard lashed out. "Ain't no way, lady! I beat you fair and square, and that's a fact."

She smiled and shook off his remark. "Nope, I let you win and that's the fact."

Howard swung out of the saddle and hit the ground laughing. "I beat you!" he cried jubilantly. Too caught up in the moment to even think, he swooped her into his arms and spun her in a huge circle. In the excitement, his foot struck a rock, which sent them tumbling into the shallow water at the river's edge. There they sat, soaking wet, and laughing like a couple of kids in a rain puddle. After a moment, the laughter ceased and they sat there just looking at each other. "You're sitting waist deep in a river," Howard offhandedly remarked.

"So are you," she responded.

Every shred of reason in Howard's mind told him to stand and walk away. But a force stronger than reason refused to let him move. He leaned forward until his lips were inches from hers. Lifting his hand to her face, he stroked it ever so gently.

A long, awkward moment passed. "Are you just going to sit there, or are you going to kiss me?" she whispered.

Howard's head was spinning in time with his pounding heart. Kiss her? Of course he wasn't going to kiss her. That was ridiculous. Howard was in love with only one woman, and that was Lori. Nothing could make him want to kiss this woman. Absolutely nothing. Nevertheless, his thumb continued to trace the line of her cheek. Who did he think he was kidding anyway? Closing his eyes, he leaned closer and pressed his lips softly against hers. His heart pounded even harder, and he wished time could somehow freeze and make this instant last forever.

"You kissed me," she said in a dazed whisper.

Howard felt suddenly very uncomfortable. "I—I'm sorry. I had no right."

After a long moment of silence, Loraine spoke, still in a whisper. "You were kissing her, weren't you? Your Lori, I mean."

At that moment, Howard searched his own soul. No one could have been more surprised at what he found there. "No," he said honestly. "I wasn't kissing Lori. I was kissing Loraine Parker."

There was another long pause before she responded, "I want to believe you." It was impossible for Howard to tell if her eyes were wet from the river water, or from her own tears. "I really want to believe you."

Howard stroked Loraine's face once again. "I only kissed Lori twice," he confessed with great difficulty. "Both were stolen kisses." His hand moved up, brushing back her wet hair. "Your kiss was different." He swallowed. "It was almost like I've been waiting for your kiss all my life."

Tears had begun to flow freely down Loraine's cheeks by this time. Backing away from Howard, she moved out of the water. Very slowly, Howard stood and caught up with her. "I do want to believe you," she said again.

Howard took her by the shoulders and pulled her around to face him. She buried her face in his chest and sobbed bitterly. "I'm so sorry," he said stroking her hair. "I had no right to kiss you." He didn't move until her sobbing had eased.

At last Loraine pulled away from his embrace. "I'm sorry, too," she said. "I don't usually act this way. It really doesn't matter who you thought you were kissing. It was only an impulse anyway."

"You're right," Howard agreed. "Just an impulse. But it was a nice kiss. Very nice."

* * *

"He kissed her, Sam," Lori said in near disbelief. "And then denied it was me he was kissing. Please tell me he wasn't lying."

Samantha shook her head. "I can't tell whether or not he's lying. Even if I am a second-level angel, that doesn't give me the right to see into someone else's thoughts. I can tell you this much, though. He'd better not be lying. Not if he wants to pass the test the higher authorities have prepared for him."

At this, Lori's heart leapt within her. She knew exactly what test it was that Samantha was referring to—although she wasn't convinced she could hold up to her end of the test. Lori looked again at the image of Howard standing dripping wet next to Loraine. It was strange seeing him like this. She was used to seeing Howard in custom-tailored suits and in complete control of every situation. It was almost as though she were looking at a different man.

* * *

Howard steadied Loraine as she slipped her foot in the stirrup and pulled herself into the saddle. "As I was saying, Miss Parker," he said, "Once we cross the river, Mesa is only five or so miles farther on."

Howard stared at Loraine, unable to take his eyes off her. Even soaking wet, she was radiantly beautiful. More beautiful even than Lori, if that were possible. He was furious with himself for the way the memory of her kiss lingered in his mind. He wondered if his sister could possibly have been right about Loraine being part of his destiny.

No! That was absurd! He forced the thought from his mind and mounted up. Settling into the saddle, he urged his horse into the water just behind Loraine, who had already started across.

The river at this point was wide and shallow, no more than three feet at the deepest point. Loraine's horse had just stepped onto the dry sand of the opposite bank when the first shot rang out. The bullet passed so close to Howard's ear he could actually feel the wind as it went by. Then a second shot sounded. This time, the bullet passed lower, very near the ear of Howard's horse. Startled, the horse reared wildly, its front hooves flailing in the wind.

If given some warning, Howard, being the horseman that he was, would have had no trouble staying with the animal. As it was, he had no warning. As the horse reared, he tumbled backward, falling haplessly into the shallow water where his head struck a protruding rock. The pain was excruciating, and his head spun wildly. He could see Loraine's mouth forming a scream, but no sound reached his ears.

"Miss Parker," he feebly gasped, fighting to remain conscious. It was no use. Blackness closed from every side, and he slid into a world of darkness.

* * *

Loraine looked on in horror as Howard's horse bounded away. She realized immediately that he had been knocked out when his head struck the rock. She steadied her own animal and looked around to see two horsemen closing in fast. There was no doubt in her mind who these two were. "I got him, Scar!" she heard one cry as they drew near. "Dead center this time."

Loraine glanced at the unconscious Howard lying face up in the shallow water. His black hat was moving rapidly away, carried by the current of the river. Her every instinct cried for her to go to him, but what good could she possibly do with these two closing in? She was on a better horse than either of them, and she knew outrunning them wouldn't be all that difficult. Her only hope was for the two of them to want her so badly, they wouldn't take time to finish the job with Howard. Reaching behind her, she grabbed the saddlebags of money and held them high for the outlaws to see. "Is this what you want?!" she shouted. "Well, come and get it!" With that, she drove her horse forward, leaning low in the saddle to avoid the gunshots she was sure would come.

* * *

"What about him?" Grayson asked, referring to Howard as they reached the water's edge.

"The devil take him!" Clay snapped. "The gal's the one with the money! After her, man! After her!"

CHAPTER 23

Crossing an untamed desert without so much as an established trail was a new experience for Loraine. She was on a good horse, and she had managed to stay ahead of the men in pursuit, but how long could she remain out of their reach? And what about Howard? She knew the outlaws hadn't slowed their chase long enough to bother with him any further, but she wasn't sure how badly he had been hurt falling off his horse. What should she do? Should she double back to check on him, or would it be better to make a dash for Mesa, where help could be gathered and sent back to his aid?

In any case, she had a problem. Unlike Howard, Loraine wasn't familiar with this desert. Howard had told her Mesa was southwest of here, but how could she be certain which way was southwest? Every saguaro she passed looked exactly like the last one. The sun was in the center of the sky by this time, making it all but useless in determining direction. Finding Mesa, or even doubling back to find Howard, could prove too much for her limited skills. Things were beginning to look very bleak.

Still not certain of her next move, Loraine crested a small hill where she received the shock of her life. There, stood a woman in her path. A radiantly beautiful woman, whom Loraine recognized instantly from the photograph Howard had shown her. What's more, this woman was holding Howard's hat that Loraine had last seen drifting down the river.

Abruptly, she brought the horse to a stop. "Annette Placard?!" she cried in astonishment. "It is you, isn't it?"

"It's me," Annette responded. "I figured it was time I met my future sister-in-law face to face."

"Your future . . . ?" Loraine's hand shot up to cover her mouth. "Oh my . . . What are you saying, Miss Placard . . . ?"

"You know perfectly well what I'm saying. And you can drop the Miss Placard thing. You and I are destined to become very close friends, Loraine. You can call me Annette."

Loraine could only stare at this woman she knew to be an angel and wonder at her own feelings. From the minute she saw Howard, there had been the strongest feeling she had known him before. Now, as she faced this angel, the feeling was the same. It was as if she had known Annette Placard all of her life. Very slowly, she dismounted and walked to where Annette stood.

"I hope you'll forgive me if I seem a little mystified," she said. "It's not every day I come face to face with an angel."

Annette laughed. "You've had a lot of mystifying things occur over the last day and a half, haven't you, Loraine? Sorry to put you through this, but it's necessary if we're to get destiny back on its scheduled path."

"Destiny?" Loraine asked. "My destiny?"

"Your destiny and my brother's destiny, too. The two of you share what we angels call a forever contract. Your contract's not in force yet, but with my help it will be in short order. And yes, I do know the feelings you have for my brother. Feelings like you've known him all your life, and like he's someone you've waited a lifetime for. It's perfectly normal, Loraine. It's all part of the destiny thing."

Loraine's heart was pounding. She wanted so badly to believe. "But—what about Lori?" she asked. "Mr. Placard is still in love with her—isn't he?"

"Never was in love with Lori. Granted, Peaches thought he was in love with her, but it's been you he's loved from the beginning, Loraine. He couldn't know that, naturally, until the two of you met."

"Peaches?" Loraine asked. "You call your brother Peaches?"

"I've called him that for years. I'll tell you the story sometime. But for now, I'm more interested in destiny."

Loraine caught her breath. "You're not one to waste time beating around the bush, are you, Annette?" she asked.

"No, and neither are you, Loraine Parker. And by the way, I like the way you handle that revolver. One of these days you and I will have to have a shoot-off. You're good, but I think I can beat you."

Loraine had to laugh. "You do have a way of putting me at ease, Annette. I appreciate that about now." Loraine grew more serious. "Is Howard all right?" she asked. "I see you have his hat . . ."

"Peaches is fine. I'll go back after him after we've had our talk."

Loraine felt the weight of concern lifted from her, and she breathed a sigh of gratitude. After a quick glance over her shoulder for any sign of Clay or Grayson, she said, "I hope you know what you're doing stopping me like this with those two on my trail."

"It was either stop you and give you some directions into town, or let you wonder around in circles here on the desert," Annette smiled. "Don't feel bad, though. I'd have been just as lost if I'd ever gone to Boston while I was part of your world." Annette pointed to the sky over toward the west. "You see that cloud there on the edge of the horizon?" she asked.

Loraine looked. "I see it, yes."

"Just keep your eye on it," Annette explained. "I put it there for your compass. It'll lead you right to the main street of Mesa."

Loraine looked at the cloud again. "Thank you, Annette," she said. "I had no idea how I was going to find the place."

Annette placed Howard's hat on her own head, then reached for Loraine's hands—taking one in each of her own. "You're going to be the most wonderful thing that ever happened to my brother," she said. "But Peaches can be darned stubborn at times. I'll be doing everything in my power to bring him around, but a lot depends on you, you know."

"What do you want from me?" Loraine asked.

"I want you to love him," Annette smiled. "And I want you to convince him that your distant niece, Lori Parker, was never meant to be part of his life." Annette gave Loraine's hands a squeeze. "It's time for you to go, now," she said. "Destiny awaits."

"Will I—ever see you again, Annette?"

"Count on it, lady. I'm trusting you with my brother. Don't ever think I'll let you too far out of my sight." Annette smiled, backed away a step, and then simply vanished.

For the next few seconds, Loraine stared after her. Then, mounting up, she urged her horse forward toward the little white cloud and didn't look back.

* * *

The six wagons hadn't even pulled to a stop when Stephanie spotted Jeremiah sitting astride a horse. She made for him on a dead run, reaching him just as he dismounted. Taking his face in her hands, she pressed her lips against his. He encircled her in his arms and let his fingers run through her long brown hair. "I've never been so frightened in my life," she cried, tears streaming down her cheeks. "Don't you ever take that stagecoach out again without someone riding shotgun! Do you hear me, Jeremiah Samuels?"

"I hear you, Stephanie," he said, pulling her head against his chest. "And you have my word, I never will."

Bill Cody was still on his horse alongside the first wagon, driven by Annie. Bill and the wagon train had been met by Sheriff Engels and the posse some miles back and brought up to date on what had happened in town. Cody had offered to send some men along with the posse, but the sheriff didn't think they would be needed.

"I'll have one of the men put Loraine's things inside the hotel," Cody said, referring to the suitcases he had picked up alongside the road that morning where they had been left the night before.

"Thanks, Bill," Jeremiah responded. "I'll see they're taken care of from here."

"Well, Annie," Cody remarked. "Looks like there's little else we can do here. I'd say we best be on our way. We've got a show to perform in Phoenix tonight."

"I reckon you're right, Bill," Annie agreed. "I'll say this for those two outlaws. They better hope they don't have to face Loraine Parker if she gets her hands on a revolver. That's the only female I ever met who could stay with me in a shooting contest."

Jeremiah raised a hand in a friendly gesture. "Much obliged, Bill, Annie," he said. "I don't know what we would have done if you hadn't happened along when you did."

"Glad we could help," Cody responded. "What about the boy, Amos? He's safe with his folks, I reckon?"

"He and his parents have gone home," Stephanie responded. "I had a hard time talking them into it, but I finally convinced them. Neither James nor Anelladee got one wink of sleep last night. They're pretty exhausted. I've promised to get word to them just as soon as I hear anything about their daughter."

"When I see Howard or the young lady, I'll get your horse from them and see to it that he gets to you in Phoenix," Jeremiah said.

"The horse is the least of my worries. If I get him back, fine. If I don't, the sun will come up tomorrow all the same." Bill adjusted his hat, then gave a wave. "Sorry to have to rush off like this, but when you're in show business . . ."

"Yeah," Jeremiah laughed. "Schedules. You forget, Mr. Cody, I'm a stage driver. I understand schedules. Believe me, I understand schedules."

"Good luck," Bill said. "I hope everyone gets home safe."

"That goes for me, too," Annie added. "We'll be praying for you."

Jeremiah wrapped an arm around Stephanie and watched as the wagons moved out. "I can't help feeling responsible for Miss Parker," he said to his wife. "She was my passenger."

Stephanie squeezed Jeremiah's arm. "I heard the story from Amos how you foiled the holdup, and how you were shot trying to protect your passengers. What was the word Amos used? Oh yes, it was 'awesome.' I'm not sure why he used the word, but I'm sure what he meant by it. You really impressed him, dear. By the way," she said, glancing at his leg, "how's the leg doing? I see you're walking on it."

"Yeah, it was just a flesh wound. I was lucky. If only Miss Parker could have been half so lucky."

"Stop blaming yourself, Jeremiah. You did all you could do. Have a little faith, the posse will find her. Scott Engels is at the head of it, and you know he's the best."

Jeremiah sighed. "I wish I could believe the posse will find her, Stephanie. But by the time the posse reaches the place where the wagons camped last night, the trail is bound to be pretty cold. I'm sorry, I wish I could hold out more hope. But—"

"Look!" Stephanie shouted, pointing up the road toward the end of town. "It's a rider coming hard! It's a woman, Jeremiah. Do you suppose . . . ?"

Jeremiah quickly turned to look. "It's her!" he shouted. "It's Miss Parker! I'd recognize that red dress anywhere. And—she's riding Cody's horse. The last time I saw that horse, Howard Placard was riding him out of camp to look for Miss Parker and the kidnappers."

Jeremiah stepped to the center of the road. Removing his hat, he waved it over his head. "Miss Parker!" he cried. "Over here!"

* * *

Annette had told the truth, the little white cloud did lead Loraine straight to the streets of Mesa. Not slowing her horse the tiniest bit, she hit the street on a full run, heading straight for the center of the small town. And that was when she spotted Jeremiah Samuels, the stagecoach driver. There was a woman with him, and Loraine assumed she was his wife. In less than a minute, she had reached the two of them.

Jeremiah grabbed the bridle to hold the excited horse steady as Loraine dismounted. "Thank heavens, Miss Parker," he said. "You're safe."

"What about my brother?" she quickly asked. "Is Amos safe, too?"

It was Stephanie who answered, giving her a warm, assuring smile. "Amos is fine. I'm Stephanie Samuels, Jeremiah's wife. I was here with your parents when Amos arrived."

Loraine's face showed her relief at hearing these words. "Thank you," she said, touching Stephanie's arm. "Where are my parents now?"

"They were up all night. I convinced them to go home and try and get some rest. I promised to bring them word just as soon as we heard anything."

"I know they're bound to be worried," Loraine responded. "I'd like to get word to them as soon as possible."

"Yes, of course. I'll take you there myself."

"No! I can't go just yet. Howard—that is, Mr. Placard is in trouble. I need some help. Someone to ride back with me to where I left him."

Jeremiah spotted the saddlebags still draped over the back of the horse. He pulled them down and checked inside to see the money was there. He glanced up to meet Loraine's eyes. "Mr. Placard caught up with the outlaws?" he guessed. When Loraine nodded yes, he asked, "What happened to him, Miss Parker? He wasn't shot, I hope."

"No!" Loraine quickly responded. "He outsmarted those men. We thought we had lost them, but they caught up with us as we were crossing the river. A shot spooked Howard's horse. He fell and hit his head. I rode away hoping to distract the outlaws. I believe Howard is all right, but we need to go after him. Is there a sheriff is this town?"

Jeremiah slammed his hat against his thigh, sending a cloud of dust flying. "The sheriff and every able-bodied man available are out looking for you, Miss Parker. I'm the last man left in town. If you'll lend me your horse and point me in the right direction—I'll go after him myself."

* * *

Tracking Loraine's horse across the desert had been an easy matter for Clay and Grayson—until she reached the road leading to the town of Mesa, that is. There were too many other tracks on the road for someone as inexperienced at tracking as these two were to distinguish her tracks from the rest. But it was a safe bet that Mesa was exactly where she was headed since that was the closest town, and it was only a half mile down the road from where they lost her tracks. They pushed their horses hard, and just as they reached the edge of town they spotted Loraine and the others near the hotel entrance. Quickly they dismounted and hid themselves behind the livery stable.

"I knew it," Clay said, peering around the corner at them. "I knew she was headed straight for Mesa. We got her now, Scar."

"Yeah, and we got our money, too," Grayson quickly added. "What's the plan, Clay?"

"We're in luck, they ain't spotted us yet. We can make our way around and come in from the alley side. Get the drop on 'em." Clay looked the town over good. "You know what else, Scar," he said. "This town's like a cemetery. Ten'll get ya twenty the sheriff and all the town's men are out in a posse looking for us."

"Yeah, Clay," Grayson said with a burst of gruff laughter. "I reckon you're right."

Clay grinned. "Ya know what we're gonna do," he sneered. "We're gonna get our money back, then we're gonna hit the bank fer good measure. And that ain't all, neither. We're takin' Miss-High-and-Mighty hostage. I got some unfinished business with her."

Grayson rubbed the back of his neck. "If all the men are gone, that must mean the bank is closed, Clay. How we fixin' ta rob a bank that's closed?"

"Ain't you got no brains at all, Scar? We'll break in the hardware store and get some dynamite."

A light came on in Grayson's eyes. "And blow the safe, is that right, Clay?"

"That's right, Scar. We blow the safe. Now come on, let's get movin' before those folks spot us."

* * *

Though Stephanie said nothing when Jeremiah volunteered to go after Howard, Loraine saw the look of concern in her eyes and understood her fears. "I'm not sure it would be a good idea for you to go searching for Howard alone," she said. "Those two outlaws are still out there looking for me. For all I know they may even have followed me here."

Jeremiah looked suddenly worried. "That's not good," he said. "This town is like a sitting duck with all the men gone." Jeremiah glanced at the saddlebags of money still in his hand. "This is what they're after. If I'd have let them have it in the first place, maybe we'd all be better off. Let's get inside the hotel and see if we can round up a couple of guns."

"That won't be necessary," Clay barked, stepping out from the alley with Grayson in his shadow. Both men had drawn their guns. "Just stay right where you are. If you do, we might get generous and not shoot the lot of you."

A bolt of fear shot through Loraine as she spotted the pair. Of all the times to be without her revolver. "Just take it easy," Jeremiah said, stepping in front of Loraine, positioning himself between the two women and the outlaws. "Let's talk this over nice and calm-like. There's no need for anyone to get hurt."

"Oh, we'll talk this over all right." Clay grinned. "To start with, I'll take them saddlebags. Toss 'em over here nice and easy-like."

Jeremiah had little choice. Very carefully, he tossed the saddlebags to Clay. Clay scooped them up with his left hand and threw them over his shoulder. "All right," he said waving his gun in a circle. "Everybody into the hardware store. And be quick about it!"

Loraine glanced down the street. She could see the hardware store was three buildings away. Why in the world would these men want them all in the hardware store? Then she noticed that right next door to the hardware store stood the bank. *They must want explosives from the hardware store to blast open the bank vault,* she reasoned. With her and the others as witnesses to this, what chance would any of them have of walking away alive? She had to get her hands on a revolver, but how?

"I said, move it!" Clay shouted. "Do it now!"

"I can't walk without my crutch," Jeremiah said, obviously stalling for time. "It's on the ground over there."

Clay glared at him. "You can walk, you can crawl, or I can plug you right here," he scoffed. "The choice is yours, but no more stalling. Ya got that, mister?"

Jeremiah exhaled a breath of surrender and began limping toward the hardware store with Stephanie's support.

"You, too, little lady," Clay spit out at Loraine.

Loraine, too, started following Jeremiah, still thinking that she had to get her hands on a revolver. Maybe her chance would come inside the store.

Clay was the first to reach the door. When Jeremiah stepped up, Clay shoved him inside. He wet his lips and watched as Loraine stepped through the door, but didn't attempt to touch her. Once inside, her suspicions were confirmed as Grayson kept them covered while Clay searched for the dynamite and a box of matches. Once he found what he wanted, he crammed the items into the saddlebags with the money. Next he picked up a length of rope from behind the counter. "Here," he said, tossing the rope to Grayson. "Tie up them two." He motioned to Jeremiah and Stephanie. "Tie 'em up good. We wouldn't want 'em gettin' loose to spoil the party we got planned, now would we?"

"Ya ain't gonna let 'em go, are you, Clay? They seen who we are."

"Don't worry about it, Scar. The gal in the red dress will be coming home with us. The others are about to meet with a little dynamite accident. Now tie 'em up good, you hear."

Grayson smiled. "Gotcha, Clay," he responded. "Turn around and put your hands behind your back," he growled at Jeremiah.

Searching the store for any sign of a gun while Grayson was busy tying up Jeremiah and Stephanie, Loraine eyed a glass case with four revolvers on display. But even if she could reach one of them, where was the ammunition kept? She was sure the guns in the display case wouldn't be loaded. She glanced at Clay, who had seen her looking at the guns and guessed her intention.

"Believe me, little lady," he said, his ugly brown teeth showing through an evil grin. "You don't want to try it. I'd plug you before you got halfway to one of them guns."

Once Grayson had Jeremiah's and Stephanie's hands securely tied behind them, Clay motioned toward the door. "Okay, people," he growled. "Everybody outside. We're about to pay the local bank a little visit. Me and Scar want to make a withdrawal."

Loraine glanced one last time at the display case containing the guns. It was no use. They might as well have been back in Boston for all the good they could do her. She sighed and stepped through the door.

* * *

Howard leaned against the wall on the alley side of the hotel building and watched as the two outlaws emerged from the hardware store holding Loraine and the others at gunpoint. His heart leapt from within at the sight. "Are you going to be able to help me out with this one, little sister, or have your higher authorities decreed that I'm on my own again?"

"I've given you all the help I can, Peaches. From here on out, you're on your own. And don't get the idea your life isn't on the line, because it is. But—you can still choose to turn around and walk away, if that's what you want."

Howard's face showed his horror at her suggestion. "Walk away and leave Loraine in the hands of these men? You know me better than that."

"Yes, big brother, I do," Annette smiled proudly. "I've never been more thrilled to call you my brother. Now get in there and give those guys what for. I may not be able to help, but I'll be in your corner cheering all the way."

Howard took a deep breath for courage, then walked back to his horse, which was tied a few feet away. Opening the saddlebags, he removed Loraine's holster and revolver. Then he discarded Loraine's belt from the holster, loosened the buckle on his own belt, and slid the holster on. After re-fastening his belt, he wrapped the leather straps at the bottom of the holster around his leg, and secured them in place with a bow knot.

Lifting the shiny chrome revolver from the holster, he pulled back the hammer and spun the cylinder, making certain there was a shell in every chamber. Satisfied, he shoved the revolver back in the holster. "All right, Annette," he said. "It's show time." Hearing himself, he grinned and added, "Appropriate words for an old producer like me, eh? There certainly have been lots of show times. But never one quite like this."

"I talked to Loraine, you know," Annette said, causing Howard to stop and look at her. "I was the one who showed her the way here to Mesa."

"You talked to her, sis? She actually saw you?"

"She loves you, Peaches. You do know that, don't you?"

"Annette!" Howard's voice held a trace of fear. "You didn't call me Peaches so she could hear, did you?"

Annette ignored his question. "You love her, too, big brother," she said. "If you'd just admit it, we could get things put in place like they should be."

Howard's eyes narrowed. "You did let her hear that stupid name! How could you do this to me, Annette?"

Annette snapped her fingers in Howard's face. "You're running out of time, Peaches. Get with it! Take a look at where the outlaws are now." Howard looked around and saw that they had reached the front of the bank. "If you let them get inside the bank, you're a dead man for sure. You'd better make your move now."

Howard took another couple of quick breaths, then forced himself to relax. Stepping into the street, he began to walk slowly and deliberately in the direction of the outlaws. Instantly, they spotted him and froze in their tracks. Howard kept walking until he came within ten feet or so of them. There he stopped. "Good afternoon, gentlemen," he said. "Fixin' to do a little banking, are we?"

"Mr. Placard!" Loraine cried, her voice shaking with emotion. "You're wearing your hat! Annette did go back after you!"

"Hold it right there, mister!" Clay shouted at Howard. "I've had about all of you I can stand. You ain't walkin' away from me again."

Howard ignored the man and spoke directly to Loraine. "Yes, Miss Parker. Annette came back for me. Led me straight to my horse. She also told me I'd find you here."

"That's my gun you're wearing. How did you—"

Clay pulled off his hat and slammed it against his leg. "I'm talking to you, mister! You better be listenin' to what I'm sayin'."

Still Howard paid no heed. "It ended up with my saddlebags," he explained, "after your little demonstration with the pebble last night." He paused, then added, "I know you've seen and spoken with Annette. She told me." Again he paused. "She said something else, too, Miss Parker. She said—you love me."

Loraine brushed away a tear. "She told you the truth, Mr. Placard. And she told me you had similar feelings. But I'm not sure I can believe her. I'm not sure it's me who holds your heart—or Lori."

That was all Clay could stand. Grabbing Loraine, he put her between himself and Howard with his gun pointed at her head. "Drop that gun belt, mister!" he growled. "Or the gal gets it right here!"

Howard glared at him, but refused to back down an inch. "You know what I'm betting, mister?" he stated coolly. "I'm betting I can have this gun out of the holster, put a bullet dead between your eyes, and have it reholstered before you could ever pull that trigger."

"Horseradish!" Clay responded. "Ain't no one that good with a gun."

Howard locked the fingers of his hands and pushed down on them, cracking the knuckles. "Let me give you a little demonstration, Clay," he retorted. "I just might be able to change your mind."

One eye squinted. "What demonstration?" Clay asked.

Howard smiled. "This is something," he responded, "I once learned from a friend by the name of Dusty Lockhart."

Before Clay could get the question, "Dusty who?" out of his mouth, two shots rang out, followed by Grayson's scream of pain. It all happened so fast, Clay hardly even noticed Howard's revolver coming out or returning to its place in the holster.

"He shot me!" Grayson screeched. "I'm bleeding!"

Clay's eyes moved to his partner, and he was shocked to see that the two bullets had grazed Grayson's face, one on each side. To make matters worse, Jeremiah and his wife had bolted through the open door into the hotel during the commotion. Clay's eyes settled back on Howard. "That's impossible," he muttered. "No one's that good with a gun."

"I beg to differ with you, Clay," Loraine spoke up. "It seems Mr. Placard is quite skilled with a gun. Personally, I'd say you're in a lot of trouble, little man."

"The lady's right, Clay," Howard agreed. "Only in your case there will be only one shot, right between your beady little eyes. I suggest you let her go before I can count to three."

Howard's heart pounded like a base drum in a marching band. He was facing not one, but two cold-blooded killers. He was fast enough to beat them, he knew that. But could he pull the trigger when the chips were down? Could he find the courage necessary to save this lovely lady's life? There was no time to consider that now. He had already reached the point of no return. There was a short pause, then the air was split by his voice coldly uttering a single word. "One!"

Clay pulled Loraine all the tighter against himself. His eyes nearly bugged out of their sockets as he heard Howard's intimidating, "Two!"

* * *

Samantha snapped her fingers, and to Lori's astonishment, the scene with Howard and the others instantly froze. "What are you doing, Sam?" Lori screeched. "You can't put time on hold now! This is like a commercial break at the hottest point in a TV thriller. Have a heart. I want to see if Howard can do it!"

"Had to put time on hold," Samantha explained. "It's time for your part in this story, lady." With this, Samantha proceeded to explain exactly what it was she expected from Lori.

Lori felt the blood rush from her face. "I'm not sure I can do that, Sam," she argued.

"Destiny's depending on you, Lori," Samantha replied. "I'll be right there with you, all the way."

"And so will I," Brad said, moving over to Lori and sliding an arm around her. "It's okay, babe. We both know the time has come for us to forgive and forget. It's the only way we can get on with things without Howard's shadow hanging over us the rest of our lives."

"You heard what Sam wants me to do, didn't you, Brad?"

Brad's voice was steady. "I heard."

"And you're okay with it?"

"I'm okay. Sam wouldn't ask this of us if it wasn't important. Go get 'em, Lori."

For a long moment Lori looked into her husband's understanding eyes. "All right, Sam," she managed at length. "Let's do it."

CHAPTER 24

Howard was on the verge of saying three when something very strange happened. He instantly realized that time had been placed on hold. But why now? Right in the middle of this crisis. Out of the corner of his eye, he caught sight of a movement. Supposing it was Annette, he turned to face her. To his shock, it wasn't Annette at all. It was—but no—how could it be? "Lori?" he gasped, his heart beating wildly at the sight of her. "Is that you?"

Lori fidgeted with her hands nervously. Her response came with obvious difficulty. "Yes, Howard, it's me. I've been sent here with a message for you."

Howard looked first at Lori, and then at the motionless image of Loraine. It was as if he were looking at the same woman. Here, with both of them in front of him, the resemblance was even more profound than he had supposed. From where she was standing several feet away, Lori hesitated to look him in the eye. After gathering his wits, Howard stepped over to her. Very gently he touched her chin, fully expecting her to flinch and pull away. To his surprise, she didn't. Instead, she looked up, nearly burning a hole through him with those fascinatingly beautiful blue eyes. Eyes filled with a look he found impossible to discern. Was it fright, or anger, or possibly frustration? He just couldn't tell. He withdrew his hand and asked, "What message, Lori?"

Lori backed away a step and folded her arms. "Actually," she said, struggling to keep her voice firm and steady, "I have more than a message for you. Sam has sent me here to honor the offer she made you yesterday on the island."

Howard forced a smile. "I knew that woman had to get involved again before this was over," he said. "Why couldn't she face me herself, Lori? Why did she send you to do her dirty work?"

"Believe me, Howard, I didn't want to come," Lori admitted. "But Sam convinced me it was the only way."

"And you say she sent you here to honor her offer." He shook his head very slowly. "Just before time went on hold, I was probably a heartbeat away from death. And I assume I'll be back in that position as soon as time resumes. Personally, I'm not sure this is the perfect time for Sam to be honoring her offer to send me back to where I was a year and a half ago, do you?"

Lori brushed a hand nervously through her hair. "You can have it all back, Howard. Just like she promised. There's just one stipulation."

Howard laughed again. "We're down to the bottom line now, are we? So what's the one stipulation. That I live through the gun battle I'm facing?" Howard kicked at the dirt with his toe. "I wasn't born yesterday, Lori. I'm not naive enough to believe I'll ever be restored to my former lifestyle." He looked into her face and said softly, "I'm not saying I don't deserve what's happened to me. I understand much better now how much I hurt you and Brad."

Lori sighed and looked Howard straight in the eye. "Will you let me get on with this, Howard? I'm not having an easy time of it."

"Get on with what?" Howard asked.

"Sam sent me here with a message that you can have it all back. But only if you turn and walk away from Loraine."

"Walk away from Loraine?" Howard retorted unbelievingly. "Leave her in the hands of those men?"

"That's the stipulation, Howard. Sam will honor her end, if you honor yours. And to honor your end, you have to deny you love Loraine Parker and walk away from her right now."

Howard's hands grew sweaty, and his legs felt like limp plastic. How could he turn his back on Loraine when she needed him so badly? "And if I do choose to defend Loraine," he asked, "does that mean forfeiting my life in a gun battle? Is that how it will play out?"

"I don't know that for sure, Howard. Sam hasn't made that part clear to me." Lori ran her hands down her dress, smoothing it. "This much I do know. You're facing the biggest choice of your life. You can walk away from Loraine and have everything you lost restored before the sun goes down tonight. Or you can deny you ever loved me and go back to Loraine and possibly your own death."

A cold chill gripped Howard as he realized the full extent of the choice facing him. He brushed a sweaty palm across his brow. His eyes shifted to the image of Loraine still in the outlaw's grip. He studied every line in her face. Could he leave her in the clutches of these men, even if it did mean returning to his former place of power in society? "Can you tell me this, Lori? If I do go to Loraine's aid, will I be allowed to save her life?"

"You will," Lori affirmed. "That point's clear to me."

Howard looked at Loraine one more time. "I don't understand this," he said, speaking more to himself than to Lori. "Yesterday I didn't even know this woman. Why am I so drawn to her now?"

"Only you can answer that," Lori said. "And before you attempt an answer, there's something I have to do." Catching Howard completely off guard, Lori stepped in and kissed him. It was a short kiss, but one that left him dumbfounded. Twice Howard had stolen kisses from Lori, but never had there been even the slightest hint that Lori would ever return his kiss. "I—I don't understand," he stammered. "Why did you kiss me, Lori?"

Lori took a hurried step backward. "Because it was required as part of your test," she answered.

"Test?" he asked, completely confused by all this.

"Yes, Howard, a test. For years you pursued me relentlessly. You nearly destroyed my marriage. But now the time has come for all that to change. An angel has brought you face to face with another woman, Howard. A woman you had always mistaken me for. It's time for you to face the facts. You're not in love with me at all. Not now and not ever. The woman you love is standing right there." Lori pointed to Loraine. "An hour ago you shared a kiss with her. Now you've shared a kiss with me. Think about it, Howard. You can only be in love with one of us. Which of our kisses touched your soul?"

Howard's mouth went dry. His stomach burned with the pain of a thousand piercing needles. "I don't understand it," he said in confusion. "All my life I've wanted you to come to me with your kiss. And now that you have, all I can think of is Loraine's kiss."

Lori's face burst into a smile. "All right, Howard!" she exclaimed. "You're halfway there! Now finish it! Tell the world you don't love me. Tell them the one you love is Loraine Parker!"

Howard wasn't sure how to respond. "I—I . . ."

"Just say it, Howard! Sam's always believed in you. Go ahead, give her a victory salute."

Howard reached out and took Lori's hands in his own. "It's . . . true!" he cried at last. "I am in love with Loraine Parker. Go back and tell Sam she's won." Howard grew solemn, and looked again at the frozen scene. "Tell Sam she can do with me as she will. I can't turn my back on Loraine, even if it means giving up my own life."

There were tears in Lori's eyes. "I don't have to tell Sam. She already knows. I—I have to be going now," she said. "My part in this plan is finished. But there's just one more thing before I go." She drew a quick breath and just said it. "I want you to know that I forgive you, Howard, although I'm not saying it's been easy. And I wish you and Loraine all the best."

Lori turned to walk away. "Wait!" Howard called after her. She paused and looked back. "My sister—Annette—told me I was being watched in one of those holographs the angels come up with. It was you watching me, wasn't it, Lori? You and Brad?"

"Yes, Howard. Brad and I have watched it all, ever since your day started with a visit from Sam. I saw a different side of you today, Howard. A side I didn't realize existed. That's what made it possible for me to forgive."

"I see," Howard observed. "I won't be seeing you again, will I?"

She shook her head. "No, I don't think so."

"There's something I'd like to say. Will you give me the chance?"

"Go ahead, Howard. I'm listening."

He took a deep breath. "I've been a fool, I see that now. Except for my blind insensibility, you and I could have been good friends. I've always envied Brad, but never so much as at this moment. He's a lucky man to have you, Lori. You're a great lady. Greater than I ever imagined. Please tell Brad I said that. And tell him . . ." Howard's voice trailed off as he searched for the right words.

"I understand," Lori spoke up warmly. "I'll tell him. Now you get back in there, Howard. Fight for her, the woman you really love. And do it with my blessing."

Howard looked first at Lori Douglas, and then at Loraine Parker. No question about it, they could have been mistaken for identical twins if it weren't for the fact that a century separated their lifetimes. And yet, they were two totally different women, with totally different souls. Lori was right when she observed that one of them had touched his soul with her kiss.

"And you get back to the man you love, Lori Douglas," Howard said softly. "And you do it with my blessings, okay?"

And thus it was—the two of them parted—as friends.

CHAPTER 25

Just as quickly as the showdown scene with Clay Derringer and Grayson Hobbs had frozen in time, it now returned to action. The count of "three" clung to Howard's tongue like a leopard ready to pounce on its prey. The events of his meeting with Lori pressed on his mind, and he knew without the slightest question what his course had to be.

Howard was confident in his ability with a gun. He was fast and his aim was sure. But the life of the woman he loved hung in the balance of this shot. His eyes focused on the small part of Clay's face not hidden behind Loraine's, and he wondered—was he really this good? Two inches off the mark, and he could put an end to the very life he was trying to save. And there was one other problem. Except for Grayson only seconds before, Howard had never fired at a living target. His targets had been red bull's eyes printed on paper, or cans on a fence post. Could he actually bring himself to squeeze the trigger, even knowing the consequences if he failed? The answer to that question loomed over him like a sickle in the hands of death.

His eyes shifted between the two men, carefully evaluating what he was up against. Grayson stood just to his left, gun drawn and ready. Clay and Loraine were directly in front of him. The barrel of Clay's revolver touched the side of Loraine's head. The hammer was cocked. There would be little time for Howard to take him out without his getting off that fatal shot. A mere fraction of a second.

"Please, Sam," Howard whispered under his breath. "Help me out here. All I ask is that you let me save Loraine."

It all happened so quickly, there was no time for thought. Loraine's arm suddenly flew up, striking Clay's gun and brushing it aside just far enough that the discharging bullet whizzed harmlessly into the sky. In one swift motion, she pulled free from Clay and dove headlong for the dirt. Even before she met the earth, Howard's gun was free from the holster and blazing away amid the sound of returning gunfire from both men. In less than three seconds, it was over—and everything became ghostly silent.

* * *

Clay opened his eyes to realize he was lying face down in the dirt road. How in the blazes did he get down here? In the midst of all the gunshots, he must have taken a nosedive without even realizing it. Spitting out a mouthful of dirt, he scrambled to his feet to find himself looking right into the eyes of Grayson Hobbs.

"I guess we showed that fellow a thing or two, didn't we, Scar?" he said. "What do you say we get on with robbin' this bank before the men of the town get back?"

"Yeah, Clay. Let's get to the bank."

An inquisitive look came over Clay's face as he stared at Grayson. "Your ear," Clay remarked. "It's there. So help me, Scar, I'm looking at the ear that worthless mule bit off all them years ago."

Grayson felt his ear. "What the . . . ? What do you make of that, Clay? Ain't no way that ear's supposed to be there." Grayson's eyes focused on someone standing behind Clay that he hadn't noticed before. "Who's that fellow standing behind you, Clay?" he asked.

"Huh?" Clay grunted, turning to look. He aimed his gun at the stranger. "Who are you and where'd you come from?"

The fellow smiled. "Gabe's my name," he responded without the slightest hesitation. "I'm here for a pickup."

"A pickup?" Clay snarled, moving his gun to the fellow's nose. "Don't be playin' no word games with me, pardner. I'd just a' soon part your teeth with a hunk of lead as look at you. Now one more time, what are you doing here?"

"Oh, my," Gabe said. "Looks like I got myself a difficult one this time. I hate getting stuck with this sort of thing. Let's start by explaining that gun of yours is useless over here on this side, friend. What the heck. Let's just get rid of it and be done with it."

Gabe snapped his fingers, and the gun simply vanished from Clay's hand. "Wha—what happened to my gun?" Clay asked, looking around to see if he'd dropped it. "Shoot this guy, Scar," he cried. "He's up to no good. I feel it in my bones."

"I hate to mention this," Gabe shrugged. "But you don't have any bones. Not anymore."

"Shoot him, Scar!" Clay shouted out again. "Shoot him now!"

"I can't shoot him, Clay. I've lost my gun. It just dropped out of my hand, and I can't find it nowhere," Grayson said helplessly.

For the first time, Clay noticed someone lying on the ground at his feet. He took a close look. "It's me!" he screeched. "I'm lying there on the ground like I'm asleep."

"You're lying on the ground," Gabe smiled, "but you're not asleep. Like I said before, I'm here for a pickup. It's not the most pleasant job in the universe, picking up the likes of you two, but someone's got to do it."

Clay's hand shot to his mouth. "You mean—I'm—I'm . . ."

"That's right," Gabe replied. "Now are you two fellows ready to come along peacefully, or do I have to do this the hard way?"

A look of horror crossed Clay's face and he hurriedly backed several steps away from the body. "I'm dead, Scar! Did you hear the man?! I'm dead!"

"I'm dead, too!" Grayson screamed. "What are we gonna do, Clay?! I ain't never been dead before!"

"There's nothing to it," Gabe explained. "The two of you just come along with me, and I'll see to it you get checked in with no hassle at all."

"Checked in?" Clay gasped, his eyes wide in terror. "Checked in where?"

"There's a place especially prepared for guys like you and Grayson," Gabe went on to say. "It's a place where you can start paying back some of the debt you incurred here in your misdirected mortal life. I don't expect you'll like it all that well, not at first anyway. But—you can put your mind at ease on one count. It's not as bad as lots of folks on this side make it out to be. Now are you coming along peacefully, or do I call out the artillery?"

Neither man moved. "Okay," Gabe said. "Let's start with a small demonstration and hope that will be sufficient."

Suddenly the thunder rolled, and right out of the cloudless sky a lightning bolt flashed, striking the ground not two feet from the two startled outlaws. Their chins drooped and their eyes opened wide as the smoke from the lightning strike slowly cleared. "Shall we go now?" Gabe asked calmly, "or do I bring on a stronger incentive?"

Clay took one last look around. He looked at himself lying on the ground. He looked at a frightened Grayson Hobbs standing next to him. He looked at the saddlebags of money and at the bank he had planned to rob. Funny how meaningless these seemed now. His chest rose and fell in a symbol of defeat. Then, like a sheep following the shepherd's lead, he moved out in the direction Gabe was pointing. Just as he had done in mortal life, Grayson followed closely behind.

* * *

Loraine hit the ground with a thud. For the next few seconds the air was shattered with the sound of gunshots. Then everything grew silent. She glanced around to see someone lying next to her. It was Clay Derringer. Quickly she scrambled to her feet and backed away from him. Next she spotted Grayson where he had fallen. She spun to face Howard. He was still holding her smoking revolver. All the color had drained from his face, and his left hand was clutching his chest. Panic gripped Loraine as she noticed blood oozing between his fingers. "Howard!" she screamed. "You've been shot!"

Feebly he turned his head toward her. Their eyes met. The gun fell from his hand. His knees buckled, and he rolled to the ground. In an instant Loraine was at his side, cradling his head in her arms. "Are they—dead?" he weakly asked.

"Yes," she said, tears filling her eyes. "You got them both. You saved my life."

Howard swallowed painfully. "Good," he choked out. "You deserve to live. You deserve happiness. I'm so glad the angels gave me the strength to save you."

"Howard, please don't die," she sobbed. "Hold on. The doctor will be back soon, I just know it."

Howard closed his eyes and coughed. "No, Loraine. I don't belong here in your century. The angels have only allowed me to be here this short time." He opened his eyes and looked into hers. "But I'm so glad they did. You're an amazing woman, Loraine Parker. I can't help feeling if fate had dealt us different hands . . ."

Loraine was crying openly now. She buried her face against Howard's chest. "No!" she sobbed. "Don't talk like that. You do belong here with me. I feel it, Howard. I feel like I've known you all my life." For a moment, her voice refused to overcome the sorrow of her heart. Fighting back the grief, she spoke again. "I feel I've loved you all my life. Now that I've found you, please don't leave me. Please, Howard Placard, don't leave me now."

Howard coughed again. "I have no choice," he gasped. "I made a deal with an angel to save your life. She kept her part of the bargain; now it's my turn to keep my part. She's free to do with me whatever she will." Howard moved his hand to Loraine's face, then stroked her long flowing blond hair. "Will you—kiss me just once more?" he whispered.

Loraine moved her head just far enough to press her lips to his. "Thank you," he said, seconds later. "I want you to know . . . I was kissing you—and not Lori Douglas."

"I know, I know," she said. "I don't know why, but I just know."

Howard groaned and cleared his throat with great effort. "Please," he said, the words coming with difficulty now. "Don't ever forget me, Loraine. Promise . . ."

She burst into a flood of tears. "I promise!" she said through quivering lips. "I'll never forget you, Howard Placard. I'll never forget you."

He let out a final breath, and she felt him go limp. "No!" she cried, her face pressing against his. "Please, no!"

For a long moment she lay sobbing. Then, as if being sung by the lips of angels, the words of a song came softly to her ears.

> *From this valley they say you are leaving.*
> *I will miss your bright eyes and sweet smile.*
> *And they say you are taking the sunshine,*
> *That brightened our way for a while.*

Still she remained with his head in her arms—and she cried. At last, she stood and after a moment leaned down to pick up her revolver. "I'll never forget you, Howard Placard," she solemnly promised. "And I'll never fire this pistol again."

CHAPTER 26

As Howard's mind cleared, he realized he was no longer on the streets of Mesa in the year 1885. He had returned to his own time and dimension, and of all things was right back on the Caribbean island he had left yesterday morning. Or was it this morning? Or had any time elapsed at all while he was gone? He just didn't know, and it just didn't matter.

He checked himself for a gunshot wound or blood. He seemed to be okay. He glanced up to see Annette, whom he hadn't noticed before. "Hi, sis," he said. "You here to gloat over your victory?"

"Hey, big brother. It was your victory, too, you know."

Howard paused, lowering his eyes. In a moment he raised them and looked at her again. "I need you to do something for me, little sister. I'd like for you to pass along my thanks to Sam—for letting me save Loraine's life. I told her she could do with me as she wished; I won't protest now."

Annette smiled. "You really are in love with Loraine, aren't you?"

"I think you know the answer to that," Howard chuckled. "I think you knew the answer long before you took me back in time to meet her. I don't claim to understand how any of this works, sis. But I do know I've loved Loraine all my life. It's like I've known her since before I was even born."

"You have no idea how close to the truth you are, big brother. And you have no idea how much she loves you."

"She loves me? Wonderful. If only we could have lived our lives in the same dimension, maybe that would have meant something."

"Personally, I think it means something the way things are right now, Howard."

Howard's eyes shot open as he stared at his sister. "You called me Howard!" he exclaimed, shocked. "What's with you, little sister? Are you sick?'

She smiled. "I called you Howard because you've earned the name now. The name Peaches just doesn't fit a man of the caliber you've become, big brother."

This brought a smile to Howard's face. "Now that's really something," he acknowledged. "I've reached a point in life where my sister uses my real name. I don't care what it was I had to go through for this, it was worth it."

Annette's grin stretched to fill her whole face. "I have a surprise for you, Howard. Close your eyes."

"What?" he laughed. "Close my eyes? Why?"

"Just close your eyes, big brother. It won't be a surprise unless you do it my way."

Howard shrugged and closed his eyes. He could hear footsteps. Whoever it was, they moved around until they were right in front of him. "Okay, big brother," Annette said. "You can open them now.

Howard opened his eyes to the shock of his life. "Lori?" he gasped. "Why are you here?" Howard looked back at Annette, but she only smiled. His eyes shifted back to Lori, who stood directly in front of him.

"I, uh—I'm sorry," Howard stammered. "This is a little awkward for me. I didn't expect to ever see you again."

"This was my idea, Howard," she answered. "I just felt there were some things we needed to talk out."

Howard cleared his throat. "Listen, Lori," he began. "I know I did some terrible things. I realize saying I'm sorry doesn't excuse the pain I've caused you and Brad. But I am sorry. More sorry than you can possibly know."

To Howard's astonishment, she didn't answer or say a word. Howard stiffened as she moved closer, stopping only inches from him. She took hold of his lapel and straightened his collar. He stiffened even more when she touched his face, raising it until their eyes met.

"Lori! What are you doing?!" he asked sharply. She lifted her other hand and placed it on the other side of his face, then leaned toward him. "No!" he protested. "We made this mistake once! We won't do it again! You're a married woman, Lori!"

Completely ignoring his objection, she pressed her lips to his—and instantly, he knew. "Loraine," he said softly as their lips parted. "But how?"

Rather than answer, she kissed him again, sending a flood of warmth to the depths of his very soul. He placed his hands on her shoulders, pushing her back ever so gently until they stood facing each other. "Annette," he said, not looking away from Loraine. "You've brought her to me this time, haven't you? Is she going to stay here with me—in my time?"

"Why ask me, big brother?" Annette smirked. "Ask her, she's the one in your arms."

"I'm here," Loraine whispered. "And we'll never be apart again, I promise."

Howard placed a finger to her lips, slowly tracing their outline. Suddenly, this dreaded island came alive with a splendor defying Howard's imagination. The song of the birds had never sounded so sweet. The air had never felt so fresh. And the smell of wild flowers filled his nostrils as never before. Moving his hand behind her head, he pulled her into the kiss he had waited a lifetime for. And just as in his movies, an orchestra played—if only in his heart.

Howard suddenly realized Loraine was crying. "What is it?" he asked, brushing away a tear from her face.

"I—I'm sorry, Howard," she said. "It's just being here with you now. It's something I've dreamed of for such a long time."

He didn't understand. "What do you mean such a long time, Loraine?"

She tried to smile through her tears. "I've dreamed of this moment my every waking hour for more than a century now, Howard."

"But that makes no sense," he responded in disbelief.

"I'm sure that to you it seems only minutes ago that we said good-bye on the streets of Mesa," she explained. "But that wasn't the case for me, Howard. I lived out a whole lifetime since your dying kiss."

Howard struggled to understand. "You—you lived out your lifetime?"

"I did," she smiled. "And I've been anxiously waiting on the opposite side of forever for what seems another lifetime. I kept my promise, you know. I never forgot you, Howard. I lived ninety-five wonderful years. Long enough to see all the things you promised I would—automobiles, motion pictures, airplanes, television . . . It was exciting seeing all the new advancements I knew you had seen before me." She paused before adding, "Those would have been unbearably lonesome years if it hadn't been for Annette's promise."

Howard's head was spinning from all this. Loraine had lived her lifetime since that kiss that seemed only minutes ago? "Annette's promise?" he repeated, glancing at his sister.

"I went back to Loraine again, big brother. On the same day you were shot. I explained several things to her, like why your body would have to disappear."

"My body?"

"Yes," Loraine explained. "Your body couldn't remain in my time, since you were from another century. The story got around that some of Clay and Grayson's friends stole your body in an act of revenge. I never refuted the story, even though I knew it was Annette who took you away. It was Annette's promise that kept me going all through the years. She said you and I would be together again. She even allowed me to look forward and see this day, Howard. I was allowed to see you kiss me, the way you just did."

Howard shook his head. "This is amazing," he said. "You lived to be ninety-five." A question came to mind he just had to ask. "Did you—ever marry?"

"No," she answered with a soft laugh. "I never married. But that was all right. I found love and meaning in my brother Amos' family." She paused to laugh again, lightly. "In fact, I was there when Amos proposed to Brittany Ann. It was at a dance. He and Brittany were on one side of the room and I was on the other, but I heard what he shouted when she said yes. Care to guess what it was he shouted?"

Howard stared at her. "I wouldn't know."

"You should, Mr. Placard. You taught him the word."

Howard laughed. "Awesome?" he guessed. "Is that what he shouted?"

"It is. Amos never forgot that word. And he never forgot the man who taught it to him, either." She paused, then went on to say, "Believe it or not, I lived long enough to see Amos' grandson David celebrate his tenth birthday. David Douglas Parker was a wonderful child, my favorite of all Amos' grandchildren."

"David Douglas Parker?" Howard echoed. "David Douglas Parker is Lori's father."

"That's right, he is. Incredible isn't it? That I was able to live long enough to become quite well acquainted with David. It was his idea, you know—naming Lori after me."

"I didn't know," Howard said, stunned.

"Remember the medallion that saved your life when Clay Derringer tried to shoot you?"

"I remember."

"Amos gave the medallion to David on his tenth birthday. That same day I gave David my revolver that I had mounted in a trophy case."

Howard's eyes lit up. "And, in turn, David passed those things on to Lori," he observed. "And we know the rest of the story about them, don't we?"

"I never fired the gun again," she went on to say. "And I wrote the book we talked about, *An Angel in Time.* I gave the manuscript to your sister on the day I died. She's the one who came for me."

Howard laughed. "You really did write our story?"

"Every word of it," she declared.

Howard felt a sudden surge of excitement at the thought of Loraine's book. "What about the gunfight? You included that, didn't you?"

"You're darn right I did. I couldn't leave that out."

"Oh, wow," Howard said. "What a fascinating story. What wouldn't I give to turn it into a motion picture? I wonder if Sam might allow me to do just one more?"

"No, Howard. You can't produce another picture. But Sam assures me she'll see to it someone else does it for you."

That's when it hit him. "I—can't produce another picture because I'm . . ."

"Yes, Howard," she grinned. "You are. Exactly like me."

Howard patted himself down again. "I don't feel any different," he said.

"Amazing, isn't it? Getting used to it took me a while, too. And now it's *my* turn to tell you of a dimension where they have things to rattle *your* imagination, Howard Placard. Things that make cameras, television, and airplanes look like children's toys. A place waiting for us just across the way. Any second now a brilliant conduit of light will appear. When it does, I'll lead you through it on our way home. And think about this, Howard. Today is the first day of the rest of our forever."

Annette smiled at Howard. "Now it's time I set you straight on another matter," she said. "I'm not Annette Placard anymore. My Mr. Right is waiting just across the line, and I want you to meet him. You're going to love him, I know. You know darn well one of the things attracting you to Loraine is that she reminds you of me, and turnabout's fair play. Scott reminds me of you, so there."

Scott? The name rang through Howard's mind like chimes from an organ. "His name is Scott Engels, isn't it, sis? I don't know how I know that, but I do. I'm right, aren't I? That is his name."

"That's his name," she beamed, "and the reason you know the name is because you and I are inseparable twins. I always knew in my subconscious that you and Loraine were destined for each other, and you always knew the same about Scott and me. Just the sound of his name was enough to pull the knowledge out of your subconscious."

Howard nodded slowly. "You're right, sis. For some reason I do know that a fellow named Scott Engels is the one destined for you. But I can't remember where I heard the name."

"You heard it from Jeremiah, when he told you about the sheriff of Mesa. That's why I couldn't tell you his name while you were back in 1885. A slip of the tongue could have brought problems. Scott didn't know about me in 1885. He was to learn of me a year later when I would appear in his world as a first-level angel. I'll show you the story in a holograph after the ceremony."

"What ceremony?" Howard asked, confused.

"What do you mean what ceremony, big brother? The ceremony for you and Loraine, naturally. I realize you haven't popped the question yet, but I'm sure you won't let much angel moss grow between your angel toes before you get around to it."

"And I will say yes, when you ask," Loraine happily added. "I want Annette for my bridesmaid, and I think Scott would be a great best man."

CHAPTER 27

When Lori returned to her family room after meeting with Howard, she found only Brad waiting for her. Samantha was nowhere to be seen. Brad took her in his arms and kissed her.

"You did good, babe," he said.

"Did you see it?" she asked.

"I saw it all, right down to the gun battle. That's when Sam excused herself and left. But she left us this letter."

Lori wiped away a tear with the back of her hand and took the letter from Brad, reading it aloud.

Lori and Brad,

Sorry to have ended things on such a sudden note, but Jason and I had other work to finish on the case. I'm sure you're wondering where things were headed for Loraine and Howard. You both watched as Howard saved Loraine's life. He was pretty brave, wasn't he? You've probably guessed we had to bring him back to his own time. As for Loraine, well, she lived a very long and happy life. You can read all about it in her manuscript. Speaking of the manuscript, I'm asking a special favor from you, Brad. I'd like you to turn it into a movie . . .

"A movie?" Brad said, interrupting Lori. "She wants me to make a movie out of Howard's story?"

"Howard and Loraine's story," Lori corrected. "And it says Sam wants the movie dedicated to their memories."

"Memories? Does this mean Howard is no longer with us?"

Lori read further in the letter. "Oh my," she said. "It says here they'll find Howard's body on the island. It will appear he's been murdered. Shot through the chest with a 45-caliber bullet."

"A 45-caliber?" Brad echoed. "That was the most common caliber used during the late 1800s. Good grief, Lori! Do you suppose . . ."

"Yes," Lori said. "Howard really did give his life for Loraine. Sam explains it here in the letter."

"Well," Brad observed. "I'm not going to say this movie was based on a real event, even though it was. Who'd believe it?"

Lori caught his eye. "You're going to do the movie, then?"

"Yeah, why not? And you know what else? I have the perfect lady in mind to play the part of Loraine Parker."

Lori's mouth dropped open. "Brad, you're not hinting . . . ? No! Forget it! I have no acting experience."

"Hey, with a director like me coaching you, we're talking Academy Award material here." Not giving Lori time to respond, Brad changed the subject. "The revolver you have in the trophy case—do you suppose if we had it fingerprinted we'd find Howard's prints on it?"

Lori broke out laughing. "You're crazy, Brad Douglas, you know that."

He took her in his arms again. "Yeah, but you love me anyway. What else does it say in that letter of Sam's?"

"It says to end your movie with the line, Loraine and Howard lived happily ever after."

"They are together now, aren't they?" Brad remarked thoughtfully. "Loraine lived in her time, Howard lived in his, and still destiny wasn't cheated."

"Yeah. It sort of reminds me of how things worked out for Sam and Jason."

"You're right," Brad smiled. "I love it."

"Are you going to include that in your movie?"

"You're darn right I am," he laughed. "You know me. I always want a happy ending."

Lori shoved a finger to Brad's chin. "That brings us to another point," she grinned. "There's some news I've been dying to tell you. And now seems like the perfect time."

"All right," Brad said. "So tell me, pretty lady. What's your news?"

Lori presented her news in the form of a question. "If we have a daughter, can we name her Loraine?"

Brad caught his breath. "If we have a daughter? Lori Douglas, are you trying to tell me something?"

She smiled. "Or if we have a son, we could . . ."

"No!" Brad shouted. "We won't name him Howard. I may have forgiven the man, but I'm not naming my son after him!"

She smiled. "I was going to suggest the name Brad."

Brad lifted her and spun her in a full circle. "I'm going to be a daddy!" he shouted. "I love you, Lori Douglas." Pulling her into his arms, he kissed her.

* * *

"Sort of gets to you, doesn't it, Jason?" Samantha asked as they watched without revealing their presence. "And I'm sure Lori will love having their daughter named after her."

Jason's eyes narrowed as he looked at his wife. "Their daughter?" he asked. "You've been snooping into their future, haven't you, Sam?"

"I asked Annette. That's her department, you know."

"You know the higher authorities frown on that sort of thing, my sneaky little wife," Jason grumbled.

"Not if it pertains to one of our cases, they don't," she said loftily.

"That's digging pretty deep, Sam. Lori and Brad's case is headed for the 'completed' file and you know it."

"Don't be such a stick-in-the-mud, Jason Hackett. There's a good chance we'll still be Special Conditions Coordinators when Loraine Douglas grows up. And there's a good chance she might become one of our clients." Jason shook his head, but he dropped the subject.

Samantha sighed. "I suppose we should be on our way, Jason. I need to stop by home to change into something a little more drab for the occasion, and then it's off to the chefs' convention. You won the bet fair and square, and I won't renege on my part of the bargain."

Jason grinned and waved a finger in front of Samantha's face. "There is no chefs' convention. I made it up."

"You what?" Samantha asked sharply. "What do you mean you made it up, Jason Hackett?!"

"I just wanted to have a little fun with you, lady. So I tricked you into the trumped-up bet. There is no chefs' convention. On the contrary, I just happen to have six front row tickets for the Elvis concert."

Samantha's anger suddenly softened as the color drained from her face. "Six tickets to the . . . ? Are you serious, Jason?"

"I'm ghostly serious," he laughed. "I've invited Gus and Joan to join us, along with Maggie and Alvin. I'd say you'd better dress in something other than the drab outfit you had in mind for my convention."

"You're taking me to the concert?!" Samantha shouted. "With Gus, Joan, Maggie, and Alvin?!"

"Gotcha," Jason said, his finger pointed right at her.

"Jason Hackett!" she cried. "You are the most despicable ghost I know! Playing a trick like that on me!" Her face broke into a huge grin. "The most despicable and the most wonderful ghost I know! We're going to see Elvis!" She rushed forward and gave him a giant kiss. Then, taking him by the hand, she started through the angelic door leading to the far side of forever. "We have to hurry, my sweet little husband. We've got to make a quick shopping trip, and you can help me pick out a new dress!"

* * *

Howard stared at Loraine, his eyes filled with love. A lump formed in his throat as memories flooded into his mind. Memories of times at home on his father's ranch. Memories of his days as a powerful producer. Memories of the way he nearly ruined Lori's marriage, and of how wonderful it felt hearing her say she had forgiven him. But his best memories were those of his trek back through time to the year 1885, when he came face to face with his true destiny.

Suddenly, something caught his eye. It was a tiny light, opening up as a crack in the sky over the breaking waves of the nearby surf. As he watched, the light grew in size and intensity until it outshone the noonday sun. Looking into the light, he could see it led off into the far distance. "Come on," Loraine said, pointing toward the light. "It's time to go home."

"In a minute," he responded, taking her in his arms and kissing her tenderly. "There's one last thing an old movie producer like me has to do." Turning for one final look at the island, he called out, "CUT!!! THAT'S A WRAP!!" He grinned back at Loraine. "Now we can go," he said. "I've officially put the story to bed." He put his arm around her as they moved toward the light.

"Wait for me," Annette said, stepping over to them and sliding her arm through Howard's other arm. "I think it's only fair I get to help escort my big brother home."

Howard laughed. "A beautiful woman on each arm. What an entrance I'm about to make." He turned to look at Loraine. "How soon before we change your name from Loraine Parker to Loraine Placard?" he asked. Her only answer was a smile as, together, the three of them stepped into the light.

EPILOGUE

Brad's movie was a huge success. He produced it, directed it, and even co-starred in it. He had to co-star in the film; it was the only way Lori would agree to play Loraine's part. Playing Loraine proved easier than Lori had anticipated, and the part came off almost without a hitch. Her one problem came in playing the second role as herself, when she had to kiss an actor pretending to be Brad. That she didn't like at all. But the parts where she played Loraine kissing Howard were no problem—since his part was played by her husband, Brad.

As great as the release of *An Angel in Time* was, an even greater day preceded it by nearly a year. That was the day when Lori presented Brad with his first daughter. By mutual consent, they named her Loraine Parker Douglas. And they all lived happily—forever—after.

ABOUT THE AUTHOR

"I've lived a storybook life," says Dan Yates. "Just like in all my stories, I met and courted the woman of my dreams and—with the help of a few angels of my own—convinced her to join me in a forever contract. As a result, we now enjoy four sons and two daughters, eleven grandsons and eight granddaughters—and oh yes—three cats.

"I've always loved being thought of as a storyteller. I'm so grateful to Covenant Communications for giving me the chance to have my stories published. I'm especially grateful to my 'ever so patient' editor, Valerie Holladay, who keeps me honest and smooths out all the rough edges I tend to miss."

Dan's previous writing efforts have resulted in Church productions and local publications as well as six previous best-selling novels in the *Angels* series: *Angels Don't Knock, Just Call Me an Angel, Angels to the Rescue, An Angel in the Family, It Takes an Angel,* and *Angel on Vacation* as well as *An Angel's Christmas.*

A former bishop and high councilor, Dan now lives in Phoenix with his wife. He loves receiving e-mails from his readers, and he does answer them all. He can be reached at *yates@swlink.net.*